A Puhaka Books Selection

puhakabooks.com

# Endangered Species:
## Let the Game Begin

**W. B. Martin**

# Also by W. B. Martin

# A Story of Science Fiction

Printed by permission of
Puhaka Publishing

Printed in the United States of America

Edited by T. Johns

Cover Layout by Morwenna Rakestraw

Version 1.3

ISBN-13-978-1-940554-10-5
First Edition April 22, 2014

*To Johnny B.*

# Chapter 1

The sound of the ocean washing onto a beach permeated the woman's senses as she lay half asleep. It was warm and her mind shifted from one thought to another as she hung between sleep and awakening. She listened to the soothing sound of waves crashing onto a beach, a white noise in her mind.

"Thump." The sound stirred her consciousness slightly. The soothing white noise of the ocean caressing the beach put her mind back into sleep mode.

"Thump." Again the loud sound interrupted the mesmerizing sound of wave on beach. Her mind focused slightly on the intrusion in her methodical wave noise. Her eyes twitched as her mind focused slightly on another sense. Her nose registered a fragrance that she had smelled before but wasn't expecting.

It was a strong smell of flowers and vegetation mixed with sea air. Her mind added the new sense to her feeling of being near a tropical ocean beach. The dream was very real as she lay enjoying such a pleasing sensation. Her mind drifted off once again with the white noise background now enhanced by a 'white smell' easing any concerns. She slept contentedly with her thoughts.

"Thump." Her eyes twitched behind closed lids. She moved slightly and her touch sensation made her stop, startled. Still groggy, her entire body registered that, except for the thing she was laying on, her body wasn't in touch with anything but a warm breeze.

Her mind focused behind closed eyes evaluating her situation. She definitely was laying naked on something firm while warm air caressed her body. Her ears tuned in more closely and put the ocean white noise aside. She heard trees rustling from the wind, then suddenly, "Thump."

Her eyes snapped open at the intrusive sound close by, blinking repeatedly to adjust to the bright light. She looked around at the blazing yellow nylon tent she was in. Then lowering her gaze, she looked at her exposed body which was alone in the tent. In fact except for her and the sleeping pad she was lying on, the tent was empty.

Her mind raced now. How had she ended up in such a state and in such a place? She worked her mind as to where the last place she had been. Her mind was blank. But she knew it hadn't been in a tent someplace warm and she would never have been naked.

Not that she had never been naked in a tent on a tropical beach. There was that time in her past. She closed her eyes to try and clear her thoughts. Was she still dreaming? The ocean still crashed on shore and the trees still made their rustling sound from the wind. And the warm air stirred her. She definitely hadn't been anywhere warm recently.

"Thump." The sound brought her back to reality. The sound was much closer this time. And more threatening. She focused her mind as she sat up.

Cautiously she looked out the small vent above the closed zippered door. The fresh sea air hit her as it flowed into the tent. The sun was making the inside of the tent uncomfortably warm now. The outside air felt cool and inviting in comparison.

She looked down to locate the zipper. As she ran the toggle around the length of the door the fabric fell away revealing a yellow sand beach with waves hitting a short distance away. The woman turned her head and saw the palm trees swaying above in the wind. The palm fronds rocked in the gentle breeze as shade dappled her tent.

Sticking her head slowly out of the tent, she surveyed to her left and right. The beach to the left headed off toward a rocky point in the distance jutting into the ocean. The curved beach looked inviting in its expanse. No one was visible. Additionally, no man-made object was in view. Just a long long lonely stretch of sandy beach.

She turned to her right. Much closer was another rocky promontory. Although not as tall or as long as the opposite point, this one was much closer: two hundred yards, she estimated.

And unlike the lack of any human life to her left, the view to the right held a house. Nestled into the land rising up that made the base of the promontory was a small house. At least it looked like a house to the woman staring from the tent.

She moved slightly out of the tent so she could see behind the tent. More palm trees stood over brush where the beach gave way to more solid ground.

"Thump." The sound startled her again. This time though, she saw the coconut that had just hit the sand roll slightly from where it had just struck. She looked up quickly to see if such a threat lingered above her tent. The tent safely sat between palm trees, but plenty of coconuts lay near her spot.

"What is going on?" she muttered to no one. Her own voice broke the tropical mood that had mesmerized her mind. "Where am I?" She worked her brain as to what she should do next.

The woman looked in vain for anything in which to cover her nakedness. Certainly not opposed to being naked, she had enjoyed many memorable outdoor trips with clothing as an option. She had even been to Hawaii with a boyfriend to spend a week on the Na Pali Coast on the Garden Island of Kauai enjoying the solitude.

But this was different. Whoever lived in the house may not be expecting a naked woman. *That is, if someone lived in the house at all,* the woman thought. In either case, there might be something in which she could at least cover up with while she tried to locate anyone who could tell her where she was. And maybe tell her how she got here.

She looked both ways again and saw no one. Crawling completely out of the tent, the woman stood up. With her arms held low in a self-conscience pose, she began to walk down the beach. As she walked, she looked in all directions as she drew closer to the house, hoping someone would appear.

Now closer to the house, details became more clear. The house was small and had the appearance of a South Sea's design. At least what she thought of as a South Sea design, if 'Donovan's Reef' with John Wayne was a good example of the South Seas. That was about as close as she'd ever been to the South Pacific.

But this house looked like many she had seen in Hawaii. It had the rusty sheet metal roof so recognizable in the tropics. A wrap-around covered porch added to the tropical allure as well as the large use of windows and glass doors between the house and the porch.

She stopped at the end of the beach when she spotted the small defined trail leading off the beach that led up the small incline toward the house. The house sat under some large leafed trees that looked like the 'Swiss Family Robinson' tree in which they had built their tree house. Only these trees were smaller. The shade they provided offered a cool respite from the hot tropical sun bearing down on the beach.

The woman looked for any signs of human life and saw none. But she did see that the large double glass doors leading into the house were open. A wind chime was ringing on the end of the porch. It looked inviting and the woman stepped up off the beach.

Still covering her private parts as best as she could, she walked slowly up the grass-covered trail leading directly to the house. She stopped short as a man walked out onto the porch. He stopped and looked down at her.

The man was Asian and short. She estimated him to be about 5'5" tall and in his forties. The woman noted that he wore glasses as his gaze scanned her naked body. She did her best to keep herself covered from his prying eyes.

A slight relief came over her as an Asian woman stepped outside. She was shorter than the man and also wore wire-rimmed glasses. She saw the naked woman and immediately disappeared into the house. While the man continued his silent stare the whole time, the Asian woman finally reappeared holding something. She walked over to the naked woman and held out a cloth wrap.

The woman gratefully took the cloth and wrapped it around her body. She pulled it tight over her breasts and tucked in on end. Now suitably covered in a sarong, the woman asked, "Where am I?"

She was taken back by the Asian couple both speaking rapidly in a language that sounded Chinese but was 'Greek' to her. Noticing that the language barrier held things back, the Asian woman stepped down, took the woman's elbow and escorted her into the house. Whatever language was being spoken, the physical sign was one of welcome.

Water was brought for the lost woman and some fruit. With her modesty secured, she ate and drank heartily as she realized how hungry and thirsty she had become. The Asian man continued to stare at her the entire time in a rather unnerving way.

The woman tried to move his attention to her concern of where she was and how she get here. But no matter how slow she spoke or how many pantomime signs she made, no information was forthcoming. But the Asian woman continued to offer hospitality in spite of the stares of the Asian man.

The woman looked around the house as she sat in frustration over the language barrier. It was a small cottage. She saw one bedroom through glass doors on the back of the cottage while a great room ran the full length of the house. She noticed a toilet next to the one bedroom and excused herself. As she closed the door, she noticed the bathroom only had a toilet and a sink. She saw no shower or bathtub.

Finishing, she washed her hands and looked in the mirror. Staring back was an image of a scared 27 year-old who was quite alone somewhere in the world. She lingered staring for quite some time trying to will herself the strength to open the door and confront her situation.

Standing at the mirror, she heard a commotion in the main part of the house. Then she heard English being spoken with the Chinese-like language answered in return. She raced to the door and flung it open.

She froze as she stepped into the main room. "Professor Brody, what are you doing here?"

The new man in the house looked up from his work cleaning fish in the kitchen. "Ms. Price, where did you come from?"

# Chapter 2

Ft. Lewis, Washington

Captain Chet Grinkis walked over to the men gathered by the obstacle course set up for physical training. He had seen it before and was determined to stop it before it went any further.

"Attention," Sergeant Aubin yelled as the captain approached. The platoon snapped to attention from their bent over position. They had just finished their morning PT, or at least they thought they had finished the morning workout.

"Ladies, that was one of the worst cases of PT I've seen in my ten years in Special Ops. I expect every man in this unit to put out 110 percent or go find another outfit. I will not tolerate the half-assed effort I just witnessed."

The men stared straight ahead as their heavy breathing continued to compensate for the oxygen drain their bodies had just expended.

"We will march back to the beginning of this course and this time we will attack it with enthusiasm. And as an added bonus, I will run the course with you."

Noticeable groans rumbled through the platoon. They had experienced PT with the CO before and it hadn't been pleasant. The captain was famous throughout Ft. Lewis as one hard ass that could outrun anyone. The men sucked in more oxygen in anticipation.

"And as an added incentive, anyone that can't beat me to the finish will be pulling extra duty. Do I make myself clear?"

"Yes sir," came the chorus. It was decidedly lackluster.

"I said, do I make myself clear?" the captain yelled at the top of his lungs.

"Hooray," the fifteen men of the platoon screamed back.

Everyone lined up at the start line and the captain nodded to the sergeant to ready the stop watch. Sergeant Aubin yelled go and the platoon raced off, the CO taking up the rear.

As Sergeant Aubin took the shortcut between each obstacle as the official observer, the platoon raced around the course. Captain Grinkis trailed along behind his men watching each carefully. At the second obstacle he started his move.

As he passed each troop, he didn't say anything. He would just smile. Soon he was closing in with the three fastest men he commanded. As he passed each in turn, the smile never faded. Crossing the finish line, he swung around to the waiting sergeant.

Captain Grinkis checked the stopwatch and noted his time. He worked on controlling his breathing as he watched each man cross the finish line. As the last two crossed together, he walked over to the collapsed crowd, all sucking air.

"That was more like it. Now Sergeant, double time this platoon back for breakfast."

"Yes sir. Fall in," the sergeant ordered. The captain took up a position beside the sergeant as the platoon began to double time back to the barracks.

Halfway back, the captain was diverted by an Army Humvee pulling up beside him. He stopped as the sergeant kept the men running.

"Colonel, you're out in the field early."

"Captain, climb in. We need to be at G2 right now."

Captain Grinkis climbed in the back seat of the Humvee and the driver took off headed toward the base intelligence center. G2 was the section in each army unit where information was gathered and evaluated.

"What's up Colonel? I'm not very presentable if we are having any formal meeting."

"Sounds big. NORAD just picked up something and has put all commands on alert. We're to await further information. From the tone of the messages we're receiving, it's serious."

Captain Grinkis sat and stared out the Humvee side window. He'd been in this position before. As Commanding Officer of a Delta Force Special Operations unit, he often spent time waiting for information on potential threats to the United States.

The driver pulled up in front of Ft. Lewis' Command Center. The captain walked beside the colonel past the security guards into the building. They turned left and went down the hall that led to the Communications Center. Again, they showed their ID to the guards and punched in their security clearance. The metal door clicked open and they walked into a crowded darkened room of computer terminals and operators.

As the colonel headed to the commanding general of the base, Captain Grinkis spotted his friend standing off to the side. As a fellow captain in the infantry, he and his friend had known each other since West Point.

"What's up?" Captain Grinkis asked his friend.

"Not sure, Chet. But from the communiqués that have come through so far, I'm not liking this."

The two captains stood and stared as the computer screens changed continuously. The enlisted men typed on their computers and information jumped onto the main screen at the front of the room. Everyone worked hard trying to interpret what was being put up on the big screen when the red phone by the general rang.

As the direct line to the Pentagon, it startled the entire room. The phone only rang during national emergencies of a military nature that were an imminent threat to America.

The general picked up the phone and talked. Or listened would be more exact. The general acknowledged the information that had been passed and hung up. He turned to the lieutenant in charge of the Comm Center and said, "Lieutenant, put what information we have on the big screen in the conference room." Then turning to the entire room he barked, "We are meeting in the conference room right now."

All the officers that had gathered moved to the adjoining conference room. The senior officers took up the seats around the table while the junior officers sat down in chairs along the walls.

Captain Grinkis sat down behind his colonel. His friend sat down next to him. They both stared in disbelief at the large screen at the head of the table. The room was silent when the general took up a spot next to the screen. He picked up a pointer stick for emphasis.

As he waved the pointer around, he smacked it on the screen. The noise startled the room. Obviously no one was willing to inform the commanding general that the days of wall charts that could take pointer abuse were over. Large computer monitors weren't so forgiving .

But as general, it was his prerogative to abuse anything in his command as he wished. And he smacked the screen again for emphasis. The screen wavered as the digital signal jumped at the physical jarring.

"We are in deep shit, gentlemen."

Captain Grinkis looked around the room. There were two women officers in the room and the general wasn't being politically correct. When the general's Chief-of-Staff started to correct his oversight, the general smacked the screen again. The monitor went to static as something gave up from the continued abuse.

The general looked at the damage he had caused and said, "The hell with that damn thing." Then thinking better, he laid his pointer down on the table, leaned over to his Chief-of-Staff and said, "Get someone fixing that thing now."

He continued, "While that's being fixed, I'll fill you in on where we're at this moment. NORAD has picked up a two-mile-wide object headed toward Earth. Radar places it just outside the Moon's orbit and headed our way. It's moving slow but it's aimed directly at Earth."

The room went deathly quiet at the news. An asteroid that large was a world killer. The scientific community had warned of such an event for years. With no ability to ward off such an assault, everyone knew that such an event was capable of extinguishing all life on earth.

A two-mile-wide object hitting the earth at supersonic speed would spew so much debris into the atmosphere that the sun would be blotted out. The ensuing 10,000-year winter would eradicate all but the most hardy life forms. As confirmation of such an event, an asteroid strike had been offered as what had ended the dinosaur age.

Any asteroid strike on Earth was serious. Just recently the Russians had been hit by a school bus-size rock. Luckily, no large population centers had been near to suffer the consequences.

But a two-mile-wide rock was another matter. The force of the impact would be felt around the world. The door to the Comm Center opened and a sergeant carrying a sheet of paper walked in.

As the general read the message, the room monitor flicked back on. The image on the screen had identifying marks that it was transmitted from the International Space Station. In orbit 250 miles above Earth, it was the home of six scientists conducting experiments in zero gravity.

Someone on the space station had trained an outside camera in the direction of the asteroid. With part of the space station visible in the foreground, the camera could just pick up an object in the distance. As the object drew closer, the Sun's shadows emphasized the objects shape and gave it definition.

"Hell, that's no asteroid. It's man-made," someone in the conference room yelled.

It was obvious now that no asteroid was threatening Earth. Instead, a very large space vehicle was slowly moving into Earth orbit close to the space station.

"Jesus, look at the size of the mother. Its huge!" a colonel said.

"I just got the report," the general said, holding up his paper. "Its 3500 meters long by 800 meters wide on the end. That is one big space ship."

"Whose is it? Nobody on Earth has anything like that," a colonel stated.

"That's the billion dollar question. Who has the capability to build something that big? Or maybe *what* has that kind of ability?"

Captain Grinkis felt a chill down his back. Who or what was in that space craft was technologically far ahead of anyone on Earth. He had seen the movies over the years of space invaders coming to Earth. The cold feeling of actually witnessing it left him numb.

The entire room watched in silence as the space station camera displayed the alien space craft coming to a stop. Whatever its intent, it had arrived over Earth.

The conference room remained silent as the camera stayed focused on the ship. As a government live feed to military centers around the world, the audio was live. The general had announced that only the video feed was being sent to the commercial TV centers. The general public made due with the network anchor describing the scene.

The commander of the space station gave live updates on the audio feed, and the room listened in.

"The space ship seems to have stopped about four miles to the east of us. It has settled into the same orbit that we are in," the space station reported. "Wait. There's something happening about one quarter the way down the long side of the ship. A door is opening. OK, there appears to be a small space craft exiting the main ship. The door is closing and the small ship is moving away to the east."

The room watched the camera follow the small space craft until it disappeared around the large ship.

"How big would you estimate that small ship to be?" the general asked.

"From the looks, I'd say about our old Space Shuttle size," someone offered. The room murmured agreement.

The Space Station commander came back on the audio and confirmed the size of the small space ship. He went back to describing the larger ship from his vantage point. It appeared from the video to be a large box-shaped vessel with a smooth surface. Dark panels were interspersed with light sections and someone in the room offered that the dark panels might be solar collectors.

As the camera zoomed in for a closer look, everyone strained to see details of the large space ship. The watch continued and the Chief-of-Staff finally suggested to the general that food should be brought into the conference room. And coffee. Lots of coffee. The group looked to be in for a long wait.

Five hours later the small space ship appeared coming in past the International Space Station from the west. NORAD reported that it had tracked the craft as it circled the Earth. It stopped its orbit in three places and appeared to be doing something. When it had moved on,

NORAD had picked up the radar signature of a small satellite that had been left behind.

The general finally spoke up. "The bastards are putting out communication satellites so they are in touch with the entire Earth. I'm not liking the looks of this."

The Space Station camera again displayed the door open on the side of the larger ship and the smaller ship disappeared inside. The door shut tight.

The Space Station commander offered, "The door is shut tight now and I see no other activity." There was a silent pause as everyone in the room saw the sudden change. "Hold on. The middle of the ship is beginning to glow. A blue light is building that wasn't there before. It's getting intense. Too intense to look at. We'll have to watch it on the monitor now."

The TV camera showed the blue light build as the aperture on the camera adjusted to the growing light. Soon, the blue light overwhelmed the camera as everything else on the screen faded to black. The camera aperture was closed down as much as possible and still the blue light grew.

"I'm turning the TV camera away from the space ship before we lose it," the Space Station reported. Then, in the background the room heard, "Get some covers over those ports now, before we get blinded." Everyone knew the alien space ship would be out of view while the intense blue light continued.

Captain Grinkis turned to his friend who was white in horror. Grinkis nudged his fellow captain who snapped out of his trance.

"What is going on? I don't understand," his friend stammered. The confusion on his face spoke volumes.

"As the general said, we're in deep shit," Grinkis offered. From what he had seen, anyone that could construct a space ship this large would probably have the means to defend it. Although the ship hadn't shown any hostile intentions, Captain Grinkis knew he and his platoon weren't about to be part of whatever was coming. He sat back to wait. The captain didn't have to wait long.

The screen suddenly flickered and jumped and the image from inside the Space Station disappeared into static. Then the screen jumped and popped a couple of times and an image of the United Nation's building in New York City came on. It was a live feed as the captain watched the flag move while people came and went about the building.

The scene changed as a person at a lectern in front of the image of the UN building came on the screen. It was a man in a suit and tie who looked to be in his fifties with gray streaks on a full head of hair. If it was possible, it looked to be Cary Grant.

"General, this image is being projected around the world from inside the space craft," the lieutenant in charge of the Comm Center announced at the door.

"We know its from inside the ship? So they look like us, huh?" the general replied.

"Or maybe they have abducted humans and have them standing in their place," a colonel offered.

"Ummm," was all the general could offer to that suggestion.

"People of Earth," the Cary Grant lookalike spokesman said. "I speak to you from the space ship that has taken up orbit next to your Space Station. But, in fact, I speak to all the creatures of Earth today. We come in judgement of all that has transpired on Earth. We represent a Federation of inhabited planets in our galaxy that keeps a watchful eye on all life-bearing planets. We have especially been interested in Earth for some time."

The entire room perked up when 'judgement' was mentioned. These were military men sworn to defend their way of life from all enemies, foreign and domestic. When someone brings up a word like judgement, it raises the fighting spirit in these individuals.

The Carey Grant lookalike spokesman continued. "Earth has been judged by the Federation to have succumbed to species dominance. We are here to correct this situation. We have seen this happen before on other planets and know the resulting disasters that nearly always take place. We will not let that happen here on Earth. We know that you are waiting for us to declare that 'we come in peace'. We won't. We have monitored all your transmissions since you began electronic communications and are quite familiar with your various cultures. You are still a young planet. We have taken on the persona of your famous Hollywood types so that you can feel more assured. Trust me, we do not look like Cary Grant."

As the spokesman paused to let the information sink in, Captain Grinkis said to no one in particular, "Species dominance to be corrected doesn't sound good." The people around him mumbled their concurrence. None of this was sounding good.

Cary Grant continued. "Now, we are quite familiar with your weapons technology. It is of no concern to us.

You may all gather at the UN and work out your attack plans. It will do nothing to us, I can assure you. This is not Hollywood where the drunk guy in a fighter jet figures out our one weak spot and gives his life for humanity. Tomorrow at noon, Greenwich Mean Time, we will demonstrate the futility of resistance. Then you will pay attention to why we are here. Sleep well Earth, for your life is about to change." The Cary Grant lookalike person disappeared from the screen.

In its place a scene from the movie 'Independence Day' came on. It was the climax of the movie where the Randy Quaid character flies his jet up into the death ray of the alien space ship to kill the 'bad guys'.

The room watched the movie clip in silence. The general stood up and clicked off the monitor. "Alright, what can we do to kick some alien ass?"

# Chapter 3

The tension in the small South Seas house couldn't have been more intense. And unknown to them were the developments in the real world. The situation in the South Pacific house was of a more personal tone.

"Professor Brody, where are we?" Karen asked.

Charles Brody stared at the woman in front of him and was lost as to how to answer. This young woman wanted answers. From the look of panic on her face, she probably wanted more answers than he could provide.

From her sarong, he surmised that she had arrived in a similar state as he had. Lying naked in the tent on the beach, he had also stumbled out into the unknown. That had been about a month ago from the calendar he was keeping.

He had discovered the answers to some things, but as to where exactly he was, he was still lost. And as a professor in geography, that was a professional embarrassment.

The best he could surmise was that he was in the South Pacific, about an equal distance south of the equator as Hawaii was north. The trade winds and temperatures this past month had been similar.

He had witnessed the Southern Cross in the sky, so they were definitely south of the equator. And from the other constellations, he placed the land they were on close to 145 degrees. But his knowledge of the stars was limited and he wouldn't bet his life on the longitude.

But he knew enough Chinese to know that the couple in the house were Chinese. Or at least they portrayed themselves as Chinese. Dr. Brody didn't have a good feeling about the couple he had been sharing paradise with up till now. At least now he had a familiar face.

Karen Price was one of his graduate students back in the real world from where he had recently been snatched. How he had gotten to this beach was a blank. He would be surprised if Ms. Price could offer any better insights.

"Ms. Price, I'm afraid I've yet to determine where we are. I've surmised some things, but nothing definitive."

"But how? How did you get here? And why me?" Karen asked.

"All good questions. All unknown to me. And our companions have no language skills conducive to answering our questions I'm afraid. Do you have any recollection of where you were before waking on the beach?"

"Did you arrive the same way?" she asked. "I can't remember anything particular before waking. I certainly remember who you are, but where I was before is a total blank."

"Same for me. I remember you and teaching classes with you in them, but where that took place is a blank. And a month's time hasn't added anything to that blank slate."

Karen sat down in a chair and lowered her head. The professor heard her begin to cry and walked over to her. He bent down and knelt beside her. He placed his arm around her for comfort. He felt her draw back slightly at his closeness. He moved away slightly.

"Now, Ms. Price. No need to get upset. We're alive on a beautiful tropical island. I do know it's an island from climbing to the highest point two weeks ago. We seem to have been supplied with adequate food. Fresh water is plentiful and we have some conveniences. The house has solar power so we have electric lights. And hot water to bath with."

Karen looked up as the tears ran down her cheeks. The corners of her mouth struggled into a slight smile. The professor knew that it was for show only. The Chinese couple saw the slight improvement in their guest's attitude and began clapping. Their smiles announced the release of concern that they had felt at Karen's demeanor.

"That's better. I think Dr. Wu might have some clothes you could have."

At the mention of her name, Dr. Wu perked up. She followed Dr.Brody into the bedroom as he led Karen toward a bureau. The professor pointed at Karen's sarong and motioned to the draws before him.

Dr. Wu appeared to get the message and escorted the professor from the room. She shut the door behind him as he returned to his job cleaning fish. A short while later, Karen and Dr. Wu emerged. Karen was dressed in a simple Chinese dress and carried an armful of other clothes.

"Thank you," Karen said. She bowed to Dr. Wu in acknowledgement of her new wardrobe.

"That's the ticket. If you head down the hallway toward the back door, you'll see your sleeping area. I slept there the first week. It's small but comfortable."

Karen walked down the hall and saw the small alcove in the corner of the house. It held a bed built into the wall. Draws had been placed under the bed. A small desk and reading lamp filled in the remaining space. Karen placed her clothes on the bed and turned to leave.

She almost ran into the Asian man standing while staring at her. She moved past him in the tight space and her breasts rubbed against his arm. As she reached the hallway, Karen noticed there was no door on her alcove.

Back in the main room she commented. "Short on privacy." She indicated the Asian man just leaving the alcove. The man left by the back door.

"Dr. Who? Yeah, he's a little strange," Dr. Brody said.

"Dr. Wu?" she asked.

"No, she's Dr. Wu. He's Dr. Who. I found a piece of paper with their names on it is the only reason I know. Dr. Wu is usually pretty nice. Especially when you get sick."

"Sick?"

"I got real sick the third week I was here. From the Wu Who team, I got that there's some parasite here on the island that can knock you flat. It's not fatal, but not enjoyable either. Dr. Wu nursed me back to health with her herb tea and Chinese chicken soup."

The professor motioned that they should take a walk down the beach for privacy. Karen fell in behind walking down the short trail onto the sand. When they were an appropriate distance from the house and any prying ears, Dr. Brody said, "Be careful with those two. They act like they don't know English, but I wouldn't bet my life on that fact."

"I've noticed they paid attention just in the little bit of conversation we've had."

"Exactly. And there's something not right about them. I can't put my finger on it, but ever since I landed here, there's been a certain feeling I've had about those two that they aren't what they appear to be."

"You said you've been here a month, Professor?" Karen asked. "And you arrived the same way I did?" She blushed slightly at the reference to her naked arrival.

The Professor noticed her slight embarrassment and offered, "Naked as a jaybird. Yep. Walked right up to Dr. Wu in the buff. But she didn't seem all that taken back now that I remember."

"Well, Dr. Who was certainly checking me out until Dr. Wu gave me some clothes to put on. He's a 'creeper', if you ask me."

"One of the reasons I moved out of the house. I had the alcove when I arrived. I found it a little too close for comfort to the Wu Who team."

"Where did you move? I haven't seen any other buildings."

With that inquiry, the professor changed direction and lead Karen back toward the house. Before reaching the short trail to the South Sea style house, he led her to the right onto a trail going back from the beach. They reached a fork and he turned left. Soon a rock cliff loomed up out of the undergrowth as they walked uphill.

They passed a small 20'x 20' shed structure. Only one door was visible on the building that had no windows The shed did have slatted vents near the roof eaves for ventilation. The same large tropical trees that shaded the house also provided shade for the shed.

Dr. Brody continued ahead as the trail got steeper. A small cabin appeared atop the cliff over their left shoulder. The trail wound up the cliff face onto an open shelf. Straight ahead lay a protected bay with two headlands coming together to form a narrow opening from the ocean.

The professor turned left at the top of the cliff and walked toward a small cabin. Like the shed below, this building was about 20' x 20'. But unlike the shed, windows wrapped around the entire structure with a large roof overhang for sun protection.

A lanai, or covered deck, was attached on the bay side of the cabin. A hammock swung in the tropical breeze. Dr. Brody walked through the open doors, leaving his sandals on the lanai. Karen followed, walking barefoot onto the hardwood floors of the cabin. It was cool inside as the trade winds moved fresh air through the windows.

"It's beautiful up here," she said. Looking down on the house nestled under the tropical canopy of trees, the beach she had arrived on was evident as it stretched out to her left in the distance. Looking to the right was another beach stretching out to a distant rocky point. The main house sat on the only high ground between these two beaches.

Unlike the main house though, the cabin sat about 100' above the beach, allowing the trade winds unobstructed access to the cabin. It felt 10 degrees cooler up here than in the main house.

"Yes, the trade winds are very constant here so the cabin stays cool all day. Even at night, I shut about half the windows and it maintains a comfortable sleeping temperature till morning. The extra heat when the sun hits the cabin acts like an alarm clock."

Karen surveyed the small one-room cabin. A queen bed took up one corner with a small kitchen in the opposite corner. A sink, two-burner stove and a small college-style refrigerator made up the kitchen. Shelves below the counter held the utensils as well as metal containers.

A bureau with draws and a short book case were along one wall. In the other corner was a comfy chair with a couch next to it. The fourth corner held a small table with two chairs. The most notable thing about the cabin was that nothing reached higher than the continuous windows. The room had an unobstructed view in all directions.

"Professor, I don't see a bathroom."

"Outside. I'll show you." He led her onto the lanai. On the other side was what appeared to be a small closet. The professor walked in to a small area with a flush toilet. The area was open toward the bay and commanded a view in two directions.

"Wow, talk about a room with a view," Karen said as she observed the ocean facing commode.

"The shower is even better." The professor led her back outside. Attached to the outside wall of the toilet building was a shower head. Two brief walls that extended from knee height to shoulder height were all the modesty offered. The third side facing the cabin was wide open.

"And there's plenty of hot water?"

"As much as you need in the daytime. We have solar panels on the roof and electricity to run the pumps. The hot water will last all night if you don't use too much. But the sun provides plenty." The professor looked at his student. "Excuse me. Where's my manners? Did you want to take a shower?"

"Maybe later, thanks. I don't think I want to be taking any down with Wu Who."

"Don't blame you there. Just let me know when, and I'll make sure you have some privacy."

Dr. Brody looked at his watch. "Excuse me again. I've forgotten the time in all the excitement of your arrival. I know I'm getting hungry. You must be starved."

"I hadn't thought about it till you just mentioned it. I am a little bit hungry."

"Splendid. We'll have lunch on the lanai. You can relax and let the whole situation soak in. I know I was in shock for a week when I arrived here. I'm still a little bit shaky on what is going on."

"Thank you, you're very kind," Karen said.

The professor noticed her eyes begin to tear up as she said it. He walked over and put his arm around her to offer some comfort. She didn't pull away this time at his physical demonstration.

"There, there. It will be OK. We English speakers need to stick together."

Karen attempted a smile and Dr. Brody noticed her body ease a bit at his show of support.

"There's a sink in the toilet room if you want to wash up. I'll throw some lunch together."

Karen was sitting at the outdoor table under the protective roof of the lanai when Dr. Brody walked out carrying a tray. Arrayed on the tray were two plates with sandwiches and two glasses with ice water in them. A slice of lemon floated in the drinking water.

"Wow, this looks wonderful! We have ice and everything. Where did all this come from?"

"The lemon is easy." The professor proceeded to point over Karen's shoulder at the lemon tree a short distance away. Next to it was an orange tree with mangos and papayas growing nearby. "Dr. Wu makes bread every other day. The tuna for the filling comes from my fishing trips twice a week. Lettuce and tomatoes come from the garden."

Again the professor pointed out the large garden growing below the cabin. Karen reacted as if it was the first time she had noticed it.

"Oh my! That's a garden all right."

Stretched out below them was a large garden flourishing with food. From the shelf that the cabin sat on, a small slope led down to a large elongated flat area. A stream flowed out from a banana grove located across the flat. A large hill climbed up in the distance that fed the stream

Once the slow-moving stream reached the end of the bench, it plunged over the cliff toward the main house. A small dam held the water back just before the drop, forming a large pond beside the garden.

"Plenty of water and sunshine. Good fertile volcanic soil. Everything grows like weeds. The corn and wheat aren't adapted to the tropical climate, but still produce enough for the few people here. All the vegetables should grow year round so we don't have to can anything. We just have to save the seeds and plant a new crop every few months."

Karen ate her tuna sandwich. She was quiet as she seemed to be thinking through her next question. "This sandwich has mayonnaise in it. Don't tell me you make your own?"

"We could. We have chickens over there by the garden. And we have stored oil. But no, this is commercial mayo. Seems that we have a number of items that were brought here sometime. They're stored in a cool dry place and seem to be still edible. Been eating it for a month now and haven't keeled over yet."

Karen smiled at the professor's attempt at humor. Her smile faded as she took another bite. The professor knew what was coming.

"Professor, I don't mean to be a nuisance, but what are we doing here?"

Dr. Brody put his sandwich down on the plate. He took a sip of cold water and let his thoughts collect before he answered. "Ms. Price, I've been dwelling on the question for a month solid. Why am I here and who brought me here? Now, I've added you to that equation. I think I need to show you something. If you're done with lunch."

Karen's expression showed that her appetite had suddenly disappeared. The way the professor had announced that he had something to show her had killed any other interest. She stood up and followed the professor back into his cabin.

He stopped in front of the bureau and opened the middle drawer. Laying there were some shirts next to some slacks.

"Dr. Wu found some clothes for you too," Karen said.

He looked at the print dress that fell from Karen's frame. It was a bit small for her. The bust area was noticeably tight and the length brought the dress to half way up her thigh.

Karen noticed the professor looking at the shortness of her dress and attempted to pull it down.

"My point. Dr. Wu is about 6" shorter than you and maybe 3 sizes smaller. Your dress is small for you, but considering the options, it works."

Karen looked at the professor with a quizzical look on her face.

"I'm sure you'll find the other clothes she gave you similarly small for you." The professor turned and pulled out a pair of pants. "Now, Dr. Who is a good 8" shorter than me. He's about as big around as me on his upper body, so the shirts should be about my size. But check this."

Dr. Brody pulled the slacks on and pulled them up. At 6' 1" in height, he had long legs. Especially compared to the much shorter Chinese male who had provided the clothes.

As Karen watched, Dr. Brody pulled the pants right up and over his nylon shorts. He snugged them shut and zipped up the fly. He stood straight and looked at Karen. Then he pointed down toward his feet. The pant cuffs were dragging on the wooden floor.

"Exact length for me, if I was wearing shoes. Now, how did a 5' 5" man have pants for a 6' 1" man? And I have more than one pair. And I have two pairs of boots that fit me like they were made for me. If you look at Dr. Who's feet, there's no way we're even close."

Karen looked up at Dr. Brody and then back down at the pant cuffs. When she looked up again, Dr. Brody spoke.

"It was as if they knew I was coming."

# Chapter 4

New York, New York

The United States Mission to the United Nations was located in a building off E. 44th St. just a block from the U.N. Building. The front of the building overlooked the East River.

Al Worthington, Assistant Consul to the U.S. Ambassador to the U.N. sat in his 8th floor office and twisted in his seat. He had his desk arranged so that when he needed time to just think, he could turn his reclining chair and see the river.

He was staring at a barge and tug plying the waters when his door suddenly opened. The U.S. Ambassador walked in unannounced. Such behavior in the diplomatic corps was not common, even if this was his boss intruding. Polite manners were more the norm in the Mission.

But since yesterday, polite manners had vaporized. Panic mode had taken over ever since the alien announcement had been made. The U.N. had been singled out for the alien announcement and the U.N. Security Council had been immediately convened.

With only one more hour remaining until the stated alien demonstration as to their intentions, the U.N. members had retreated to their respective missions. The entire Security Council had been meeting non-stop since the challenge had been thrown and the U.S. Ambassador was due to return to the council shortly.

"Al, do we have anything to work with yet?" the ambassador asked.

One of Al's jobs was to liaison with the U.S. Department of Defense, and he had been in constant contact with the Pentagon since the alien announcement. Along with a three-star Army general who had suddenly shown up at the Mission, the two had tried to find some answers to the dilemma facing Earth. Any threat to Earth would naturally include the United States.

Even the Russians and the Chinese were suddenly being noticeably agreeable. The antagonistic attitude toward the U.S. that had prevailed for years was suddenly missing. The aliens had brought all the countries together in one quick motion.

"Madam Ambassador, I'm afraid not. The general and I have been busy in the Comm Center reviewing all traffic from our various units. The Space Station report is still the most informative. But since they shut down any observation due to that blue light, we have little that's new."

"No readings on any other electronic searches?"

"We've got everything we have attempting to probe the main ship. No scans are getting through. Those satellites they deployed are active and sending signals back to the main ship. But we haven't been able to break into their transmission links. They seem to have some very sophisticated encryption going on. It's far above anything we've ever dealt with," Al offered.

"So, no news is bad news, in this case. We just have to wait and see what 'species domination' means and what 'correction' will entail. Not a good situation."

"No Mam'. But at least the Commander-in-Chief is secure," Al said.

"We can hope. Cheyenne Mountain was designed to withstand a Russian nuclear attack. Having the Rocky Mountains over your head should do the job. We have a direct feed to the Comm Center there so we can relay between the Security Council and the President. If these aliens continue to choose to deal with the U.N., that is."

"Yes, I guess we'll see what noon in London brings us," Al said. A noon announcement in London where Greenwich Mean Time originated, meant a 7 AM announcement in New York.

"Get your things. I want you with me when we hear the news. Bring the encrypted laptop computer so we can check with the Comm Center."

Al gathered his papers and stuffed them into his computer bag. He checked that the secure laptop was in the bag and zipped it close. Putting on his coat and pulling the bag strap over his shoulder, he followed the ambassador out of the building.

Security personnel joined them for the short walk to the U.N. Building. Already large crowds had gathered in the blocked off streets. Police kept the people behind the barricades that never seemed to leave the U.N. area.

But unlike the typical protests that always seemed to be occurring in front of the U.N., this crowd was subdued. These people had come to see what fate awaited Earth in the form of creatures from another world.

A large plasma screen had been installed on the sidewalk so that the crowd could receive the broadcast if the aliens made their announcement public. Many in the crowd voiced their concern that only the members of the U.N. would be privy to any message. That seemed to be how government worked lately: the ruling elite making decisions for the masses. And this crowd was acting as though they were ready to end 'business as usual'.

The police kept a close eye out for trouble when the U.S. Ambassador and her staff walked up.

"Keep the people informed," someone in the crowd yelled.

"Yeah, don't do your usually back-room deals hidden from the people," a man yelled.

"We want the truth," another screamed.

"That chickenshit President has already hightailed out of here with his family. He's safe in his bunker. What about the rest of us?" a woman barked.

The police shifted to this new threatening tone. Al keep his gait strong and headed to the opening in the security fence leading to the U.N. grounds. The ambassador ignored the taunts and jeers as she led the delegation to the secure area.

One of the crowd finally yelled in good New York fashion, "Fuggedaboudit. Those shitheads will save themselves first. We're on our own, people." A cheer went up from most of the crowd at the man's words.

The police moved toward the man as he slinked back into the crowd. The crowd closed ranks to restrain the police while the man slipped away.

Once inside the General Assembly building, Al offered, "I'm not sure that we will be able to walk back to the Mission, Madam Ambassador."

"I think you're right. Call and have them ready the Suburbans. We'll use the parking garage entrance when we leave."

Al stopped and called the Mission, the remaining group continuing on to the Security Council chambers. Al caught up and took a seat along the wall behind the ambassador. He pulled out his laptop and turned it on. Working through the security, he finally connected with the Comm Center in the Mission. The general in charge acknowledged his connection.

The entire Security Council eventually filled the room where they sat quiet, watching the clock. A large screen on the front of the room was switched on but only carried the blue and white image of the U.N. logo. Due to the early morning hour and the late night sessions, everyone was subdued.

It was evident that the other countries had come up with nothing on the alien invaders. It had been agreed that if any one country came up with more information, then the council would meet during the night to discuss the findings.

Coffee cups were evident throughout the room as the members and their staffs fought fatigue and nerves. None knew the consequence of the alien visit. They waited anxiously to find out.

The second hand on the large clock marking London time swept around to 12 noon and the screen image jumped. It flicked a couple of times and then changed to the image of the UN building on the East River. An empty lectern sat in the middle of the screen image.

A person appeared on the edge of the screen and walked to the lectern where they turned and faced the camera. It was a double of Betty Davis today. The Cary Grant character was gone.

The Betty Davis double began, "Earthlings. We announced yesterday our intent to demonstrate our power today. We have monitored your feeble attempts to interdict our communications. We commend you on the wise decision to refrain from immediate nuclear attack on our ship. That would have been futile and would have only antagonized us further. For showing such restraint you will only receive half of what we intended."

Al looked around the Security Council. Everyone was transfixed on the image. Having Betty Davis, or whoever or whatever she really was, lecture them on restraint was interesting.

A total nuclear attack had been the first thing discussed right after the first announcement. It had taken a lot of diplomacy to check the 'attack first' crowd. But the group that had wanted a major nuclear strike against the main ship was still active. Hearing that the aliens had recognized the Earth's inaction and would reduce the demonstration seemed to lift the appeasement crowd.

Betty Davis continued her speech, which broke Al's thoughts. "After today's demonstration you will have five days to think about what you have seen. We will then set our program for 'species adjustment' before you." The screen flickered and Betty was gone. The blue and white U.N. image took her place.

The room exploded, the members all talking at once about what they had just heard.

"And what the hell is this 'species adjustment'?. It doesn't sound good," the U.S. ambassador yelled. She turned to her staff to see if the demonstration had shown up yet. Al shook his head to indicate that there was no news of anything happening.

The chairman of the Security Council banged the gavel and the room went quiet. Then he turned to the U.N .staff to enquire of any news of a demonstration. The staff shook their heads.

It was a very pregnant thirty-minute wait until Al's secure link to U.S. military command chatted to life. The noise of the buzzer he had set to warn him of arriving news startled the room. Everyone turned their gaze to him.

He quickly read the message. It was brief and was followed by a second message, the buzz sound announcing its arrival. Everyone in the room sat anxious for the news.

"Madam Ambassador, will you please read these two messages? I believe they're suitable for the entire room," Al offered. He knew he should be careful with U.S. military communications, but under the circumstances he would risk censure.

The U.S. Ambassador took the laptop and read the two messages to herself. She wanted to make sure no vital U.S. secrets were contained in either note. Confident that none existed, she said, "Both messages originate from U.S. Far East Command, Seoul, Korea. The first message states: Frontline commanders on the DMZ between North and South Korea report no visible sign of life on the opposite side. Moving to investigate."

The Chinese Ambassador demanded, "What are they saying?"

The others shushed him quiet. The chairman asked what the second message said.

The U.S. Ambassador continued. "The second message says: All North Korean troops have abandoned border. U.S. and South Korean commanders have moved over the border into North Korean positions. Unable to find a living soul. All vehicles still parked but no people."

"This sounds like an imperialist trick. We will support our North Korean brothers in their struggle against the West," the Chinese Ambassador yelled.

"Mr. Ambassador, I can assure you this is no Western trick. We need to wait for further reports," the American ambassador said.

The council seemed to be satisfied with that suggestion. They would have to wait an hour before the buzz sound startled everyone.

Al again read over the message on the laptop before he reluctantly handed it to his boss. His boss took the diplomatic advice.

"Before I read this next message, I want to get something straightened out. We have alien beings hovering over our world threatening us with 'species adjustment'. We cannot play our usual accusatory games between ourselves. We either face this together, or the aliens will destroy us all."

"Who says the aliens are here to destroy us all?" the French Ambassador asked.

The entire room turned toward the U.S. Ambassador. The chairman broke the silence. "Madam Ambassador, I will speak for everyone in this room to say that we look to the United States and its world-wide resources. At least for information at this time. We will refrain from any further accusations if you will share what is going on in the world."

The U.N. information people were noticeably quiet. Their computer links hadn't provided any news. Nor had any of the other nations present in the room. Only one country had a world-wide reach.

Looking directly at the Chinese Ambassador, the U.S. Ambassador said, "Very well. With those assurances, I will read the latest message. It's from the U.S. Commander to Headquarters, Far East Command, Seoul, South Korea. It reads: Have reached outskirts of Pyongyang. Have encountered no human life. Entire population seems to have disappeared. Cars and trucks are sitting in road with motors running. No drivers. Live farm animals in fields. No dead human bodies encountered. Advise."

Just as everyone was about to ask what it all meant, the door opened to the hallway. A Chinese staff member quickly walked in and handed a note to the Chinese Ambassador. He read the note and turned white. The room waited.

Through the translator, they learned the contents. "From Supreme Headquarters, People's Liberation Army, Beijing. Our Party Chairman announces that the night time darkness near the North Korean border was broken by a blue beam of light. The source came across the sky from alien satellite to satellite from the main ship. It crossed China and then came to Earth over North Korea. Our border units report that the blue light quickly scanned the entire country and then stopped."

"It's that blue light we saw from the Space Station. Is that all the reports says?" the French Ambassador asked.

"No, there's more. Chinese border guards report no North Korean guards at their posts after the blue light. They have moved into North Korea to investigate and report no people seen. They've all disappeared."

The U.S. Ambassador had slid her chair back to consult privately with her staff when Al's alarm went off. The ambassador read sitting next to Al. It was more news from the Korean Peninsula. The Security Council waited.

"New report. One of our special biological warfare units was at the DMZ. It has driven into North Korea. It reports that it has tested a white powder found in numerous homes of the local people. The powder was found in the beds of the locals, under the blankets," the US Ambassador stopped. The full Council waited, assuming there was more. "I'm afraid the quick tests confirmed human DNA in the dust. The medical officer describes the dust as 'freeze dried humans'."

"Ladies and gentleman," the British Ambassador announced. "I think from what information we have so far, we can assume that the entire population of North Korea has been vaporized. Twenty-five million people have been wiped out as a demonstration by the aliens."

"Then this means war!" the Russian Ambassador screamed. He had been the leader of the 'attack first' group on the Security Council.

# Chapter 5

Colorado Springs, Colorado

The word of the North Korea demonstration spread throughout the world like wild fire. Evidence followed as Chinese, U.S. and South Korean forces searched in vain for any human life. Even the vast underground tunnels that the North had constructed in anticipation of an attack were empty.

Plenty of the now-infamous white dust was found in the tunnels, proving that the blue ray could reach anywhere. DNA samples confirmed that the dust had previously been living, breathing human beings.

And everywhere throughout the former North Korean territory, live healthy animals roamed at will. None showed any ill effects from the blue ray that had decimated the human population.

Open rancor raged between the countries that wished to retaliate for North Korea's slaughter. The opposing group continued to council caution. The comment from the Betty Davis character that the demonstration had been reduced in recognition of Earth's restraint on aggression was repeated. If the aliens could vaporize an entire country in about thirty minutes, who could project what the blue beam was capable of destroying?

Captain Chet Grinkis sat at his new post and contemplated what exactly he was supposed to be doing. His sergeant sat nearby at his desk, busy with paperwork.

Both had been flown out of McChord Air Force Base shortly after the first Cary Grant announcement.

The entire platoon of Special Ops had been transferred to Colorado Springs. Their stated mission was to provide additional security to Cheyenne Mountain.

*But how much more secure could Cheyenne Mountain become?* Chet wondered. A NORAD missile command base dug deep under the Rocky Mountains, Cheyenne Mountain represented the epitome of secure facilities. Designed to withstand a Soviet nuclear attack in the Cold War, the underground command center was about as secure as it got.

A company or two of Special Forces sitting outside the mountain sure didn't up the security much in Chet's mind. But with the President and his family arriving shortly after his unit had, the Defense Department was pulling out the all the stops. *Total waste of everybody's time,* Chet thought.

If the Commander-In-Chief wanted to feel better with a couple complements of Army Special Forces teamed up with some Navy Seals, who was he to question it? It had been like 'old home week' over the last few days as units continued to show up.

Warriors that he had trained with over the years as well as other Special Ops personnel were all getting caught up on personal news. With the President under 5,000 feet of granite, there wasn't much else to do.

"Sergeant Aubin, you have the PT schedule all set for the men. No need letting the time be wasted while we screw the pooch sitting here."

"No, Sir. We're ready to hit it hard tomorrow. The chief for the Seals and I have worked out a course. Seems like we're about to start some inter-service rivalry. Or continuing, I should say. We've already informed the men that unit pride will be on the line starting tomorrow. Loser gets the shitty end of the stick, whenever we figure what the hell the stick is," Sergeant Aubin said.

"Good work. Does that challenge include officers?"

"Affirmative, Sir."

"Should we take the men through the course this afternoon then? A little recon seems in order."

"Way ahead of you Sir. Already got the men on that one. We move out at 1400."

When Chet's outfit arrived at the nearby golf course, they were surprised to find the Navy Seal unit already there. The two commanding officers greeted each other.

"Seems we had similar plans. A little recon on the objective," the Navy lieutenant said.

"Well, since we're both here and the competition doesn't start till tomorrow, what do you say we perform a more casual recon together?"

"Sounds good. My chief has explained the course to me, so why don't I lead out?"

"Then lead away. Sergeant, you and the chief will observe that this is a friendly jaunt today. No extracurricular activities will be allowed," Captain Grinkis offered.

The Navy lieutenant led off with Captain Grinkis beside him. The men of the two units filled in behind their commanders as they ran over the undulating ground on the golf course. While not an obstacle course that each unit would be more familiar with, both units enjoyed the workout. And with the high elevation of Colorado Springs, the thin air added to the work load.

"I hear the Air Force Academy has a course. Maybe we should check that out?" the Seal lieutenant said.

"You think those flyboys have anything like what we're used to?" Chet asked.

"Certainly not. But it might be more challenging than a golf course."

As they rounded the 10th tee headed out for the 'back nine', they ran into a bevy of suits with ear pieces. The military men quickly recognized a security detail from the Secret Service. Chet looked around as to why the Presidential protectors were out here on the golf course.

Then it hit him. *I haven't seen any other golfers since we started our run,* he thought. Chet progressed to the point where he concluded that it couldn't be happening. That was when the runners were stopped by a man in a suit talking into his sleeve.

"Sorry men. You can't go out on the back nine. We let you have the front nine for your run, but you can't go any further."

"What are you telling me? That the golf course is in use?" Captain Grinkis inquired.

"I'm not saying anything, but you can't go any further. Just turn around and run to your hearts content on the front nine."

"Come on, men. Our Commander-in-Chief has priority for the back nine. We'll do another lap around the front," Chet said with a certain exasperation showing. He looked at his Seal counterpart and got a similar exasperated look in return.

# Chapter 6

It had been four days since someone had somehow deposited her on the beach. And she had had enough of the weird Dr. Who by the second day. Without any means of dividing off her personal space, sleep was impossible in her small alcove in the main house.

It seemed that each time she had to change clothes or use the toilet, Dr. Who was standing nearby watching. And even in her sleep, she always had the feeling that he was close by watching her.

The only relief had been Dr. Brody's offer that she could use his outdoor shower. With the tropical heat and work required to keep the garden producing food, a shower at the end of the day was necessary. Thankfully, the professor ran interference while she took her shower.

It seemed that the professor had impressed on Dr. Who that the cabin area was off limits. In the short time she had been on the island, she had witnessed Dr. Who working hard to avoid ever going near the professor's cabin. Dr. Wu would politely ask if she could approach the cabin and the professor was cordial most times to allow it.

Karen had reached a decision after careful consideration. Today would be the day she would broach the subject with Dr. Brody. They seemed to be getting along well as they tended to the tasks of living their isolated existence.

With only two of them speaking English, it wasn't as if they had much choice. Karen had estimated the professor to be in his early 60's. From her time taking his classes, the talk of the other students had been that he was a widower. It seemed that his wife had died some time back from breast cancer. The other news she knew about Dr. Brody was that he had three children, all married and living somewhere away from the professor.

But for a man of his age, a month in the sun working in the fields and eating a clean diet had certainly leaned him up. She had never seen him in their past life in shorts without a shirt, but over the last three days she would admit that the professor was a good looking guy.

He had a strong upper body that now sported a dark tan. His legs were muscular as if he had worked out during his teaching career. She had seen lots of men the professor's age with sagging chests and accumulated fat in the middle. The professor had none of these signs of old age.

Dr. Brody even had a good head of hair. It was gray, but that just added to his distinguishing features. And he hadn't let the island life get to him by letting himself go. He shaved every day and kept himself and his clothes clean. *For being stuck in wherever the hell she was stuck, things could be worse,* she thought. *Like having Dr. Who being your sole companion. That would bite.*

Karen straightened up from the row of lettuce she was cultivating. She surmised that it must be close to lunch time. The professor had been prompt each day announcing lunch. It would be the perfect time to broach the subject. She arched her back to get the kinks out and lifted the wide brimmed hat she had taken to wearing while in the garden for protection from the blazing sun.

All four wore long pants, long-sleeved shirts with wide hats while working. The tropical sun beat down mercilessly and required a mid-day break. The typical day consisted of field work for a couple hours in the morning, a siesta during midday, followed by more field work late afternoon. It made for a long lunch break and Karen was determined to use it today to her advantage.

"Lunch," the professor yelled. The Wu Who couple had already disappeared down to their house. Karen carried her cultivator tool over to the small tool shed by the garden and hung it on the tool rack. She climbed the short hill to the cabin.

The change in the air was divine. While the garden sweltered in the small depression between the large hill and the shelf that held the cabin, here the trade winds relieved the heat. The sweat on her body felt cool as the wind caused it to evaporate.

She sat down after washing up in the expansive toilet room. "Don't tell me, tuna sandwiches again."

"You'll be surprised." The professor walked out with his tray. He placed the ice water down and then served the plate. The expected sandwich bread was visible but no lettuce was protruding.

Karen picked up the top slice and exclaimed, "Fried egg sandwich! That's a welcome treat." She began to eat while the professor placed a green salad down. "Aren't we getting fancy? Salad and a sandwich. Do we have dressing?"

Without saying a word, the professor placed a small bowl on the table with a white creamy sauce in it. "Don't tell me." Karen dipped he pinky finger in the sauce and tasted it. "Well, I'll be, fresh Ranch dressing. How did you ever . . ."

"The ways of the island are mysterious somedays. Just enjoy the treat."

Karen complied with the professor and ate heartily. The combination of sun and work in the garden had increased her appetite since her arrival. The two enjoyed their lunch sitting under the cover of the lanai roof. The trade winds kept the temperature on the warm but comfortable range.

Karen knew the time was ripe for her to broach her question. She took a long sip of ice water and looked at the professor.

"Dr. Brody, I have something I've been meaning to discuss with you."

The professor stopped eating and placed his sandwich down on his plate. His expression turned to one of concern from the tone that Karen had asked the question. "What is it, Ms. Price?"

"Please call me Karen. Since we're a captured audience so to speak, I'd like it if you could call me Karen."

"I'd be happy to, but only if you call me Charles."

She stopped short on his request. She had only ever thought of him as the professor or Dr. Brody. She wasn't even sure that she had known previously his first name.

"Yes, I can do that, Charles." The name came out of her mouth with a certain hesitance to it.

"Good, now that we have that settled, what's on your mind, Karen?"

The sudden informality of the situation threw her off her task. She hesitated to re-focus on the main issue she wanted to discuss.

"Charles, you'll agree that Dr. Who is a bit strange. And you said yourself that living down at the main house when you first arrived was difficult."

"Yes, I did say that. I lasted a few days before I moved up here."

"Well, I hope you can imagine how much worse it is for a female living down there with Dr. Who as my constant companion. I woke up the other night with him sitting in my alcove staring at me."

"I'm sorry for that. Did you let him know in your tone that such behavior wasn't acceptable?"

"I tried. I screamed and made enough hand signs I hope he got the message. With the language barrier, I'm not so sure I got through to him though," Karen said.

"I'll try to get to him if you'd like. He's gotten the message pretty well that this cabin is off limits."

"That's the point I wanted to bring up. Is there any way you could see yourself letting me stay up here in your cabin?"

The words had been put out. Karen closed her eyes and prayed that she wouldn't be rejected outright. She didn't know how much longer she could stay in the main house. If her request was dismissed, she was ready to try moving to the tent on the beach to escape Dr. Who's careful care.

"Oh. Well. Hmmm." Dr. Brody cleared his throat.

"Please, Dr. Brody. I won't be a bother. I'd be happy to sleep in the hammock here on the lanai. Anything to get out of the main house," Karen said, slipping back to formalities in her excitement.

"Remember, Charles." he reminded her. "I just don't know. The cabin is very small with no privacy. Even the shower and toilet have no doors. And with just one room to live in, it would be very close living."

"I can adjust to that. We can work out a system for the shower and toilet so we don't intrude on each other. Please Charles, I'm desperate. I'm ready to move to the tent on the beach if I have to."

"Oh no, that would be worse. You'd be all by yourself out there. At least in the main house Dr. Wu is close by and can be of some help if Dr. Who gets out of line. Out on the beach, no one would hear you if you needed help."

"Then I can stay here with you. I'll help with the chores and won't be in your way," she pleaded. Tears started to well up. She didn't want to revert to the old female ploy of the emotional appeal, but she couldn't control it. She was desperate to get away from Dr. Who.

Charles stood up and walked over to offer her his hand. She relaxed at the comfort offered by the professor.

"Don't worry. We'll see what we can work out. We'll go down and get your things and move you up here. There's room in the bureau to store your clothes."

"Thank you, Charles. Thank you." Karen moved away from the professor and began to walk toward the trail to the main house. Dr. Brody fell in behind her. She glanced at the hammock as she walked by. *I guess I can sleep in that,* she thought. A recollection of some history book flashed in her brain that had the image of old sailing ships with men in hammocks stacked cheek to jowl. *If they could survive life below decks in a hammock, I guess I can live swinging to the trade winds,* she thought. She soon found out that she wouldn't have to test the swinging hammock sleeping theory.

# Chapter 7

New York, New York

Since the Betty Davis look-alike had set her timetable, the ensuing five days had been one of rancor at the United Nations. Several members of the Security Council were siding with the Russians for a nuclear attack on the alien space craft. The United States was leading the contingent of members that were calling for restraint. France was leading the remaining countries that didn't know what to do.

"Your appeasement will lead to ruin. Just as British appeasement 70 years ago led to the nightmare of Hitler. We have to strike and we need to do it now," the Russian Ambassador argued for what seemed the hundredth time.

Five days of lengthy meetings had led to nothing. Neither side could get the votes needed as the neutral countries sat and dithered. To Al Worthington, that fed into the U.S. position for not attacking. Any delay on attacking kept the status quo as it was.

"Mr. Ambassador, we have argued this issue to the point of exhaustion. We don't know if a nuclear attack will be successful. And as the aliens stated, our showing restraint saved someone a fate similar to the North Koreans," the U. S. Ambassador said.

"And we won't find out if a nuclear attack will be successful until we attempt it. If we're all going to suffer 'species adjustment', whatever the hell that is, I'd rather go down fighting."

"And if we don't take out the space ship, what will the blue light bring us. It sure didn't seem to take much effort killing twenty-five million Koreans. Will we antagonize the aliens to the point that humanity will be adjusted off the planet?"

The French Ambassador broke in the discussion. "I agree, 'species adjustment' sounds better than 'species extinction'."

"The Russian people aren't afraid to take the challenge. If this body won't approve common action, then we are ready to act alone."

The entire room had been prepared to hear the call for unilateral action by one member. Now that it had been said, all the members stopped the discussion as they contemplated the Russian challenge.

The Russian Ambassador took the quiet non-response as a tacit agreement. He stood up and left the room, his staff members following in his wake.

"Since we have eight hours till our next command performance from the aliens, I suggest we retire to our missions to await further developments. May God look down on our friends the Russians and what they are about to do," the U. S. Ambassador said.

* * *

But God must have been looking the other way as Al joined the ambassador in the Situation Room at the U.S. Mission. Sitting next to the general that handled military affairs for the emergency, Al watched the large screen as information flowed in from around the world.

U.S. intelligence sources were working overtime trying to stay on top of any changing dynamics concerning the aliens. The U.S. spy satellites had continued to function with no interference from the aliens.

It was two of these satellites that gave the people in the room a firsthand account of what transpired next. It became obvious that the Russians had been planning their nuclear attack since the first day of the alien ship arrival. It had only been a couple of hours since the Russian Ambassador's claim of independent action and now the U.S. satellites picked up the launch of six intercontinental ballistic missiles from bases in Siberia.

With the alien space ship in orbit above the equator at the time of the missile launch, the point of contact between the missiles and space ship would be over the Atlantic Ocean. Al quickly thought of the crew on the International Space Station who were about to discover that being only two miles from the aliens was going to be a death sentence.

The six missiles would be carrying multiple warheads of unknown size. Russia had kept its nuclear capacity quiet after the breakup of the old Soviet Union. *That the Russians had six operational missiles that could launch was impressive,* Al thought.

After the collapse of Communism, the Russian economy lacked the resources to sustain the large military capabilities that the Soviets had built. Ships, planes and missiles fell into disrepair. Lately, with the increased value of Russian oil and natural gas, its economy was on the upswing. The Russian military was rebuilding itself, but Al still wondered how many of the warheads would explode.

The room grew tense as the large computer screen at the front of the room showed the trajectories of the climbing missiles. At the point where the missiles opened to release the separate nuclear warheads, the satellite trackers indicated the six separate objects.

Thirty-six high-explosive nuclear bombs streaked through space, aimed at the aliens. Everyone held their breath for the expectant explosions. The general announced that both U.S. satellites were at a distance that would allow them to survive the resulting explosions. No mention was made of the nearby International Space Station and its crew of twelve scientists.

"Hey, what's going on down there?" a voice came over the audio. The screen scrolled the words in a separate box in the corner with the tag line that the transmission was emanating from the commander of the Space Station.

Suddenly a TV image flickered on a different box. It was an image of the alien space ship from the Space Station. The blue light that had blinded the camera for the last ten days was gone. An ominous red light now emanated from the space ship. Its lower intensity combined with its wavelength allowed viewing by the camera.

"Things are happening up here, and I don't think its good. I can see multiple red lights being emitted from the alien space ship, all aimed at Earth. And they all seem to be directed toward Europe. Is something going on we should know about?" the commander asked.

The audio was quiet as ground control remained mute to the commander's question.

"Hey, wake up down there! I think some bad shit is about to happen and-" His transmission stopped in mid-sentence.

Al looked at the main screen and saw the answer. But where everyone was expecting to see indications of detonations against the alien space ship, the spy satellites were showing multiple warheads now reversed and returning toward Earth. It was quickly determined that each one was being directed somehow back toward the attacker. The room waited for the results.

The satellites began recording the strikes on Russian cities as each warhead exploded in sequence. Thirty-six separate targets glowed red on the screen as three dozen Russian cites went up in smoke.

"Holy shit! What the hell just happened?" The Space Station commander came back on the audio.

"This is Ground Control. We read you. Can you give us a visual update? Those were Russian nuclear missiles that were to take out the alien space craft. It appears that the aliens tracked them back upon their attacker."

"Well, you think? No body was willing to clue us in up here? We're in the same neighborhood you dim wits. It's bad enough we have who-knows-what right next to us in that space craft, but to have a bunch of stunned mullets on the ground doesn't help our situation up here," the commander yelled.

"Sorry, Commander. We didn't know the Russians were going to attack," Ground Control lied.

"Well, try to keep us a little bit in the loop, will you?" The Commander calmed down a little. "As for our space buddies next door, the red lights are gone. The blue light is building so we'll be shutting down the camera and closing up our viewing ports."

The U.S. Ambassador stood up at the front of the conference room and asked that the audio be turned down. With everyone's full attention, she said, "Now we know that resistance *will* be futile. Whatever those red lights are capable of besides tracking missiles, I'm not sure I want to find out. I suggest a moment of silence for our Russian comrades."

Al lowered his head. If a missile attack on the aliens would only leave the attacker's cities in ruins, the alternative was to see what the aliens had in mind for humanity. And whether the Russian attack had just upped the ante for Earth.

* * *

The Security Council was a subdued group when they met that afternoon in anticipation of the alien demands. The Russian Ambassador was noticeably absent and his hawkish compatriots sat in stunned silence.

The news of the decimation of thirty-six Russian cites had hit the media. Images were already streaming into newsrooms from the areas hit. Moscow had been one of the cites flattened and TV crews from nearby citics had rushed their reporters close enough for an alarming image.

Smoke poured thousands of feet into the sky and images of refugees from the blast zone streamed by on the screen. The entire world was now aware of the Russian attempt at killing off the aliens. Everyone knew that any repercussions would be felt now by everyone.

At the scheduled hour, the blue and white UN image flickered and the familiar picture of the UN building overlooking the East River came on. The empty lectern was once again on the center of the screen.

The Security Council sat and waited for its fate. James Cagney, or at least a lookalike, walked out from the side and took up a place behind the lectern.

"You guys. You guys." The likeness to the original actor unnerved everyone in the room. "You guys want to play rough, eh? Well, we're ready for anything you got. Just try us." The mannerisms to the real James Cagney were remarkable. As he spoke, his body took on the twists and turns that had made the original screen tough guy famous. "Top of the world, Ma!"

With that final taunt, the screen went blank. Everyone looked around for someone that could offer an answer to what they had just seen.

Al stood up and everyone turned to him for an answer. The U.S. Ambassador spoke first. "Al, you have some insights as to what we just saw?"

"Two, Madam Ambassador. First, whatever life form these aliens are, they certainly have a twisted sense of humor. Second, that last comment of 'Top of the world Ma' comes from a movie called 'White Heat'. James Cagney plays a thug who is pursued by police. He attempts to escape into an oil tank field. He climbs to the top of a gasoline storage tank in the dark. When police lights locate him and sharpshooters wound him, he yells 'top of the world ma' and shoots his gun into the tank. The resulting fireball ends the movie."

"We can assume that the reference doesn't bode well for us, then?" the French Ambassador asked.

"No, I'm afraid not," Al answered. Al scanned his laptop that was connected to the U.S. Mission Comm Center. In his earbud he heard, "Hey, something is happening up here. The blue light intensity is increasing," the Space Station commander announced.

The others noticed Al's distraction as he worked the keyboard on the computer. He held up his hand to explain to the group that they needed to wait before he could inform them. The computer buzzed as message after message arrived on his email. He read furiously as each one arrived.

When the news was confirmed, he raised his head. "I'm afraid I have bad news." He shook himself since no other kind would be arriving right now. "It would appear that Iran is suffering a similar fate to North Korea. Our forces on the ground in Afghanistan report blue light streaking across the night sky toward the Iranian border."

Al continued, "But I have conflicting reports from advisors we have with the Kurds in Iraq. As you all know, we have supported the Kurds after the capture of Iraq. Advisors on the Iran-Iraq border report the blue light, but that the Kurds on the Iranian side are still alive. The Iranian border guards all disappeared, but not any of the local Kurds."

"Maybe we can get a clearer picture with daylight. I'm sure the U.S. Air Force in Bahrain will do an overflight to determine what is happening in Iran. By my watch, we have four hours to first light."

# Chapter 8

Dr. Brody had worked out a few changes in his living arrangements with the arrival of his new roommate. He had located spare hinges and had fashioned some simple wood gates. Now the outdoor shower had some modesty on all four sides. Likewise, the toilet room now had a swinging gate so that when occupied the gate could be shut.

But inside the small one room cabin, things had been a bit more difficult. Charles suggested that Karen sleep on the couch in the corner of the room. Karen had insisted the first night on sleeping in the hammock on the lanai. The next morning made it clear that it wasn't a good solution.

The professor then had insisted on her sleeping on the couch. The arrangement was still a work in progress. The professor slept naked and needed at least one toilet break during the night. After one surprise, the professor started keeping a *lavalava* on his bed to wrap around his waist on his nighttime jaunts.

Dr. Brody knew from his deceased wife that he snored, but Karen hadn't mentioned the fact. She seemed to be able to deal with the close quarters in return for a secure sleeping space. Getting dressed and undressed meant a trip to the toilet building. Karen's nighttime sleeping attire consisted of one of Dr. Wu's dresses.

But the natural male-female attraction was what was bothering Dr. Brody. He hadn't lived in such close proximity to a female since his wife. That had been some six years earlier and he had become resigned to a life of teaching college classes and going home to an empty home.

His friends over the years had attempted to set him up on dates. Some had been a disaster while some had been promising. But always something had interfered with any serious relationship developing. He had experienced physical relationships with some of his companions, but nothing ever seemed to get past the initial stages.

Now he was 'shacked up' with a twenty-something. At least shacked up in the literal sense. The emotional sense was missing. The island held limited personal companionship possibilities and the two English-speaking islanders knew that they only had each other.

The Wu Who team still occupied the main house and the two couples cooperated in food production. Otherwise there was limited social contact. The language barrier continued to hamper any close relationship. Karen and Charles had worked out some rudimentary Chinese, mostly words for food and for work.

Intense conversations between the two couples was out of the question. And even if conversation was possible, something still raised the hairs on the back of Dr. Brody's neck about his neighbors.

Over a breakfast of tea and some of Dr. Wu rolls, Dr. Brody said, "Karen, we need to get a new crop of lettuce planted today. You did a good job getting the soil ready yesterday."

Karen barely looked up from her hot tea. The professor noticed that in spite of the tan she had accumulated from the tropical sun, her face looked white.

"You don't look good." The professor suddenly knew what was wrong. The parasite that had racked him a short time after his arrival had found its way into Karen. Charles suddenly knew what his companion faced.

Karen mumbled something in response and then quickly fled toward the toilet. Moans emanated from the small room and Charles was reluctant to invade her personal space. When the moans continued, he warily stuck his head around the corner.

A prostrate woman sat on the toilet, leaning against the wall, her head down on her shoulder. She moaned louder as her body revolted at the parasite inside her. Charles backed out and waited.

When the moaning subdued, he again looked around the corner. Karen appeared to be asleep, still sitting in the same spot. He carefully put his hand under her armpit and asked, "Do you need some help getting to bed?"

"Huh, oh you. Yes please," Karen stammered. A daze emanated from her face.

Dr. Brody carefully lifted her up. Then he reached down and swept her up into his arms. Her 5'9" frame settled into Charles's grasp as he carried her out to the lanai. He adjusted his hold as he estimated her weight at 115 pounds. She was fit when she had arrived on the island, and the life they were leading had only added to her fitness.

The professor carried Karen into the cabin and placed her on his bed. She rolled over and groaned as sleep took over. He noticed the beads of sweat forming on her brow as the fever arrived.

From his fight with the parasites, he had learned the stages of the illness. And from Dr. Wu he had learned the treatment to gain his health back. He walked over to his kitchen area and started making the soup broth that Karen would need shortly.

Treatment consisted of lots of sleep and lots of fluids. He would get his soup ready and then go pick oranges and mangos for juice. He retrieved a bucket and placed it by the bed in case of emergencies.

Returning with an armload of fruit, he checked on his patient. She was sweating profusely. The professor retrieved a tall bowl and placed ice water in it. Using a small towel, he sat on the edge of the bed and placed cold compresses on Karen's neck and forehead. She protested weakly at the cold on her body but quickly continued her sleep.

Her body's reaction to the parasite would take forty-eight hours to resolve itself. Charles alternated Karen's care of cold compresses followed by liquids. He would provide either fruit juice, hot tea or soup whenever she was awake. Each time, Charles saw the gratitude in her eyes at his care.

The professor grabbed sleep whenever he could in between administrating to his patient. Asleep on the couch when he heard the early morning stirrings beside him, he raised his head to see a wide awake patient laying on her side looking at him.

"Good morning. You're looking like you're among the living again," Dr. Brody said.

"Morning. How long have I been out?"

"This is the third day. You're right on schedule. The parasite has done its worse. I'll be able to get something in you so you can get your strength back."

"Hmm, could you help me to the little girl's room? I really need to go," she said.

Charles swung the *lavalava* around him as he lifted the sheet he had been under. He swept his arms under her, one under her knees and one around her back, and lifted her up. Noticing the weight difference from when he had carried her before, Charles carried her into the toilet room.

Steadying her against one of the walls, he quietly retreated. After a short wait, an unsteady woman emerged from the room. Holding the wall for balance, she said, "I think I can walk back if you could provide a shoulder."

Dr. Brody quickly placed his arm under her arm for support to her uneasy shuffle. She flopped back into bed.

"I'm sorry I took your bed. Here, I'll get on the couch."

"Don't you move. When you're ready, we'll switch. Till then, you're under my care and you'll stay right in that bed," Charles said. "Now, let me get you some breakfast."

"Did Dr. Wu come up and help? I don't remember." Charles shook his head and Karen's face warmed. "You were with me the whole time. Thank you, you're very kind."

"It was nothing. We have to stick together." His comment had more than a ring of caretaker to it. The look that Karen returned said more also. "After I get something for you, I need to go see Dr. Who. He's been anxious to show me something. I just couldn't get away while you were sick."

"What is it that he wants?"

"No idea. But he was agitated for the last two days. As if he was supposed to do something on a certain date and my delay was causing him fits."

With Karen fed and snoozing in bed, Dr. Brody hustled down to the main house. Dr. Who was waiting for him, his anxiety showing. Dr. Wu walked in from the beach carrying coconuts. The professor knew she used them in her bread as they added the sweetness that he had learned to enjoy.

Dr. Who jumped up and motioned for the professor to follow him. They headed up the trail toward the small cabin but before they turned onto the trail leading past the cliff, Dr. Who stopped at the storage shed. He pulled out a ring with a key attached and unlocked the metal door.

Pushing the door open, the professor strained in the dark to see inside. He had never been inside the shed, although he had seen Dr. Who enter it many times and would typically leave carrying some item in his hands.

But Charles was being invited inside. Dr. Who shut the door and made sure the lock caught. In almost total darkness, Charles waited before Dr. Who hit a light switch and a bank of fluorescent lights came to life.

Blinking from the sudden change, Charles looked around at shelves covered in boxes and cans. Labels on each spoke to the contents of food and material for living on the island. But Dr. Who was intent on another door to an adjacent room. He opened it.

Dr. Brody was startled to see a complete communication center arrayed before him. The large screen attached to the wall came to life when Dr Who hit the power switch on the desk. A computer terminal clacked to life as lighted diodes announced their readiness. Dr. Who sat down at the keyboard and typed.

He moved a second chair so Dr. Brody could sit beside him. When the computer and screen were fully activated, he slid out of the way and motioned the professor to take his place.

Dr. Brody reluctantly slid his chair into place and looked at the electronics. He jumped when a face appeared on the screen. In two separate windows on the screen, Dr. Brody saw himself. Next to him was a new face.

And the someone in front of him was familiar. *What is Errol Flynn doing on the other end of this link?* he thought.

"Good day, Doctor. Welcome to our small island paradise. We have established it just for you."

"Who are you? You can't be who you look like. What is going on?" Dr. Brody asked.

"All in due time, Professor. We will answer all of your questions shortly. But first let me show you what is happening out in the world."

The screen switched to video tape taken from the U.S. Military of the original arrival of the alien space ship. With the audio of the Space Station Commander offering commentary, Dr. Brody watched in amazement at the events he had missed. With the pronouncements that Betty Davis and Cary Grant had made, the Professor started to understand.

Then the images that had been sent out of North Korea appeared with U.S. Army personnel examining the evidence of twenty-five million dead Koreans. Dr. Brody grew wary as he watched the video screen. The Russian footage of their devastated cities was shown followed by the news of Iran's evisceration. Dr. Brody's mood was set.

The Errol Flynn lookalike came back on. "As you can see, you have escaped the initial chaos that the Earth has experienced. We are-"

The professor broke in, "Who are you and what do you want? How am I involved in all this?"

"Professor. You are the key to everything. Do you recall a little computer software game you developed and sold?

"Endangered Species. What of it? It was mildly popular with the environmental crowd."

"Exactly. Well, I'm afraid to announce that we come as environmentalists on steroids. I think that's the modern phrase your people use. We took your computer game and used it to determine what course we should take in our dealings with Earth."

"So you are here as judge, jury and executioner to adjust humanity's role on Earth?" Dr. Brody asked.

"Exactly. You are a quick study and grasp the obvious. We are to adjust the human role on the planet in order to make opportunities for other species to thrive. No longer will all the other creatures on Earth take a back seat to humans. We liked your game so much, we have adopted it for our own purposes. Sorry, no royalties. But the worldwide exposure should drive sales through the roof."

Dr. Brody ignored the attempt at alien humor. He was thinking about the stupid game he had designed years ago. It had started as a geography project to map out the most important areas of the world for human development.

Each section on the flat panel display had been given a rating as to the critical nature it held for human survival.

The game aspect was easily adopted from the computer-based statistics he had researched. The game consisted of two players: one representing humanity, the other representing nature, taking turns selecting gridded squares. As the game progressed, a running total on the computer screen would announce how many humans could be supported by the selected sections.

Conversely, the player selecting for the nature side would get a running total of species saved from extinction. The human winner of the game was the person who could choose enough area on Earth to keep the most people alive. The opposing player would attempt to select enough land to permit the animal world to flourish.

In the game, a second counter on the screen would keep track of how many species were saved by the areas selected. With half the map human and half animal, each player could see their success on reaching the highest number. The professor had made a few dollars from the royalties. But he had forgotten about it soon after he had sold the rights to the game to a software company. That company provided the updates and fixes to the gaming crowd.

From the response by some of his students, he had discovered that he had a mild cult following for his role in the game's development. He had shrugged it off as a geography project that had gone viral. He had been more concerned with the real world to worry about computer games.

But it appeared his game was coming back to haunt him. If this Errol Flynn character was serious, he was about to play a deadly serious game.

"So, Professor. You've had ample time to recall your work. Let me explain how we will be playing," Errol Flynn said.

"First, a couple of questions, if I may? Why are you a lookalike for Errol Flynn?"

"Our species has advanced to the stage that we can take on the shape of anything we choose. We have watched your planet since your electronic communications started. Some of us liked your old movies and decided that it would be less stressful for Earth if we didn't show ourselves. Sort of like the movie 'Galaxy Quest' with Tim Allen. The aliens take on human form but show themselves in true shape under stress. Hollywood is quite imaginative when aliens are concerned."

"OK. I'll accept that reason. But a request--when you deal with the representatives at the U.N., forget the movie actors. Stalin or Mao lookalikes would be more appropriate," Dr. Brody ventured. He knew he was being a little presumptuous making any demands.

"I'll pass that on. You want us to be portrayed as bad guys, eh? I thought the Cagney lookalike was good though," Errol offered.

"You have a strange sense of humor, at least from my perspective, sort of black humor."

"Yes, we see that in your TV shows we receive," the Flynn character said.

"One more thing. Why is Ms. Price here on the island? She wasn't involved in the game development," Charles said. The answer wasn't what he expected . . .

# Chapter 9

Colorado Springs, Colorado

The sun was just setting over the Front Range of the Rocky Mountains. The glow of the summer sun lit the snow fields high on the mountains a deep red. The clouds held their pink as the sun retreated for the night.

Chet Grinkis and his platoon sergeant sat in the comm center that had been set up outside the entrance to Cheyenne Mountain. With the leading components of the American government ensconced deep under the granite, Chet and his special warfare unit sat for another day outside in the fresh mountain air.

They had been spending their days working out on the area golf courses and mountain trails. The Air Force Academy's physical training course was nearby and his men had mastered it easily.

Their only work had been adding to the security detail whenever the U.S. President had emerged from his bunker for a turn at the golf links. And Chet had been amazed at how often that occurred. *The man sure is casual with the fate of humanity at stake,* he thought.

Sergeant Aubin had offered that Chet had been missing the point. After the Russian fiasco trying to attack the alien space ship, everyone had hunkered down to await Earth's fate. The sergeant's attitude was that the President might as well enjoy life since there was little else he could do.

And that was Captain Grinkis's attitude also. He'd like to go enjoy life a little instead of providing security to a 12,000' mountain. *It sure didn't make sense keeping heim and his men sitting here for some hole in the rock*, he thought.

The Navy Seals posted nearby felt the same way. During their daily training sessions, the two commanders exchanged jaded views of their current assignment. *Maybe today, with the alien announcement, they would find out more*, Chet thought.

Navy Seal Commander Lt. Butch Goring had joined him at the comm center for the expected announcement. After Russia had upped the ante and Iran was vaporized, the original message concerning Earth's fate had been delayed. The aliens had re-scheduled the event to today.

"So you think we're going to get to do anything after this announcement? It seems the world is in a bend-over, here-it-comes position," Butch said.

"Well, my Navy Seal friend, I'm not seeing a lot of options in all this for us warriors. The level that this is all happening is way above our pay grade," Chet offered.

"I'd just like a shot at these alien assholes, that is, if they have one. Can't kick ass if they don't have any."

Chet laughed at his friend's observation. He was right. They knew next to nothing about their enemy other than the blue light vaporized people and the red light could redirect threats. The captain didn't know if there were more colored lights capable of more action. He certainly didn't want to find out. Red and blue were sufficient in his mind.

The overhead screen jumped as the image changed. The room quickly quieted as the now familiar U.N.

building image switched on. Already standing at the lectern was Joe Stalin.

"Hey, at least they got their characters right this time. Hard to have Cary Grant telling you he's going to wipe you out. Uncle Joe fills that bill," Sergeant Aubin offered.

Everyone nodded their agreement until Uncle Joe spoke. "Earthlings, the time for your judgement has arrived. The federation of planets we represent has determined that humans have overrun the planet you call Earth. Such action has caused grievous harm to the other species. Since you have ignored the Biblical warning to be good stewards, we are here to enforce such action."

Chet looked at Butch and they shook their heads about the reference to the Bible. *Where were these creatures coming off quoting the Bible?* Chet thought. He studied the Stalin character on the screen. If he could only be in the same room for two minutes with this guy, he'd show him some respect.

"For anyone familiar with the computer game, 'Endangered Species', this will be simple. For those who aren't familiar with this game, become so. We play it for real starting tomorrow. Representing Earth will be the games designer, Dr. Charles Brody. Representing the animals of Earth will be this character ..." Joe Stalin stopped and waited. The right side of the screen filled as a Giant Panda walked into view. The panda turned and sat on its backside next to the Joe Stalin character. Stalin continued. "Giant Panda will be making the selections when the game begins. He prefers to be called GP."

"What the f-" Chet announced. "What does this computer game have do with all this, and who is this Dr. Brody? And GP, that's rich. I suppose he'll be telling us what to do?" The room offered a nervous chuckle at the captain's remark.

"Captain, if I'm free to speak?" one of his platoon corporals asked.

"Yeah, Corporal, enlighten us," Chet said.

"I was home on leave and my asshole brother was playing that game. He's gone off the deep end with this environmental bullshit. He used to be a good kid till he got to college where someone did a number on him."

"And you saw this game played. What's up with it and why are these assholes loading the Giant Panda onto the pile?"

"Actually, the Giant Panda is one of the players you can choose in the game. My brother talked me into playing him. I was Thomas Jefferson trying to save humanity and he took on the character of Killer Whale, you know 'Free Willy'."

"And you and Tom saved humanity?"

"Hell no. My brother kicked my ass. The 'totalator' on the side bar at the end of the game showed me with 4.5 billion dead. I didn't go after enough squares with the resources to support the worlds population. I saved two billion is all."

"And Free Willy freed the animals?" The sarcasm was evident in Chet's question.

"Well, he knew enough about the game to reestablish wild herds of bison across the American West. He received a 92% score in the game as established by the

World Wildlife Preservation Club. The software company that designed the game operates an online gaming web site. The record score for the animal side is 98%. That translates into a 7.2 billion death rate of humans."

"Shit. That bad, eh?" Chet joined the others as they shook their heads. Human were suddenly under the gun. "So who's this Dr. Brody? How's he the lucky bastard to be playing for the humans."

Sergeant Aubin joined in. " I got his biography up on the computer. He's a Geography Professor at a state university in Iowa. Holds a Doctorate in Geography from Northwestern with undergraduate work at Cornell. Has a couple of books published on economic geography, whatever that is. His stint at computer gaming seems to be tied in with this economic geography stuff."

"Does it say where he is now? Maybe we should go pay him a visit. He might like some company. If he has the fate of the world on his shoulders, things could get a little dicey for him."

"Too late, there's a newspaper article online about the disappearance of one Dr. Charles Brody under mysterious circumstances. Seems he had dinner out with friends who dropped him off at his house. Two days later, when he hadn't shown up at work, the university went to investigate. The house was undisturbed except for a pile of clothes that the professor had worn the night of the dinner," the sergeant said.

"OK, maybe we can go and add out expertise to finding where he went to. Beats the hell out of sitting here waiting for the next Golfer-in-Chief appearance," Captain Grinkis said.

"Sounds like a great idea. I'll go and make my request," Butch added. "The Navy Seals aren't about to have Delta Force get the only excitement around here. Especially if it means getting away from the clowns here in their mountain bunker."

* * *

The C-130 transport plane circled over the small Iowa college town for its final approach. Sitting on one side of the cargo bay were Butch Goring and his Navy Seal unit. On the other side of the plane sat Captain Chet Grinkis and his Delta Force platoon.

On the tarmac, the two units loaded up into four Suburbans. The Seals would reconnoiter the campus for information on Dr. Brody. Chet and his troopers would scour the professor's neighborhood.

The decision to send such highly trained professionals on a police matter was easy. Dr. Brody had just been named the man of the millennium by the invading aliens. The entire world wanted to know everything about the person who would be deciding their fate. The Pentagon had jumped at the Special Ops request.

Chet had half his men with him while Sergeant Aubin had the remainder. The sergeant would check the investigation records at police headquarters and radio his findings. They would all meet up later to share information.

Chet's Suburban pulled up to a typical Midwest home that had probably been built in the 1920's. Close to campus, the neighborhood was home to many of the professors who worked at the university. The street had

Americana written all over it. Chet met the police officer that had been sent to open the house for the unit.

Captain Grinkis ordered his men to fan through the neighborhood knocking on doors. They were to ask about the professor and any information a neighbor might have on his location. Chet followed the officer into the foyer.

"Everything as you found it officer?" Chet asked.

"No one's been in here since we first investigated Dr. Brody's disappearance. Even his clothes are still in a pile where we found them."

"Show me please," Chet said.

The two walked up the stairs leading from the foyer. The house was a large two-story house with a hip roof. The foyer led off to a living room on one side and a parlor on the other. From the foyer Chet could see through the door that led to the kitchen in the back.

From the layout, he assumed that the house had four bedrooms upstairs. The officer confirmed the four bedrooms along with two bathrooms. One of the baths was off the master bedroom. But that wasn't where the pile of clothes were found.

As the two reached the top of the stairs, they turned left toward the front of the house where the master bedroom lay. The police officer stopped. In the hallway next to the stairwell railing were a small pile of men's clothes. A pair of shoes protruded from the pile.

Chet looked down at the pile. He crouched so his face was inches from the clothes. He sniffed for anything unusual. Nothing registered. He took a pen and carefully lifted up the shirt. Underneath were the professor's pants and underwear. He lifted each up, looking for any clues.

Moving them slightly, he uncovered the shoes. Socks sat limp inside the shoes. Chet used his pen to pull the socks out. There was nothing in the shoes that was unusual.

"The FBI Forensic Team will be here from Washington this afternoon. You have photos of all this I assume?" the captain asked.

"Yes Sir. We didn't run any tests as our budget isn't the best. We didn't see any signs of forced entry or foul play. From talking to his daughter that flew in, there's nothing missing in the house. I guess the guy has a large gun safe downstairs with a valuable collection. I'd assume there would have been attempts at opening the safe if any bad guys had been here," the officer said.

"Kind of a strange place to disrobe if you ask me," Chet said.

"That's the only strange thing about the whole case, unless he met a woman right here and they went for it."

"Was the professor known for his dalliances?" Chet asked.

"No, he was a widower. Age 61. Kids all grown with lives of their own not around here. His friends said he had the occasional tryst with some local women, but nothing kinky, if that's what you're trolling for."

"Not trying to smear the professor. Just attempting to figure his whereabouts."

The two waited by the front door for the FBI to show up. Captain Grinkis's platoon members slowly drifted in with no news. The neighbors they had contacted had neither heard nor seen anything. At close to two months since his disappearance, memories of that night were fading.

The police had canvassed the neighborhood immediately after the disappearance and had turned up nothing of significance. After the FBI Forensic Team arrived, Chet loaded up his men and headed to the Campus Conference Center. It had been designated command central for the Federal agents.

Chet greeted his Seal counterpart as he entered the room. Everyone gathered around the table to compare findings. With copies of the police reports, there was nothing new that offered a solution to the missing professor.

Then Butch dropped something. "While we nosed around campus we did hear about one of the professor's students who disappeared from her house about a month after Dr. Brody."

"Did you pull the police file on the case?" Chet asked.

"Yeah. They considered that the two might be related but never did much on the second case. Not much to go on. We went by the house where this Karen Price rented a room. It's since been rented to someone else, so nothing to see there now. But we have photos from the police investigation."

Chet took the file and laid the photos out on the table. They were of the house and the inside rooms. Shots of the outside of the house showed a typical two-story house. But the shots of her bedroom showed something.

Located in the middle of the room was a pile of clothes with shoes sticking out, just like the professor's pile of clothes. Except the woman's clothes weren't out in the hallway. *But with other people in the house, if someone grabbed her they would have done so in the privacy of her room, not the hallway,* Chet thought.

"How was she related to our Dr. Brody? Anything romantic there?" Chet asked.

"No. The police also tried to link the two. Seems she was just one of his graduate students working on her Master's Degree. He was on her Thesis Committee, but that's about how personal it got."

"Did the professor go for any coeds that we know of?"

"Not according to all his colleagues. We even impressed upon them the seriousness of this whole thing and they didn't change their story. Seems the professor was involved slightly with some older women after his wife's death but nothing before, and never with any students."

The two commanders agreed that it was time to get some sleep. The FBI team might come up with something but that would have to wait until morning. The campus hotel had been made available to the two teams and Chet walked his platoon across the street after locking up the conference room.

# Chapter 10

The next evening the news hadn't changed. The professor's clothes had been bagged by the FBI Forensic Team and flown back to FBI Headquarters in Washington D.C. for analysis. The early reports that had come back were negative. Nothing unusual was showing up. The rest of the house was clean, confirming that no foul play had happened inside the house.

Chet and Butch sat in the conference room contemplating their next move. They sure didn't want to get stuck back in Colorado on golf patrol. They were working hard on what they could do next to keep out of the prying eyes of higher command.

"Captain, the TV is saying that the opening moves are about to be broadcast. You might want to check it out," Sergeant Aubin yelled from the other room.

Chet and Butch strolled in and took up a chair among their men. The corporal who had played 'Endangered Species' on the computer walked up to them followed by a reluctant younger man with long hair.

"Sir, I took the liberty to contact my younger brother at college. He was close by in Nebraska. He drove all night to get down here. He was sort of hesitant at first, but then I told him I'd take my buddies up there and we'd C-4 his dorm. That got him in gear. Captain Grinkis, my younger brother, Mel."

Chet stood up and reached out to shake the young man's hand. Mel flinched at the motion but recovered enough to shake Chet's hand.

"Your brother tells me you're an expert at this thing that's starting. Care to sit with me and enlighten me."

"I don't know what my brother told you, but I'm no way near Sabretooth Tiger level. I'm in Mastodon level but at least I got out of Unicorn level."

"Excuse me? You lost me there Mel," the captain said.

"The higher up you go on the proficiency scale you move into levels named after extinct animals. Sabretooth Tiger is the top of the scale. Those guys are like way good. They just cream humanity."

Chet looked at the corporal and then at Butch. This was a different world to him and he wasn't sure it was a healthy world. People were playing games and betting against the humans. And now with the aliens actualizing the game, humanity was suddenly out of the virtual world and on the line for real. Reality was being forced on the world's population.

An ad for powdered soap ended and the television in the conference room switched to blazing graphics of animals and humans falling across the screen. Everyone in the room tensed up as the alien show began.

The opening graphics soon faded into a sports center type set with three people sitting behind the desk. On the back drop was the lettering that stated 'Endangered Species: Animal vs. Human'. A man in a suit and tie who appeared to be the host spoke first.

"Ladies and gentleman, welcome to tonight's opening show. In the next hour we will start the process of dividing Planet Earth between the humans and the animals. We will outline how that will all proceed in a minute. First let me introduce you to our two analysts who will give us a blow-by-blow description of what is taking place. With me for the duration representing the animal kingdom is David Brower, founder of Friends of the Earth. Providing insight into the human side of our contest will be President Reagan, former American leader in the late 20th Century."

Chet looked at his sergeant. *President Reagan, how did he get put on this thing?* he thought. Then he realized that it was the aliens once again playing funny man to the planet. The whole setup looked like an ESPN Game Day Show.

The show's host continued. He explained the rules of the Endangered Species game to the TV audience. Each side would pick a roughly 500 mile by 500 mile area marked on a giant map of the Earth. Each night the show would be broadcast worldwide at 6 PM local time. The first half hour of each show the host and his analysts would review where each side was in dividing up the world.

The second half hour of the show would entail the selection of the next area by each side. Two selections each night would be made with each side having 5 minutes to make their selection. After half the world was selected, the number of moves would increase to six per night, but the total twenty-minute time allocated for selection would remain the same.

The last ten minutes of the hour show would be wrap-up by the analysts as to how the new selections fit into the previous choices. The show would continue until the entire flat panel dispay was equally divided into a human half and an animal half.

"Now that we have the rules set down, how do you both see this shaking out?" the host asked.

David spoke first for the animals. "Brian, nothing could be more exciting for all the people who spoke of the preservation of the Earth for all these years. Finally, man is about to be put in his place. I'm just sorry we weren't capable of reaching this stage in our development as a species without outside intervention."

"Well there you go again, David. This whole action is being forced down our throats by a ruthless foe from God only knows where. Our friends, the Russians, paid dearly for standing up to these sadists and I can only offer my protest to these proceedings," President Reagan, or at least an excellent lookalike, said.

Brian, the host, shot back. "President Reagan, you volunteered for this position and we can find a substitute if you find the job distasteful."

"I stand with my fellow humans in this travesty and will not be silenced. I paid for this microphone and I intend to use it fully," the former President boasted.

The remaining portion of the show was taken up with a discussion on the shows rules. Without any areas yet chosen to add to the discussion, the half hour was filled with talking heads. Finally, the host announced that the show would be switching to the arena for the first selection.

"Far out. I can't believe this is really happening," Mel exclaimed. He moved up to the front edge of his chair in anticipation of the opening gambits. "Do you guys mind if I pull out my laptop and load up the game? I can do a better job following along then."

Mel's brother looked at his captain and got the nod that it would be OK. Mel's laptop was quickly loaded up with the Endangered Species software while he adjusted the parameters of the game.

Chet watched the whole time and then asked,"What are you doing changing the grids?"

"Every time you play you have to set the scale that divides the Earth up into the grid pattern. The aliens are playing on a 500-mile grid. The game can be played tight with 100-mile grids or loose with 2500-mile grids. They have set the scale in the medium range."

"Is that important?" Chet asked.

"At 100-mile spacing, the game takes forever. The Earth is roughly 25,000 miles in circumference. At a 500-mile grid, that's 50 moves just to get around the equator. Add in the moves taking you up to each pole and we'll have about 2,000 moves. We'll be here forever at that rate."

Chet jumped in, "Then that's why at the half way mark we speed up the process. The really important stuff will have been picked and we'll be down to ocean and polar regions."

"Correcto mundo," Mel blurted out. He looked at his brother and caught the threat in his face. "Sorry sir. Yes, the oceans are important but not as much as the land. The opening moves will tell us a lot."

A headache medicine ad ended and the show came back on, this time in a large indoor arena. It looked to be a copy of the 'Who Wants to be a Millionaire' set with dramatic lighting and music for affect. A large, brightly lit flat panel display of Earth floated in midair in the middle of the set. As the light flashed down onto the center stage, Bob

Barker, of TV game show host fame, perked up. Once again, it appeared to be an exact lookalike of Bob.

"Good evening, everyone. Welcome to the first of what I expect to be many exciting evenings. Tonight we start the selection of two separate areas: one human, one animal. Lets meet our contestants. First, for the animal world, let's give a warm welcome to our contestant, GP."

The audience sitting behind the Giant Panda roared its approval at GP representing the animals. The camera panned across the crowd.

"Holy shit, they're all there!" Mel exclaimed.

The others in the room were lost in his observation. About three hundred people appeared on screen, none familiar to the soldiers.

"What do you mean by 'all there'? You know these people?" Chet inquired. He was afraid of the answer.

Mel started to explain that he knew most of the people shown. They were all famous humans in the environmental movement, at least ones that were dead.

"There's Rachel Carson, of 'Silent Spring' fame. In the front is John Muir and Aldo Leopold, early visionaries of man's destructive nature. I assume that is Thoreau and Walt Whitman beside them." He continued through a litany of early environmental people that had started the move to a nature-centered understanding of the world versus a human-centered view.

"How do you know all this, brother?"

"We study it in class. Plus the computer game has many of these people that you can choose for your persona in the game. Each one has different strengths when you play the game."

Chet was mystified. He stared at the giant panda that had taken its place on one side of the floating flat panel display, sitting in an overly large recliner that had been lined with bamboo branches. In front of the animal was a small table with a large joy stick on it. On the opposite side of the large display, a second video display floated in midair.

Bob Barker continued, "And from a secure location, we have our contestant representing the human world, Dr. Charles Brody. Please put your hands together and give it up for the person holding our fate in his hands." A large crowd seated behind this second video display cheered wildly as it flickered to life. "How are you tonight, Professor? Ready for Earth's ultimate challenge?"

"I'm ready Bob," the professor said from the floating video screen. Chet noticed the body language of the professor. In his Special Ops training for hostage rescues, Chet had been trained to recognize a captive's actions and mannerisms. The professor was giving off expressions that he was a less-than-willing participant. Chet put that into the back of his mind for further research as the show continued.

"Good, then lets get started," Bob announced.

The TV camera panned across the audience that had taken up their positions behind the screen with Dr. Brody's image on it. They were cheering for the game to start.

"Who are these people? Recognize anyone?" Chet asked to anyone in the room.

His troops all shook their heads. Unlike the animal side, no one in the arena representing the humans was particularly famous. Mel didn't offer up any help in identifying anyone. The game continued.

"Before the show started, we flipped a coin and GP gets the first selection. What will it be GP? The Amazon rain forest? The Serengeti of Tanzania and Kenya with all those herds of magnificent animals? Or maybe the lagoons of Mexico with their whale sanctuaries. The world is waiting."

The giant panda reached its paw out and manipulated the joystick. As he did, 500-mile chunks of Earth would highlight on the floating flat panel display. As he slowly maneuvered the cursor around the map he would stop briefly on famous locations of wild animals. The crowd behind him roared their approval as each grid was illuminated.

Finally the cursor swung around to Southern China and a 500-mile square lit up. GP pressed down on the joystick and the lighted square turned a greenish hue. It was now an official animal domain. The rooters behind him roared approval.

"Our first selection goes to the animal world, the grid labeled Sichuan in South Central China. As the software tells us, GP has just selected the native habitat of the giant panda. A 'natural selection' considering pandas are one of the most endangered animals on Earth," Bob added with a wink.

"A bit self serving if you ask me," Chet commented to the room.

"OK, Dr. Brody, the gauntlet has been thrown. How does the human side answer this first selection?" Bob asked.

Dr. Brody worked his mouse at his secret location. On the floating flat panel display of Earth lighted squares flicked on as he moved. The camera in the room where Dr. Brody was stashed followed his face as he made his first selection.

Suddenly Chet noticed cheering and groaning from the next room as the cursor moved around the world. Sergeant Aubin went to investigate. Before he returned, a large cheer went up when the professor clicked and highlighted the 500-mile square that included the mouth of the Mississippi River. The entire area took up a good portion of the States of Louisiana and Mississippi. A red hue denoted the first human grid space.

"Sir. There's a large group of college students in the next room. They're watching the show and were registering their approval for the human side," the sergeant reported.

Before the captain could say anything, Bob was back.

"A good choice by the professor to start. New Orleans is important to North America. Should make the Big Easy happy knowing they're on the good side."

Chet suddenly realized the potential effects of this show. If people panicked over the selections being made, there would be social chaos. *How were those inhabitants of Amdo Province in China taking the news that they were now living in animal-only land?* he thought. He didn't realize that he was about to get the answer.

GP swiveled the joystick in his right paw and the cursor danced across the world map. Highlighted square after highlighted square rang up as the panda swept across the globe. With much jeering by the pro-animal crowd behind him, the panda seemed to be enjoying the torment he was inflicting as one grid after another lit up.

Chet could hear the crowd next door cheer as the cursor swept over Africa and South America. When the cursor swung up onto North America, the cheering stopped. Moans could be heard as the panda's joystick slowed over the United States.

The cursor came back to a square of eastern Colorado. The light came on the large display indicating that this square was now in the panda's sights. The groans from his own troops matched the noise from next door. The panda pushed on the stick and the square turned green.

"Son of a bitch. There goes Denver," one of the soldiers yelled.

"Well, that will set the Americans on edge. Denver and the eastern range land of Colorado just got moved to the animal world. What will be Dr. Brody's response to that challenge, ladies and gentlemen?" Bob smiled.

The uproar from the next room was drowning out any conversation in the secure conference room. Not that any of the troops were talking. Everyone was staring at the large green square that had just been chunked out of the United States, and they were powerless to stop this attack.

The TV cameras panned across the arena audience. The animal side was jubilant. Two 500-mile squares set aside for the animal kingdom, no humans allowed.

The human supporters were subdued. They awaited the professor's next choice.

"Dr. Brody, you have one minute left to choose."

The cursor had been stuck motionless over the center of the Atlantic Ocean after GP had made his selection. As the clock wound down on the 5 minutes that the human side had to make a selection, Dr. Brody's appearance was one of stark terror. The last selection had hit home for someone who had been living in Iowa. The camera in the room held a motionless professor staring at his computer screen.

"Thirty seconds Doc or the humans lose a selection."

The noise from the other room was suddenly roaring its encouragement for a man who could not hear it. But it was as if the entire human population was yelling encouragement. Even the audience in the arena was now alive with its cheers.

The human side needed every 500-mile section it could take. To lose one at the beginning of this game would be catastrophic.

As if willed on by seven billion individuals, Dr. Brody's cursor moved slightly. It continued to move east toward Africa. The squares on the globe lit up as the cursor crossed one square and then the next. The second hand swept down to zero as the pointer moved over Egypt. The square containing the Nile Delta lit up and then turned red just as the time buzzer sounded.

"Well, that was close Professor. But you snuck in there just in time," Bob said. "A good choice. That grid certainly holds the cradle of human civilization and the Egyptians certainly will be happy."

"Yeah, what about the rest of the world, asshole? We have to put up with this bullshit for how many nights to see whats going to happen. A load of crap if you ask me," Sergeant Aubin added.

Captain Grinkis never got to see the wrap-up of the Endangered Species Show. The secure line to the Pentagon that had been set up rang and took him away. He listened as his men all stood waiting.

"Load up. We've been ordered back to Colorado Springs. That last selection included Cheyenne Mountain. We're on protection duty again for our Golfer-in-Chief. It seems he's suddenly trespassing on animal land."

# Chapter 11

Dr. Charles Brody lowered his head onto the desk when the little red light switched off indicating that the show was over. The second monitor showing the arena had been switched off. The monitor with the map of the world remained on.

He lifted his head and looked at the red and green selected squares. Four selections from the two thousand or so yet to do. *I'll never survive this,* he thought. Denver was gone now. Lost to the other side. And he felt the loss personally. *How many million people just lost everything?* he thought.

Dr. Brody didn't know if the aliens meant to clear the selected areas of humans right away. Things hadn't been explained to him fully and the anxiety of not knowing consumed him. He had to get away from it all and think.

He pushed himself away from the desk and switched off the computer. He staggered over to the door and stepped into the storage area. The outside door was closed and locked. He twisted the knob and light streamed in, energizing him.

He closed the storage shed door and locked the deadbolt with the key Dr. Who had given him. He placed the lanyard holding the key around his neck and started walking up the hill to his cabin.

At the top of the cliff, he turned right, away from the cabin. He followed the cliff top as it led him west. About 200 yards from the cabin, the cliff jutted out toward the bay below, creating a point.

The professor scrambled over the rocks as he scampered out to the point. One-hundred and fifty feet below him, the bay slapped against rocks at the base of the cliff. The professor stood on the upper edge of the cliff and looked down. *It would be so easy. Just a slight nudge forward, a short fall and it would be all over,* he thought.

Dr. Brody stood motionless as the trade winds rustled him. The winds seemed to add their voices as they buffeted his body toward the drop.

"Dr. Brody, what are you doing?" the voice yelled.

The professor continued to stare at the rocks below.

"Professor, don't move," the voice said, now closer.

Dr. Brody scanned the bay for an answer. The rocks seemed to be his only answer. He leaned forward.

A hand clutched his shoulder. It was a small hand, but it firmly held him. The winds threw a small gust at him and he rocked slightly. The hand pulled on his shoulder.

"Dr. Brody, why don't we both back up a bit?" The voice offered a soothing comfort to his duress. The gentle tug on his shoulder seemed to take his mind off the rocks below. He stepped back one step.

The voice continued. "That was good. Now, how about another small step?"

The professor complied. *This voice seems to care,* he thought. *I need someone to care for me right now. I can't do this alone.*

"Charles, can we just sit down and talk?" The voice was soothing. The hand on the shoulder pushed his body down slightly and he complied. *Yes, I'm tired. I want to sit down,* he thought.

As he sat down on the rocks on the cliff top, the weight of the world seemed to be relieved. Two arms came around him and pulled him into a warm place. He closed his eyes. *I want to be safe from all this,* he thought. His head rocked back and bumped into something. Whatever it was, it smelled good. He turned his head slightly and buried his face into the smell. *Make it all go away,* he thought.

* * *

Karen had been looking for Dr. Brody after lunch. He had eaten and then disappeared. As the afternoon grew late, she had given up waiting. She took an outdoor shower and put on clean clothes. After three days of fighting the parasite, she was feeling alive again.

She wandered around looking for the professor. *It was unusual for him to disappear like this,* she thought. In the time she had been on the island, he had always been close. She grew worried as the day grew later.

She scanned the area from the perch the cabin afforded her. The windows took in the entire area as the island stretched out below. Her eyes stopped at an object she had never seen before. Nestled in the large tropical trees that shaded the main house was a satellite dish. At least it looked like the satellite dishes she had seen on numerous houses.

*What could a satellite dish be doing on the island? And if there was a satellite dish, there would be communication with the outside world,* she thought. She was standing at the cabin window when she saw Dr. Brody emerge from the storage shed. She watched as he locked the door and hung the key around his neck.

When she observed the professor heading up the trail to the top of the cliff, she rushed over to the edge of the lanai to greet him. It was there that she saw the professor reach the top of the cliff and turn right. She waited, anxious as to where he was going.

When Dr. Brody reached the point overlooking the bay, she acted. She ran across the rocks to reach the professor just as he seemed ready to fall off the cliff. Her hand on his shoulder had stopped him. Her voice seemed to soothe him

As he stepped back from the edge, she pulled the professor down to the ground. Wrapping her arms around him for safety, he leaned back into her chest. His head swiveled and came to rest against her neck, her hair hiding his face.

Karen didn't know what to do. The two just sat entwined as the trade winds blew against them. As evening came, the warm air swirled as the sun set over the ocean west of the bay. On any other occasion, Karen would be content. A beautiful evening overlooking a tropical locale holding a special man. *As romantic settings go, it doesn't get any better,* she thought.

But this was more than a romantic setting. The strong vibrant male that she had known at college and had seen in action on the island was anything but that now. She sat holding the professor contemplating what had changed since this morning.

*The shed,* s*omething in the shed,* she thought. In the time she had been on the island, she had only seen Dr. Who enter the shed, and he had only left with things in his arms. Things they would eat or needed to live on the island.

She moved her hand up to the professor's neck. Dr. Brody just seemed to linger, content in her arms. She lifted the lanyard that held the shed key up and over the Professor's head. He moved easily as the key slipped off his head. He resumed his restful position.

Karen placed the key over her head and stuffed it down inside her dress. *I will look in the shed later and maybe find an answer,* she thought. The professor was too close to going over the cliff when she had interceded. She wasn't about to lose her only friend on the island.

Dr. Brody continued leaning against her as the sun set over the ocean. Stars came out and the cliff edge disappeared into darkness. Karen looked around and could barely make out the top of the cliff. She would have to be careful getting the two of them back to the cabin.

As she twisted around to check her path, the professor stirred. She felt his head jerk. His arm came up and his hand caressed her head. She leaned into his grasp and the hand stopped.

"Oh, I'm sorry. I didn't know where I was." He leaned away from Karen's clutch and turned to look in her face. There was just enough light for the two of them to see each other. "What happened? Where are we? How did I get out here?"

"Professor, if you're ready, we should carefully walk back to the cabin."

She unwound her body from the professor and stood up. Her joints ached from the long spell on the hard rocks and she shook herself to get some blood flowing. Karen reached down and helped the professor stand. The two of them backed further away from the cliff edge.

When they were safely standing away from the cliff edge, Karen took Dr. Brody's hand and carefully led him back to the cabin. She sat him down on the lanai. Reaching inside, she hit the electric light switch and the cabin was suddenly bathed in a warm yellow glow.

"Why am I so tired?" the professor asked.

"Dr. Brody, you've been up for the past three days taking care of me. You haven't slept."

"I see. I forgot. How are you feeling?"

"Much better. Thank you for all your care. I don't know what I would have done without you."

Dr. Brody acknowledged Karen's sincerity and then looked out at the evening. A moon was coming up over the eastern horizon.

"Charles, when I was sick, all I could think of was crawling into the ocean and letting the waves wash all of it away. I haven't been in the sea since I got here. I think tonight would be a splendid time for a swim."

"Are you sure?"

Without waiting to answer the professor's question, Karen stood up and went to her side of the bureau. She opened the top draw and retrieved a small cloth object.

"One of the items Dr. Wu gave me when I arrived was a bathing suit. I think it will fit." She disappeared into the toilet room and soon emerged, still in her dress. She reached out with her hand and took ahold of the professor.

"Let's go."

"If you insist. I guess I can swim in my shorts. Let me grab a flashlight."

The two followed the light beam down the cliff trail and past the main house. They could see the Who couple through the windows, sitting in the light, reading. They quietly passed the house and stepped down onto the beach.

Leaving their flip flops, they walked barefoot down the beach. Waves lapped up the beach and soaked their lower legs. Karen felt the warm ocean water on her feet.

As the moon rose, more light shown on the beach, revealing small waves crashing onto shore. A third of the way down the beach they both stopped. The professor peeled off his shirt and threw it onto the sand. He stepped toward the water.

Turning back, he watched Karen disrobe. Pulling her dress over her head, she watched the professor as it moved up her body. The bikini that Dr. Wu had given her was small to start with. That it was Dr. Wu's size made it seem infinitesimal on Karen's larger body. She noticed Dr. Brody register the scanty covering that remained. The dress landed on the beach next to the shirt.

Karen walked over and took the professor's hand. Facing the waves, they ran into the surf. A large wave caught them, knocking them over. Floundering in the water, they both scrambled to the surface.

Swimming out to deeper water, the two stood in the water, barely touching bottom. Facing each other, Dr. Brody reached out and grasped the lanyard around Karen's neck.

"What are you doing with this?"

Karen froze. She had forgotten about the shed key she had lifted off the professor. She stammered to answer.

"This isn't something you should be involved in. You don't know what's at stake here," Dr. Brody barked.

"But Professor, I saw you come out of that shed. Then when you went to the cliff and..." She stopped. She saw the eyes of her friend widen at the mention of the cliff. He was remembering now. What he had tried to shove into the recesses of his brain was boiling back to the surface.

A wave crashed into them, knocking them over. Karen felt the professor's body against hers. There was that same sensation she had felt at the top of the cliff. She wrapped her arms around him as they reached the surface.

"Please let me help. Whatever it is, we can do it together. We're all we have," Karen pleaded.

Karen saw the professor's eyes in the moonlight. The light reflected off his iris as tears formed. Soon his eyes were swimming in liquid. She held him tighter. Another wave swept over them and they both struggled for footing on the sandy bottom.

Finally Dr. Brody clutched her body and lifted it up over his head. He lowered her and she slid down his front, her breasts rubbing down his face. She felt a hot flash come over her. When her face reached level with his, he stopped her slide. Their mouths were inches apart as they stared in each other eyes.

Karen reacted to the closeness as tears streamed down the professor's face. Karen's eyes watered up. She leaned and kissed him on the mouth. The kiss was returned as the two bodies rubbed in the smoothness of the seawater.

A new antagonist crashed into them as they fell over into the water. Apart, they each swam to the surface to find their embrace again. Their mouths met as their bodies slid together. The wonderful sensation that Karen had been holding back let loose. She put her hand behind his head and held on tight.

The next wave took both of them under, but not apart. They floated underwater fully embraced until the now shallow water retreated. Laying on the sand, they continued their kiss. Another wave washed over them, pushing them further up the beach.

Neither one noticed the change. They were intent on clinging to one another as much for support as for lust. Both were a long way from civilization, together on a tropical island. Karen didn't want the night to end.

She could tell that Dr. Brody was physically aroused by their surf play, but there was something else more important. She wanted more, but something held her back.

They were holding each other for more than lustful desires. The loneliness of the island had overwhelmed each of them. Something even more basic was present as they lay in each other's arms. A human need for companionship trumped all other human desires.

"From Here to Eternity. I finally remembered the movie." Dr. Brody broke the spell. Another wave lapped up their bodies as they lay entwined in the sand.

"What?" Karen asked.

"Burt Lancaster and Deborah Kerr. Romantic embrace in the surf while the Japanese bomb Pearl Harbor."

"Oh, right. I remember that now. Famous surf scene with two lovers," Karen answered.

The professor lifted himself up as the next wave washed over them. "I'm sorry. I guess I got caught up in the moment."

Karen panicked. *He's pulling away and I want more,* she thought. *I especially want some answers. Like what happened this afternoon.* She reached up from her prone position and pulled the professor back down. She kissed him. The kiss wasn't returned, at least not like it had been a minute ago.

"We need to get back. We have a busy day tomorrow." Dr. Brody stood up and offered a hand to Karen. She reluctantly took it and was pulled up. They walked up the beach to their clothes.

They were soon in the cabin. Each took a separate shower to remove the sand and salt. With her sleeping dress on, Karen headed to her couch. Dr. Brody was already asleep on the bed.

# Chapter 12

Dr. Brody woke with a start. It wasn't quite daybreak yet, but he was in a panic. He reached around his neck and found nothing there. He ran his hands around his bed and found nothing. He looked up and in the lingering moonlight saw Karen sleeping a short distance away.

Then he remembered. She had the lanyard with the key around her neck last night. He strained to see if it was still there. Karen had her head away from him and a sheet pulled up for protection from the slight breeze that was blowing.

The cabin seldom was cool enough for anything other than a sheet. Tonight was typical as the professor crawled out and wrapped his *lavalava* around his waist. He retrieved a flashlight from the table nearby and flicked it on.

Making sure the beam wasn't aimed in Karen's face, he quietly stepped over to where she was sleeping. He knelt down next to the couch and carefully pulled on the sheet. As it slid down her body, her neck was revealed.

Dr. Brody let out a sigh of relief to see the lanyard still around her neck. He sat back on the floor and relaxed slightly. *There would have been big trouble if I had lost the key,* he thought. But he realized he didn't exactly have it either. He debated what he should do.

Last night, the surf had stirred emotions in him that he thought he had suppressed. But the feel of her supple body had broken down many barriers in his mind. And her responsiveness to his touch last night said volumes.

*But he was old enough to be her ... He was also the only one who could .... If you discount Dr. Who, that is,* he thought. Male possibilities were certainly limited, as were female choices. They had been thrust together, more on purpose than Karen might believe.

*But the key, I have to get the key back,* he thought. He moved to see if he could remove it from her neck without waking her. As he grew close, his nose flared at her scent. He stopped. The senses hit his brain as he remembered the smell of her hair on the cliff edge.

He had been ready to end the alien game, at least his role in it. Let someone else represent Earth. From the scores he had seen from the players that lived for his software, there were many more proficient at saving humans. He had never even tried the final game, but knew he couldn't score high enough to set any records.

Dr. Brody might have designed the basic concept of the computer game, but the company he sold the rights to had designed the software. And the parameters of the game held the quirks to scoring a high score. He wasn't a geek and would have no idea how the nuances of the software allowed high scores. *Let someone else do the alien's bidding,* he thought.

Just as he was about to reach for the lanyard a low voice asked, "Is that you, Dr. Brody?"

The professor stopped cold. Two beautiful eyes opened just in front of his face. They blinked several times as they focused in the low light. Before he could say a word, she spoke again.

"We need to talk. And I think right now is a good time."

"About last night. That wasn't me out there on the beach."

"We'll talk about that later, Charles. First we're going to talk about why you were trying to take this key off my neck just now. What is in the shed that drove you to the top of the cliff last night?"

Dr. Brody didn't immediately answer. He knew what he'd been told. No one else was to know about the shed. The aliens had been very explicit about that item. If he told this woman lying in front of him, what fate would he seal for her.? *I can't do that,* he thought. No matter what the aliens had told him, he had strong feelings for this woman.

"Professor, we're talking here. It's not me talking and you sitting there like a lump. Something in the shed made you want to end it all. Whatever it is, we can take it on together."

"You mustn't know what's in the shed. It could be very bad for you."

"By who? Dr. Who? Is he the one directing this all?"

"I can't tell you. If you find out ..." he stopped.

Karen sat up on the couch and turned to face the professor. The sheet slid away revealing her naked body. She sat up and pulled Dr. Brody into her. His head nestled between her exposed breasts as she caressed his back.

"Whatever fate has in store for us, we will be doing it together. You aren't going to get away from me."

Charles relaxed as his mind let go. Her caresses eased the tension away from him. If she wanted to be a part of this, he would make it work. They were probably doomed to never leave this island anyway.

The first rays of the sun lit up the cabins interior. The two inhabitants moved to the bed to embrace. Still, the human need for companionship outweighed the bodily desire. By the time they realized it, the sun was high in the sky.

"Dr. Brody. Are you there? It's getting quite late."

The two were startled by Dr. Who's voice speaking English. They leaped out of bed and raced to get dressed. Each watched the other with pleasure as they threw their clothes on. Dr. Brody stepped out onto the lanai. He saw Dr. Who standing below in the garden, keeping his distance.

"Dr. Who. You speak English. Why haven't you spoken before this."

"Dr. Brody, that's not important. I hadn't seen you yet today and the noon hour is approaching. There is a one o'clock deadline you know. Each day you need to be ready."

"I'll be ready. Now, please excuse me, I'm quite busy."

Dr. Brody watched as Dr. Who retreated down the garden trail leading to the main house. It allowed access to the garden without passing the cabin on the cliff. Dr. Brody had made sure that the Wu Who couple had learned to use it after he had moved into the cabin.

"What's with Dr. Who speaking English all of a sudden?" Karen asked.

"As I told you. Those two are not what they seem."

Karen and Charles stared at each other and the implication of what Charles had just said.

"Well, I'm starving. How about eggs and toast for brunch?" he asked. Karen nodded her agreement that she also was starving, still recuperating from her fight with the parasites.

Charles had noticed when he saw her naked that the sickness had leaned her out significantly. He would have to put some weight back on her. *If she's serious about doing this together, she'll need all her strength,* he thought.

* * *

After eating, Dr. Brody took Karen down to the shed. He retrieved the key off her neck and unlocked the metal door. As they stepped into the darkened storage side, a voice caught them.

"Dr. Brody. She can't go in there. That is not allowed."

"Listen, Who. We have decided that we are doing this together."

Karen looked a little startled and overwhelmed. All he had told her so far was to be strong and to not let anything she was about to see rattle her. He still wasn't sure if they would live through what was coming, but they were about to find out.

"That is not why she was brought here. You are the chosen one, not her. You must fulfill your role on Earth. We have written it so. She is nothing."

Karen looked back at Dr. Who. The professor imagined what was running through her head. She must be thinking all sorts of things by what Dr. Who had just said. *No time for answers,* he thought. He gripped her hand harder and she responded.

"Get this straight right now. If she is not part of this, then I'm not part of this. Are we clear on that?"

"We must call in. I can't allow this. She'll have to wait outside ."

"Wrong answer. We are going in and calling. You may observe if you wish."

The professor opened the inner door and hit the power switch. The lights and the computer came alive. Charles looked at a wide-eyed Karen as she scanned the displays. A large map of the world sprang up with four color squares marked. She sat down next to Charles.

The second monitor flicked on and Errol Flynn was sitting, waiting.

"What's this? The woman is in the shed with you. You know that's not allowed. She was brought to you for other reasons. Now that she's seen everything, I'm afraid she'll have to be-"

"Nothing," the professor barked. "You will do nothing to her. She is my partner in this and I demand that she be included."

"Dr. Brody, you are hardly in a position to demand anything. We can end this all with a quick beam of light."

"Fine then, do it. Find another to make your picks. There are plenty, most better than me."

"Maybe we shall. You are irritating me."

"Get used to it or get another guy. You picked me for this for some reason. I'm assuming that reason is important enough that the woman doesn't affect your plans at all. For me, she affects my humanity greatly. And you don't understand that part, do you? Humans still baffle you. We aren't just what you see on our satellite feeds."

Dr. Brody glanced at Karen as she tried to take all of it in, but had a look of total confusion. She didn't know about aliens and vaporized cities or humans struggling for survival yet. Those things would come soon enough and he would see what this woman was made of. She had certainly helped him last night reach a decision to fight as long as he could.

"Do not threaten us. You have seen what threats get you."

"Then take this as a human trait. If you've seen enough old movies, and you seem to relish in them, then maybe we can reach a compromise."

"I'm listening."

"You have no doubt seen that every Batman has a Robin, every Lone Ranger a Tonto. It is common for our heroes to have a sidekick. I can give you countless examples of how the sidekick saves the day," the professor said.

"There is no option to save the day, Professor. The Earth will suffer division and no sidekick will stop that."

"Fair enough. But for the TV spectacular that you have resorted to, and I have no idea why, but for that, the audience will understand," the professor lied. He had no idea what appealed to the common masses. Charles had never watched any of the reality shows but knew they were quite popular.

The aliens were attempting a similar show for whatever reason. *They could just as easily divide up the*

*Earth, vaporize those in the wrong quadrant and move on,* he thought. But they hadn't chosen that option, and maybe that was where his strength lay. He wasn't sure, but he was betting both their lives on a hunch.

Errol Flynn sat for a long time before speaking. "Very well, you may have your sidekick. But no more interruptions, or I promise you-"

The professor cut him off. "We have a lot to do to prepare, so if you'll excuse us." He hit the switch cutting the camera feed.

Dr. Who, who had been watching the whole exchange said, "You risk fate, Dr. Brody. No one has ever-"

Dr. Brody stood up and interrupted Dr. Who. He took his arm and escorted him to the outside door, pushing the door shut in his face. Sitting back down next to Karen, he took her hand. "I told you it would be dangerous, but it's too late to turn back now."

"And why was I brought to this island?" Karen asked.

"Later. I have to bring you up to speed on all the other things."

He spent the next hour explaining everything to Karen. Her eyes got bigger and bigger as he told her of the alien ship holding the Earth hostage. By the time Dr. Brody was done he sensed that it was all beyond her comprehension. *Luckily, she's totally forgotten to ask again why she had been brought to the island,* he thought.

Charles leaned over and kissed her to bring her back to some reality. "OK, ten minutes to showtime."

"What do I do?"

"Tonight, just look beautiful. There will probably be four billion in the audience for tonight's show. I'm sure every human being on earth is scrambling to a television for this show.

"What? Four billion people are going to see me like this? No way." She started to get up and leave.

"No time. Just sit and act natural. It will be over in twenty minutes."

Karen fought slightly to retreat but gave in to the moment. From her expression, she was overwhelmed by it all. *Hell, I'm still overwhelmed,* he thought.

The second monitor flicked on and the scene from Game Central came on. The three talking heads greeted one another and started into the hype. They described the previous evening's show and which side was looking stronger.

The hype that they interjected was laughable. This wasn't a sporting contest between athletes, but a life and death struggle between species for survival. The first half hour finally ended and it was time. The blank screen in the shed would be filled by ads on each TV station, making the whole thing more bizarre. Charles waited, holding Karen's hand. She attempted a squeeze of support but he knew it was bravado showing through.

The little red light by the bottom of the large monitor came on just as the second monitor clicked to the arena. The reaction was immediate.

"Dr. Brody, what's this? An assistant?" Bob Barker asked before he even did his opening hype.

"Yes, this is my assistant Karen Price. She was a graduate student of mine whom I've asked to help me."

"Well, OK Professor." The leer in Bob's comment showed. *Could the man be any more suggestive?* Charles thought.

Bob continued. "Good evening, everyone. Here we are at our second nightly selection. Its human versus animal. Which one will prevail tonight? Back with us is GP. Are you ready to stick it to the humans?"

The panda didn't answer but his rooting section sure did. By their enthusiasm, it would appear that they would be happy if the entire Earth was converted to strictly animal habitat, leaving humans with nothing.

"And I'll assume the Professor and Mary Ann are ready. Oh sorry, Karen, my oversight." The human side of the arena broke out in boos at the obvious host put-down. The host appeared rattled by the response.

Bob carried on through the catcalls while the panda crowd tried to encourage the host. He finally spoke. "Last move was by Dr. Brody. That means GP makes the next selection. Start the clock."

The giant panda reached out for the joystick and the cursor began to move around the large globe. Once again each grid section lit up when the cursor entered the area. GP moved around the Earth, letting his five minutes of torment settle over the humans.

Where the cursor settled would become animal territory. The professor still didn't know if humans were being immediately eliminated or if they would be given time to move to a human section.

The panda used up four of his five minutes before settling on an Amazon River square. He pushed down on the stick and the grid turned green. His supporters roared approval.

"Good solid choice. The Amazon Jungle has the most diverse animal population of any place on Earth. Dr. Brody and Karen, your turn."

The human cheerleaders went wild. They knew from the professor's performance the previous night that he had almost succumbed to the pressure. They certainly didn't know what had transpired after the show, but the appearance of a young woman by his side spoke volumes.

Dr. Brody knew which two sections he wished to add today. He just had to be patient. *One at a time,* he thought. The panda's choice of the Denver square had rattled him. It was a logical choice because he knew that in historic times the North American Plains had supported huge concentrations of animals. The bison herds were just one example.

But today he was playing politics a little. He would make sound choices, but he knew he had to move them around. The cursor stopped on the square next to the first animal selection, the section that included the Yangtze River and a large chunk of Chinese farmland along the coast. The grid section turned red as he made his selection.

"Another solid choice for Dr. Brody. Plenty of humans live in that area, thats for sure," Bob Barker added. The 'totalator' on the side of the screen rolled up by millions. It was indicating how many people had just been added to the human total.

Watching the 'death' totalator yesterday when Denver had been placed into the animal column was disconcerting. Now the 'live' human total vastly outnumbered the 'death' total.

GP went to work on his joystick. After much taunting and at the end of the five minute limit, it settled on a square over northern Kenya. The section turned green on the world map.

"Again, a solid choice by GP. That section holds the majority of the Serengeti and is famous for its animal herds. Well played." Bob seemed to be a bit biased in his host job.

The professor ignored the host's rantings and took the mouse on a mission around the world. Following the panda's lead, he taunted the crowd up till the end before finally settling in a large section of France. The area turned red.

"An interesting choice. As we can see from the game software this grid holds the farmland along the Loire Valley. Unfortunately for the French, Paris lays just east of that grid. Some Frenchmen will wonder at that choice."

The camera swung into a close up of Bob Barker as he closed his portion of the show. "Tomorrow night we'll see if your neighborhood stays with the humans or gets converted to wilderness. Stay tuned for our wrap up show featuring our talented analysts. They'll explain what happened tonight. See you all tomorrow night."

Charles turned off his camera feed as Bob finished. He didn't need the hype and he certainly didn't need the talking head analysis. Having designed the game, he knew enough to get the best for the human side. He turned and faced Karen.

"Are all the people in Denver already dead? It sort of dawned on me what those little green squares mean on the map."

Dr. Brody turned around at the big monitor displaying the divided land. He reached and turned it off, then took Karen's hand. "We need some fresh air."

# Chapter 13

The two geographers sat and held each other for most of the afternoon. After their session of 'Humans vs. Aliens' for international TV broadcast, they had made their way out to the point where Charles had contemplated ending his involvement in the whole deal. Sitting away from the cliff edge on a large flat rock, each was lost in their thoughts.

Karen waited for the professor to break the silence. The way he had recommended that they both get some fresh air made her hesitant to pursue her concerns. She knew that the man sitting beside her had much on his mind and needed time to process the days events.

They both sat and admired the view of the bay. Off in the distance, beyond the two headlands, the tropical blue waters of the open ocean expanded to the horizon. No other land intruded on their world.

Charles finally broke the quiet. "Are you doing OK? This is all very stressful, and we need to be aware how each of us is handling it."

Karen thought about Dr. Brody's question. She was still in the dark about what was really happening. But she wasn't sure that the professor knew much more than she did. She hesitated in adding to his worries so decided to use a different tack.

"Charles, the problem I'm having is what to call you."

"Huh?"

"Well, we've moved past 'Dr. Brody' as well as the 'Professor' even though I'm comfortable with those since our time at college. But I know we have a different relationship now. We need to be less formal if we're to see this thing through together."

"I agree Karen."

"But Charles just comes off as still too formal to me. I don't know what it is, but I almost prefer Dr. Brody to calling you Charles. I can't explain it, but its too stiff to me."

"I see. What about Charlie? I haven't been called that since high school, but that would be fine."

"No, not Charlie. Where I grew up the next door neighbor's dog was called Charlie. And it wasn't a very nice dog."

"Chuck?"

"Oh no. You are not a Chuck," Karen pleaded.

"Well, what do you suggest?"

Karen now felt stupid even bringing up the issue. *What's in a name?* she thought. *The man is dealing with the end of humanity and I'm busting him on his name.*

The two sat in silence when an idea hit Karen. "I have it. We're fighting aliens, correct?"

"Correct," Charles answered.

"Star Wars' is coming into my brain, and-"

Dr. Brody cut her off. "And you want to call me Darth Vader? Just what I need."

Karen turned red from embarrassment. This wasn't going well. She needed to get things back on track. "No, not him. But I was thinking of someone a little more on the good side. Captain Han Solo maybe."

"Well, that sounds a little better, putting me in the same category as Harrison Ford. Any male sure wouldn't complain at that."

Karen relaxed a little bit. "So you wouldn't mind if I called you Han then? Just between us, of course."

"Would I have to call you Princess Leia?"

"If you wanted, that would be fine."

"No, I like Karen. Its a beautiful name," Charles stopped. Karen could tell the professor was thinking. Then he added. "Han... I like that. Sort of goes with the Errol Flynn theme our game buddies are running with."

"Well, if you do think of a character that you'd like to call me, let me know."

Han answered by turning to face her. He reached out with both arms, pulled her close, leaned in and kissed her mouth. The suddenness of the embrace took her a little off guard, but she recovered fast.

She had been waiting and imagining this moment since their evening on the beach. Returning his kiss, she slid her arms around him and pulled him into her to pass the message that his action was welcome.

The kiss became more passionate. The trade winds swirled around the entwined couple. Shifting on the hard rock, Karen felt a hand on her breast.

"Oh Han." She moaned as she kissed him again. A sharp pain shot through her leg as she leaned into the embrace. "Ouch. Maybe we could find a more comfortable spot than this rock."

Han backed off and a redness came over his face. "Yes, how thoughtless of me. Allow me." He stood up and gently pulled Karen to her feet. He swooped down, gathered her up into his arms and began carrying her toward their cabin.

"Han, how romantic." She placed her hand behind his head and gently pulled it to the side where she kissed him.

He stumbled as his attention was distracted by the head movement. "You better let me get you over these rocks before we continue."

"I'm sorry." Karen settled down and let her man carry her back to a soft bed. He gently placed her down. She slid to the side as she pulled him down on top of her.

The two embraced. Karen twisted her legs up and around the professor. "Can the Wookiee come out and play?" she asked as she moved her hand down his stomach.

"Only if Princess is ready," Han answered as he returned the motion. His hand found the top of her shorts and slid under them.

"Princess has been ready longer than you know," Karen said as she arched her back and thew her head to the side. The two explored each other as the Wookiee and Princess met for the first time.

By evening, the couple lay exhausted in the dark. Trade winds caressed their naked bodies as the wind chimes danced outside their window. The sound played across the room as the two lay half awake.

"Are we doing something wrong?" Karen finally broke the mood.

"What are you asking?"

"Here we are laying naked in a tropic breeze after a wonderful afternoon of closeness, and out there in the world people are-"

Dr. Brody stopped her. She knew it probably wasn't the time or place for such subjects, but the nagging knowledge of humanity's struggle for life wasn't pushed aside easily. Even by such intense physical activity. And it had been intense. She hadn't experienced anything quite so intense ever in her life.

She had been with men before, but nothing like Han. Whether it was the situation or the man, she didn't care, she would just enjoy it while it lasted.

Karen rolled over onto Hans. She shifted her body. "Sorry for breaking the mood. Princess seems to want more attention."

The Wookiee come to attention and she moved to place the Wookiee and Princess back into close contact. She kissed Han as he pulled her down on top of him. The wind chimes took over and muffled the sounds coming from the bed.

* * *

Al Worthington sat and shifted in his chair. The Security Council of the UN was on its fourth straight hour with barely a break. Food had been brought in as the members continued their heated discussion.

"This situation is totally intolerable," the Chinese Ambassador yelled. Al noted that it was probably the eighteenth time he'd said it since the meeting had started.

The Security Council had watched the third installment of 'Endangered Species' on TV like the rest of the world. This meeting had developed soon after the episode in response.

The Chairman of the Security Council looked over his fellow members and added, "I agree with the Chinese Ambassador. Who is this Dr. Brody and why is he playing this most dangerous game with the aliens? And now this woman is involved, a Ms. Karen Price. What do we know about her?"

Al drifted off from exhaustion. *Whoever she is, I'd like her sitting right behind me,* he thought. Then he changed his thoughts. *I could even think of better places she could be sitting.*

He had stared at her through the whole twenty minutes that she and the professor were on the screen. The woman was late twenties and quite beautiful. He couldn't tell from the camera angle how tall she was, but compared to the professor, she seemed above average. And she appeared to be well built.

She certainly had improved her looks from the first night she had shown up. She had gotten rid of that dumpy cotton dress and switched to something decidedly more revealing.

He closed his eyes and remembered the tan body that her loose chamois top had exposed. And the cleavage she let show indicated plenty of womanly attributes under the chamois.

If her tan was any indication, the two were someplace far from the Iowa cornfields. The professor was tan and fit from his image on the screen, but without any background other than the room they appeared in, Al couldn't determine where they were located.

But wherever it might be, the couple on the screen seemed to be thriving in the situation. *I don't think the aliens have them locked in a cell somewhere,* he thought.

The ambassadors of the member countries droned on as Al drifted off to daydream of him and Ms. Price alone on some tropical island somewhere. His head began to droop and the motion brought him back to reality.

"And furthermore, I demand that we assert our right as the duly appointed representatives for the United Nations to be involved in the selection of the human sections."

Al blinked his eyes to focus on the task in front of him. As his mind switched from images of romping naked on the beach with that woman, something clicked. "My God," he almost yelled.

The entire room stopped and turned to the noise from the back row. Al froze as an intense gaze landed on him.

The U.S. Ambassador turned and looked at his employee. "You have something to add?"

Al stammered as the situation pressed on him. "Maybe Madam Ambassador." He looked around at the other people in the room. His thoughts suddenly switched to security. *I need to confirm what I just thought before I pitch it to the entire Council,* he thought.

"Then please enlighten us."

"If I may be excused. I need to go review the tapes of the last two episodes." Al jumped up and left the room without any further explanation. The room exploded in questions as he hit the door.

Returning to the U.S. Mission, Al Worthington, Consul to the U.S. Ambassador to the U.N., grabbed the general.

"I need someone who knows Morse Code."

The general looked at Al in confusion. He hesitated at this strange request. Morse Code was a hundred-year-old form of communication that had been superseded by digital blips traveling the speed of light.

"General, a Morse Code expert, right now," Al demanded.

The general stammered and headed to the Comm Center. Al followed along and heard the general ask for a Morse Code-qualified personnel. One private raised his hand.

"You, with me." The general turned and bumped into Al. "Ok, what do you need him for Mr. Worthington?"

Al led the two into the Conference Room. He picked up the phone and asked the technician to run the past two alien shows.

"Sit," Al indicated to the two. The flat screen TV monitor on the wall turned on and soon the blue was replaced by the talking heads introducing the show. Al requested the tech to fast forward to when Dr. Brody came on the screen.

"Now private, I want you to watch the woman's eyes. Tell me if she is trying to send a message."

The three men sat and watched. The private took a tablet of paper and began making notes. Al watched the woman intently. There seemed to be a non-random blinking taking place. Somewhere in his sub-conscience it had registered when he had first watched. His dreaming of her in less-than-professional ways had brought it out from where his mind had buried it.

The screen switched back to the talking heads as Dr. Brody's part of the show ended. Al leaned forward and tried to look at the private's notes. The general spoke first.

"Anything? I sure sensed a decided pattern in there, but it's been too long since I've done any Morse Code crap."

"Yes, sir. There's more than crap there. I got a definite message," the private offered.

"Well, good God man, spell it out," the general demanded.

"Yes, sir. S-O-U-T-H_H-E-M-I-S. She kept repeating it."

"Huh, south hemis. What's that?" the general asked.

"Southern hemisphere. It has to be. She's telling us that they're in the Southern Hemisphere."

"How do we know if this woman even knows Morse Code? For all we know she just randomly blinked out a message."

Al offered to check on her background. With her disappearance from Iowa and her subsequent reappearance with Dr Brody, no one on Earth was being more scrutinized. Except maybe Dr. Brody himself. Al ordered the third show's tape run. The three sat back as the tech found the beginning of the selection segment.

As the two watched intently, the private wrote his notes. They recognized that Ms. Price seemed to repeat her blinking pattern. The talking heads came on and the screen went blank.

"Come on, man, what is it this time?" the general ordered. Al noticed the strain produced by such a superior officer barking at a lowly private. Al spoke to offer some support.

"Its OK, private. What was the message this time?"

The private seemed to relax just a bit. "1-4-5-W-L-O-N-G_0-2-0-S-L-A-T_A-P-P-R-X."

"Well, I'll be, she gave us longitude and latitude coordinates. Where's a map?" Al said.

Al ran out and quickly returned with a globe that the Mission kept by the receptionist. The two spun the globe around as Al traced his finger along the Latitude line denoted by 20 degrees South. He stopped when he got to the 145 degree longitude line.

"There." He held his finger on the spot.

"What's the 'a-p-p-r-x' on the end mean?" the general asked.

"If I may, sir. That would be an abbreviation of approximate. She is telling us she isn't exactly sure of where she is," the Army private added.

"But we know she was a geography major working on her Master's Degree. She should be familiar with longitude and latitude."

The private returned to his communication room duties as the other two men went to work. The general was soon on the phone to the Pentagon ordering up detailed maps of the thousand-mile circle around the coordinates they had been given.

Al dove into the task of confirming that Ms. Price knew Morse Code. Even though it seemed evident that she did, they needed to confirm it.

The general's detailed map arrived by computer and was on the room display just as Al got his phone call. After a brief conversation, he hung up.

"That was my secretary. She tracked down Ms. Price's brother. With all the FBI agents scouring the country trying to stay on top of this, he was readily available. It seems that Karen had helped him learn Morse Code when they were kids. He was going for his First Class Rank in Boy Scouts and had trouble with it. He says she knew it better than he did by the time they were done."

"That confirms it then. But the coordinates she gave us is open ocean. There's no land anywhere near her spot. Its a wild goose chase, I'm afraid," the general said.

Al looked intently at the large circle that had been placed around the specific coordinates. The general was right. He could see nothing but the South Pacific within 500 miles of the center. As his eyes roamed across the map, he noticed something.

There appeared to be a small island outside the 500-mile circle. He moved in to examine it closely. "Can we get this section enlarged?"

The general worked the computer and the cursor moved across the screen. Suddenly the island grew larger. The general stood and joined Al, looking at the island. He picked up the phone to the Pentagon.

"Might as well get something to eat. We have a couple of hours to wait," the general said as he hung up.

\* \* \*

The men of Special Operations Delta Force sat in the ready room near Colorado Springs. The occupants of the Cheyenne Mountain underground bunker had been evacuated yesterday and Captain Grinkis was waiting for new orders.

With the aliens selecting the 500-mile square that included the Colorado Springs area, the Pentagon had decided that it would be prudent to move the national leadership to an area already selected for the human side.

Air Force One had flown out bound for Greenville Air Force Base north of New Orleans. The nation's command structure would be safe in the only American square so far selected for human habitation.

Unfortunately, thousands of Americans had a similar idea. Already the roads leading to the 500 mile section were clogged with people heading to what they perceived as safety. Captain Grinkis was anticipating orders to follow Air Force One to New Orleans for added security when Sergeant Aubin announced a phone call.

"Captain Grinkis," he answered.

Standing beside him was Lieutenant Butch Goring, US Navy Seal Commander. Butch moved closer to see if he could pick up any of the conversation.

There wasn't much to hear as Captain Grinkis listened, offering the occasional 'uh huhs' to indicate agreement. After a short time, the captain hung up.

"Get your guys ready to move, Butch. You'll be getting your call soon, but we've both being deployed to Kaneohe Marine Base on Oahu. We are to be brought up to speed when we arrive," Chet said.

"Nothing more to go on than that?" Butch asked.

"Just that something is up in the South Pacific. We are being tasked to find out what."

The Special Ops officer turned to Mel, the 'Endangered Species' software gaming expert who had 'volunteered' to offer advice. "You won't be going home soon, Mel. Seems you will be traveling with us."

"Ahh man. I got classes I'm missing." Mel turned to his brother. The corporal had sucked him into this and he did his best pleading to get out of it.

"Sorry brother. If the captain says you're with us for the duration, you pack your bags," the Army corporal said.

"I don't have any bags. I didn't plan on spending more than a day playing Army."

"Mel, I'm sure we can come up with some duds for you. But I'm afraid they'll be camo. At least you'll look the part."

Mel sighed in resignation to his situation. Somehow he knew that if he tried to skip out on these guys, it would be the last thing he probably would ever do, at least with his joints still functional.

"I know what you're thinking dear brother. And you're right. If you did, it would be the last functional body experience of your life." Mel fell in behind the captain as they all headed to their quarters to pack.

# Chapter 14

The morning sun streamed into the cabin atop the cliff. The trade winds had died down during the night and the room was unusually stuffy. With the low rays coming in under the large roof overhangs, Dr. Brody noticed the extra heat.

The warm still air made the heat between the two human bodies more noticeable. Each of them moved to relieve the slightly uncomfortable stickiness. Karen rolled onto her back and looked up at the items hanging motionlessness outside by the window.

Normally the wind chimes would be announcing their presence, but all was quiet. And with no trade winds carrying the sounds of the surf up from the beach, the cabin was exceptionally quiet.

She turned her head toward a sleeping professor and looked down his naked body. The warmth of the room had forced the bed sheets to the floor. Both of them lay totally exposed, seeking some coolness.

Charles' eye lids moved as he turned his head. Their gaze met in sleepy haze as both adjusted to the morning light. The smile that overcame his expression told her everything. Even after last night, she wasn't totally sure of their relationship.

She continued to dwell on their seemingly captive status by the aliens. Although both of them were taking advantage of their personal situation, the real world still hung over them. She couldn't dismiss that while they were enjoying each other, people out in the world were tormented as to whether today would end their existence.

Karen reached over and took her companion's head, pulling it toward hers. They kissed and embraced. Her stomach broke the mood as it announced its protest. She suddenly realized that she was extremely hungry.

"Oh, excuse me. Seems one part of me isn't being nourished by your sweet attentions."

"You should be starved. We missed dinner last night in all the excitement. Why don't you go shower while I get breakfast. I'll meet you on the lanai."

Karen headed to the toilet before turning on the shower. She purposely left the swinging doors open on both. She noticed the Professor watching her intently from the kitchen as she washed her body. Rinsing off, she turned off the water. She wrapped a towel around her and sat down at the outdoor table.

"The water helps with the heat. I finally feel cool and refreshed," Karen said.

A *lavalava* wrapped chef soon emerged from the kitchen carrying a tray. Charles placed two plates of egg and toast on the table. He put a dish of raspberry jam down and a bowl of fresh tropical fruit he had sliced.

"Smells wonderful. We can eat, then why don't you take a shower. It's marvelous."

"You know, we haven't been in the garden lately. We can't forget our chores to keep us going on this island," Charles said.

"Let the Wu Whos take care of things for awhile. We're busy," Karen purred.

Dr. Brody seemed to take the hint. He raced through breakfast and headed to the shower. He left the swinging door open as Karen watched intently. She worked her pieces of fruit enticingly around her lips for her partner to witness. It definitely did the trick of reviving the Wookie.

Soon a wet Wookiee was greeting a still moist Princess as the two captives spent the rest of the morning drying off. When they were done, they headed to the shower together to get reinvigorated.

"I need to head down to the shed. I've got some questions for Errol Flynn before the show starts."

"And I need to get ready. I have an audience of billions to prepare for." She knew that the past day's activities would radiate across every TV screen. After Charles had left, she looked in a mirror and confirmed the news. Any perceptive female out there would recognize the look. Karen decided to forgo any make up and let her natural blush show.

By the time she reached the shed and the small TV studio it held, Charles was off the air with Errol.

"Good news," Charles announced as she walked into the room. "No one needs to move until the end of the game. All selections will be made first. Then unlike the computer game, a trading period will take place where we can trade sections to try and reach logical groupings for each side."

"So no more deaths."

"I didn't say that," the professor stopped her. The pause struck her hard.

"What do you mean? I thought people were going to be able to move to human sections at the end of the game."

"They will." Karen watched Dr. Brody carefully. He didn't want to offer more and she didn't know if she should press. The man was already under intense pressure with what he was attempting to do and she didn't want to add to that stress load. Karen had worked hard the last 48 hours trying to relieve the professor's stress and it seemed to have worked, at least until now.

No more information was forthcoming so Karen left the issue alone. *He will tell me when the time is right,* she thought.

"More good news. I bargained and we get Sundays off. I explained that many on Earth worship their spiritual powers on that day and that they shouldn't force the game on them. They reluctantly agreed but said they would run a wrap-up show for an hour each Sunday night. A sort of go over the weeks selections," Charles said.

"One day off a week would be nice. We can catch up on our chores."

\* \* \*

By the time that Captain Grinkis and his troops reached Hawaii, four more days of the 'Endangered Species' show had taken place. Chet sat down with Mel, his resident expert on the game. The Special Ops troops would wait at the Marine Base Hawaii at Kaneohe for orders from headquarters.

Captain Grinkis wanted an update on the status of the selections that Dr. Brody had made along with the selections the panda had made for the animal world. The map in the Situation Room was slowly filling in as the participants made their two selections per day.

"OK Mel, give me your analysis. Do you see a pattern forming yet?"

"Oh yeah, man. Dr. Brody is opening with the John Deere Gambit. Nothing flashy, but it gets the job done," Mel offered.

"John Deere Gambit? Enlighten me," Chet asked.

"Some players go right for the big cities. Save as many people as possible. The numbers on the 'totalator' look good for awhile. They get pumped and keep the big city thing going."

"I assume that's not good."

"Hell no, man. As the game goes along, those cities suddenly become albatrosses around the players neck. He finds out he's been too busy running his human population numbers up and forgot about resource squares he needs to support them."

"Like farm land and minerals."

"Hey, you're smart about this. Cities are incredible resource hogs. If a player doesn't grab enough farmland and other resource squares to support all those cities, the 'totalator' starts making its calculations and the 'number dead' total starts zooming up. The opponent will have grabbed all the prime food squares before the human player can adjust."

"And the results are..."

"Brutal. Humans die like flies," Mel said.

"So the professor is going for the farmland?" Captain Grinkis asked. He noticed that they had gathered a crowd during their discussion.

Mel's brother, the corporal, then asked the obvious. "But what if he never has a chance to get to select the big cities? Seems like that its all farmland and no live bodies living there."

"Yeah brother, that's the downside of the John Deere Gambit. It's like a fine line between food and people. We just have to see how the Doc balances it."

"But does the game allow people to move to human squares at the end of the game?" Chet asked.

"No flipping way. Those on animal squares are liquidated. That's the appeal of the game man," Mel said.

The room went quiet as the occupants all stared at Mel. His answer didn't sit well with soldiers sworn to defend people, Americans in particular.

The attitude of the human-hating crowd mystified them. The environmental movement had done a successful job indoctrinating many into the belief that animal life trumped human life. It was a view that few in the military held.

Mel slid down into his chair trying to disappear from the gaze of the soldiers. His brother walked over and whacked Mel in the head.

"Hey, what's that for?"

"For being such a dumb son-of-a-bitch."

The troops all nodded their approval. Chet took his troops' leadd and shook his head in disgust. *Where do these people come up with such anti-human ideas?* he thought.

He knew the answer was in the easy life to which so many had become accustomed. Easy living led to complacency as to the reality of the world. Humans had suffered disease and war through millennia and learned to turn to God for solace.

Over the last century, life had turned more agreeable. Modern medicines solved diseases and living standards had raised people's lives above subsistence existence. Many in the Third World still struggled daily, but in the Western world, young people had no concept of any struggle for life.

The alien invasion and their attempt at dividing the Earth between human and animal would certainly change all that. And as Mel had said, if people caught on the wrong side of the dividing line were vaporized, things would get testy on Earth.

Butch Goring walked into the room and announced, "We have a target. Its lock and load time."

The room exploded in commotion as all the troops tried to talk at once. Butch walked over to Chet and motioned that they had a meeting to discuss their mission.

"OK, Mel. I guess you're done with us. I'll see to your transport back to the mainland."

Mel smiled at his release from the clutches of Special Ops. Chet was about to find out he had misspoken. Mel wasn't about to leave for civilian life...

# Chapter 15

New York City lived with the ignominy that it had not yet been chosen by Dr. Brody to be part of the human world. It was a dubious consolation that no other large city had been selected yet either.

But New York had always considered itself different from every other city on Earth. With the United Nations headquartered on Manhattan Island, New Yorkers took on the airs of the World's Capital City. And they were pressing as to why they were still in limbo.

Inside the Security Council, a similar attitude was evident. The French, British, and especially the Chinese all fought for an answer as to why their capital cities were still unselected.

"This Dr. Brody might have designed this game, but he sure doesn't know how to play it. I'm hearing from my citizens daily who play this 'Endangered Species' software. They tell me they could be doing better than the professor," the French Ambassador said.

The Chinese Ambassador jumped right in. "We have switched our computer software experts from other tasks to solve this problem. They said they've run thousands of scenarios and they all do better than this doctor. I smell an American trick."

"Now Mr. Ambassador, the United States is working hard trying to resolve this selection thing. We also have gamers, I think they're called, that have set the high scores on this game. They say that Dr. Brody has never even played the game. He certainly has no scores listed."

"So, what can we do?" the Russian Ambassador asked. He had finally retuned to the meetings after the failed Russian attack on the aliens. "The aliens are in charge of this and we all know we're powerless to intercede."

Al Worthington sat in the back once again and listened to the discussion. He was thinking that maybe something could be done about the good professor and his nubile woman assistant. She still haunted his mind, especially after her appearance three days ago.

Watching intently for any new eye blinking, he had observed none. But then her demeanor overwhelmed any study of her eyes. Her whole facial look spoke volumes. The natural blush of her cheeks, the satisfied look on her face and the way her body seemed to radiate sex appeal.

He wasn't sure if it was the tank top that offered a revealing gaze at her upper body or if it was the glimmering tanned body. She seemed to glow. The torture he felt in his loins distracted him from his search for any added Morse Code messages.

The Army private in the Command Center could determine that later. He wanted to relish in his twenty minutes of erotic thoughts watching this woman on the screen 'assist' the man choosing life and death for Earth. The whole power equation involved made his male ego embarrassingly responsive. He had to shift each time she was on screen to adjust as his body parts grew embarrassingly large.

So tormented by the vision he was that even when told that no secret message had been sent, he took a copy of the tape home and watched it over and over each night. But just a video would never satiate himself fully.

Al had seen the satellite image of the small island he had found. When the Pentagon had tasked the spy satellite to overfly the supposedly uninhabited island, he had been in the room to view the feed.

As the satellite tracked over the island, the garden and then the small cabin came into view. The main house was mostly obscured by the large tropical trees shading it. A shed between the two houses was evident in the camera's view.

He had seen people walking. The uninhabited island had at least two people on it. They had appeared as plain as day. *Those satellites are so amazing,* he thought. When Al asked the general to replay the tape over and over he imagined Ms. Price and her sultry tan body walking enticingly through the garden.

And then he heard the answer to his dreams. The general told the ambassador that a Special Ops team was being tasked to interdict the island.

"We've picked up electronic signals at the same time each day. For a deserted island, there's a signal going up to the alien space satellites. And if you notice, whenever one of their satellites goes over this island, the electronic footprint goes way up. Much more than we'd expect from two cabins and a shed," the general had told the ambassador.

"So, are we going to do something about it, General?" the ambassador had asked.

Al sat in torment as he overheard the entire exchange. If there was a mission to the island, he wanted to be part of it. But how could he talk his way onto a Special Ops mission? Knowing he had to be on the team, he went to work on his political connections to make sure he would be part of any ground work on the island. *I'll meet Karen Price in person if it was the last thing I did in my life*, Al thought.

* * *

The trade winds were still missing as Charles and Karen readied themselves for their first day off. Sunday had finally arrived on the island, or at least what the aliens had said was Sunday.

Dr. Brody had lost track of time after his arrival on the island. The only thing he tracked was day and night. Added in was mealtime when he was hungry, and the rest was a blur. The day of the week, the month and the year were all indiscernible to him.

He had started keeping track of the number of days he had been on the island. The small X's on the side of the toilet building marked each new day. A circled X marked the day of Karen's arrival.

Charles had added a square on the X denoting when the 'Endangered Species' game had begun. Although the computer kept track of the game sequence for him, it helped keep things in front of him. He looked at the days marked as he would prepare food in the kitchen.

Karen was excited about their first official day off since the alien game had begun. Making two selections each day for the human world had piled up on him. He could only imagine the stress it caused Karen.

She put on a good face for his benefit. But when he held her each night while they slept, her frequent crying revealed pent-up emotions. He thought he knew just the thing for releasing tension, or at least he hoped it would do the trick.

He busily made lunch and packed. Karen returned from her early morning chores in the garden, announcing she was ready.

Dr. Brody went to the short cabinet that held personal items and retrieved two sets of masks and snorkels. He stuffed them into the pack along with two sets of flippers.

"Hey, where did those come from? You've been holding out on me."

"Dr. Wu gave me a box that had been in the shed. Among some other useful items were these. Get your suit on, we're going snorkeling," Charles announced.

Grabbing sun screen, towels and a blanket, the pack was bulging by the time they left. The professor explained as they walked west through the garden that he had spent his first two weeks on the island exploring.

He had mapped out the entire island by the time Karen arrived. Most of it was volcanic cliffs and steep slopes. But along the western shore the hills had eroded offering access. It was one of his special places that he had discovered. He was excited to now share it with someone.

They hiked along a side slope that sat above a cliff. The ocean crashed into the base of the cliff as the two carefully crossed the slope. They both had worn boots, with Karen suddenly finding a pair of boots that fit her perfectly.

Both had commented at the time how the island always provided just what they needed at the time they needed it.

Charles walked ahead thinking about Karen's undersized bikini that Dr. Wu had given her. *At least a new suit hadn't show up to replace it,* he thought.

The small Chinese woman wore a small sized bikini. The translation onto an above average sized Western-framed woman was not to be missed. Charles' stride sped up.

"Hey, what's the hurry? We have all day."

"I'm just anxious to show you, that's all," Charles answered.

"You sure that's the only reason?"

"Yes," he lied.

The next ravine took them to their destination. Scrambling down the rocks, Charles dropped the heavy pack on the small beach by the water. He sprinted back to the top to help Karen safely negotiate the slope.

As they climbed down, a large rock outcropping blocked any view. As they came around the obstacle, their destination came into full view. Karen stopped.

Below was a lagoon of luminescent water. The color of turquoise, the shallow water held dark spots, indicating a reef. Outside the outer reef, breakers crashed onto the rocks that protected the lagoon.

"It's beautiful."

"And I've been waiting for someone special to bring here. Let's get wet."

They scrambled the last slope down onto the sand. Charles picked up the pack and took Karen's hand. A clump of shade trees half way down the short beach offered a respite from the tropical sun.

Charles spread the blanket in the shade and pulled out the snorkel gear. They sat on the blanket and adjusted the flippers to their feet. They slipped the snorkels into place on the mask strap. Then pulling on the masks, each worked the side straps to assure a tight fit.

Their equipment ready, they readied themselves. Charles hung his sweat-stained shirt on the branch so it would dry. Grabbing the sunscreen, he lathered his body from the sun. He watched as Karen pulled her top over her head then bent and slid and stepped out of her shorts

Charles stared at the minuscule suit that barely covered anything. Karen noticed his stares, smiled and grabbed the sunscreen. She lathered it on and then turned to Charles.

"Could you do my back, please?"

Charles took the lotion and squeezed some onto her back.

"Oh, its cold."

He swiped his hand back and forth, working the protection into her back. It was warm to his touch and he lingered in his task.

"OK, don't belabor the point. Turn around and I'll get you."

Charles responded and the cold lotion hit his back. Karen's warm hand smeared the sunscreen around until he was covered.

They picked up their equipment and headed into the water. When the water reached their knees, they both sat down. Flippers went on first and then the mask. They pulled their mask down and spit onto the glass. Coating the glass in saliva would help keep it from fogging up.

With the masks adjusted snuggly on their faces, they inserted the snorkel mouth piece. Rolling onto their stomachs, they floated out into the lagoon. The world suddenly went quiet as it exploded with color.

Being, until recently, an uninhabited island, the lagoon was pristine. They both knew from previous snorkeling forays not to touch anything. Just floating along breathing through the snorkel and admiring the vast display was enough.

Tropical fish flitted away as they approached. Diverse stands of coral lay below them, some waving in the lagoon currents. Stopping to check their location, they would bob to the surface. At most stops, the snorkel dropped to the side as they embraced and kissed, their face masks clanking. The salt water combined with the sunscreen caused their bodies to rub together in a smooth slippery motion.

They continued their journey until Karen stopped with a jolt. She frantically pointed to her right. Charles swam around her to see what had caused the excitement. A sea turtle was lazily diving to the bottom to feed. They both floated motionless on the surface as they watched their new sea companion.

Motioning for shore, Charles led them back to the small beach. Reaching shallow water, he took off his flippers and stood up. Karen joined him as their masks came off and they walked to the blanket.

"I don't know about you, but I'm starving," Charles said as he dug out the lunch he had prepared.

Karen sat down beside him and took a sandwich. She announced that she had also been starving by the quick work she made of lunch. As they finished with fruit, Karen turned to Charles. Juice ran down her face, dripping onto her chest.

Charles leaned over and kissed her on the mouth. Then he licked the juice where it had flowed down her. He continued to follow its path onto her chest. Reaching the bottom of the fruit flow, he switched his attention.

The small bikini top was pushed aside. Karen leaned back onto the blanket as Charles continued his search for any spilled fruit juice. Being very thorough in his search, Karen enjoyed every lick.

When the bikini bottom got in the way, it too was dispensed with. *I'm sure that fruit juice found its way down here,* he thought. Karen offered no protest.

As the lunch break continued, the shade shifted with the sun. Soon the two of them were in full sunlight and the increase in temperature only added to the heat already on the beach.

Exhausted after their lunchtime activities, the two found the intense sun impossible to handle. Charles motioned that they should move the blanket under the shade.

Up and moving, Karen motioned that she wanted another turn in the water. Now naked, she grabbed her snorkel gear and headed to the water. Charles eagerly followed.

The freedom of diving naked was wonderful. The two swam contentedly around the lagoon. Whenever each wanted to attract the attention of the other, they would run their hand up the inside of the other's thigh.

With onlooking tropical fish, the two spent more time exploring each other than the lagoon. They didn't even return to shore before the Wookiee and the Princess were once again greeting each other. A smooth rock near the reef provided a solid spot for the strenuous activity.

Finally reaching shore, Charles flopped onto the sand. Karen rode the water up onto him. Half in the water and half on the beach, the two embraced.

"I wish we could just stay here forever. It's so easy to forget what's on the other side of the island," Karen said.

Charles nodded his agreement and bent in to kiss the woman who had changed everything. He wanted to rid himself of his other life.

But knowing the price he had paid to get Sundays off, Charles tried to shove it back in his brain. He had put in his first shift at the nasty task the aliens required. Charles was just glad that Karen would never find out what he had done.

# Chapter 16

Kaneohe, Hawaii

Al Worthington, Special Envoy of the United States President, was escorted into the large airplane hangar that had been assigned to the Special Operations Teams the government had assembled. Captain Chet Grinkis looked up from the equipment check he was conducting with his Delta Force Team. His men stopped as they watched the civilian stroll over to where they were all seated. A pile of equipment sat in the middle of a circle of chairs.

Thirty feet away was a similar circle holding the members of Lt. Butch Goring's Seal Team. They also stopped what they were doing and looked at the intruder. Butch stood up and joined Chet in meeting Al. The Marine security detail that was escorting the civilian stopped and stood ready.

"Yes sir, what can we do for you?" Chet asked.

"I assume you've received orders from the Pentagon?" Al offered.

Al had scrambled from his position as Chief Counsel for the United States Mission at the U.N. in New York City to Washington D. C. Hearing of this mission to investigate an island in the South Pacific to see if it held the now-famous Dr. Brody, he pulled out all his political IOUs to join the team. That a certain Karen Price would be with Dr. Brody was a big part of his plan.

"Yes, sir. And I would strongly recommend that you reconsider your decision to go. We have no idea what we'll be walking into down there," Butch said. He and Chet had received the news yesterday and had lobbied unsuccessfully with their commander for relief.

"Negative Lieutenant. The President has a personal interest in this mission. The members of the Security Council at the UN are up in arms that an American was selected to play this game with the aliens. And that Dr. Brody has yet to pick any of the large cities of the world has sent almost everyone over the edge," Al said.

"Great, just what we need. Politicians picking the sectors. God help us now," Mel said, standing nearby.

"Who is this civilian and what is he doing here? I wasn't informed that another civilian was part of this operation," Al said, his anger showing. *They were questioning my right to be here but had allowed some nobody a position,* Al thought. The concept rankled his Ivy League sensibilities.

Chet motioned Mel over and introduced him. Al reluctantly shook the man's hand. "This is Mel. He's the brother of one of my men and is an expert at the 'Endangered Species' software that Dr. Brody designed. We brought him along to aid in our mission."

"Well, the members of the Security Council have three of the top scorers in the world ready to take over if we can get to Dr. Brody," Al said.

Mel looked at the man inquisitively. Al recognized the challenge and continued. "You seem to want to know who that would be. Does 'Dragon Slayer', 'Vlad the Impaler' and 'Princess Die' ring any bells?"

Mel emitted a low whistle. "Holy shit. The holy trinity of 'Endangered Species' gamers. How did you ever . . ."

Al cut him off. "When the might of China, Russia and America lean on you, you come out of the shadows. They were tracked down and detained. They are each sitting in a secure location waiting to take over for this boob Dr. Brody who is on his way to disaster."

Chet looked at his resident software expert for collaboration. "Mel, is that true?"

"Dr. Brody ain't doing too well. Yeah, he's grabbing up farmland but he's going to get crucified soon. We're about done with all the recognized good farmland. And that panda has just about finished up on all the recognized important animal areas."

"That's right, we're getting down to crunch time. If that panda starts picking off the major population centers, humans are going to take a severe haircut," Al said.

"Mr. Worthington, you need to know the limits of our mission as ordered by our commanders," Butch said.

Butch went into detail on the orders he and Chet had received. Both Special Ops teams were to travel together in a submerged nuclear attack submarine to the island. They were to land by small inflatable boat at separate locations on the island and then determine if Dr. Brody and his assistant were on the island.

Chet continued that each team would then reconnoiter the island for hostiles. If the island was the center of the alien selection process, then they were to quietly contact Dr. Brody and determine if the President could intercede with the gamers the world had selected.

If the two teams were ordered by the President to involve Al, then he would be provided access. Otherwise, Al would be required to endure the stress of the operation without interference. If not, he would be required to stay out of all operations on the island.

Al agreed to the terms and was instructed to follow Sergeant Aubin to the supply room to pull his required gear. Following the sergeant, Al headed toward the supply room. As he walked by, Al noticed that Mel was packing, his brother assisting him.

* * *

The trip to the island was quick. Nuclear subs could maintain a sustained speed in excess of 40 knots. The two teams had transferred from Kaneohe Marine Base to Pearl Harbor where they met up with their submarine.

Al had finally adjusted to life underwater when he was told that Delta Force would be disembarked first. The sub surfaced that night to the southwest of the island. The inflatable motor boats were manhandled out onto the deck of the sub and made ready.

Four of Butch's Seals had volunteered to make the run into the island for the landing. The sub would submerge while the boats were away and then surface to retrieve them upon their return.

Once ashore, Chet's men were cut off from any direct support. Consequently, the Delta Team had packed food and water for an extended stay. The spy satellites had confirmed only four people on the island, so heavy weapons and extra ammunition had been left behind. The team would make do with their small arms and a normal supply of ammo.

Al stood at the bottom of the hatch as each man climbed onto the deck. Al would be inserted with the Seal Team the next night. He noticed that Mel was hesitant to leave and it took a prod by his brother to get him up and out of the sub. The Navy seamen soon closed the hatch as the sub got under way, slipping beneath the surface.

When Al noticed the motion of the sub change, he knew it was time to retrieve the boats and their crews. He waited as the gear was loaded into the sub. The Seals climbed down the ladder and reported a clean insertion. Delta was last seen loaded up and heading north.

The inflatables were stowed and once again the sub slipped beneath the waves. Al laid in his bunk as he waited out the daylight hours. He pulled out a picture of Karen Price that he had copied off the screen image from the game show. He studied her image.

Then he pulled out several more that the FBI had obtained in their investigation. He had asked for copies of her pictures, ostensibly for a proper identification once on the island. Al had been smart enough to ask for Dr. Brody photos also, but those weren't the pictures he now studied.

The FBI file had provided candid pictures of Karen from her family and friends and it was these that he studied. But it was the TV screen copies that mesmerized him. Luckily, the aliens were using high definition cameras so the details from the screen shots were wonderful.

They showed the tan woman glistening with sweat beads as she sat in whatever building from which they recorded. The combination of her entrancing looks with a body damp from who knew what tormented him. A sleepy fantasy took over.

Just as he was about to strip the last piece of sweaty clothing off her body, someone shook his foot. The dream disappeared.

His eyes snapped open. Lieutenant Goring stood next to his leg. "It's time, sir."

"I'll be right there." Al rubbed his eyes as he struggled to remember the last of his dream, the tightness in his pants lingering. *Had the Lieutenant noticed that?* he thought.

Al had his gear ready beside his bunk and slipped on his web gear. Sergeant Aubin had instructed him in the proper use of all his military gear during the journey south. Except for a light-hearted break when they had crossed the Equator, the journey had been all business.

Both teams had worked together on their plans as well as contingencies for action. Al had watched and listened so he was familiar with the goals of each team.

The part that had been plain to him was that he would be stuck on the beach until the Seals had done their reconnoiter. Since Butch had chosen to insert his team on the small headland close to the main house, he and his men would make the first observation.

Delta had to traverse the length of the island to get into position on the high ground south of the garden. Both teams would be in communication with each other while Delta carried the larger radio that could reach the submerged sub offshore. A raised antenna on the sub would allow communication between the sub, the teams, and the Pentagon.

The Seal Team scrambled up onto the darkened deck and went to work readying the boats. Al followed along next to Lieutenant Goring as they passed gear up through the hatch. When the boats were ready, Butch made sure the civilian got safely into the raft before joining him.

His men fired up the motors and the crouching Seals checked the shore with their night vision scopes as the small boats headed inland. Al looked around to see the sub slipping below the surface. After landing, they would camouflage the boats on shore at a small beach that the satellite had revealed.

Although unarmed, Al would be the inflatable's guard while the Seals moved toward the house. He would be stuck in limbo on the beach until the Seals allowed him to leave.

With the Seal Team crouched on the tubes, the four boats motored through the sea toward the island. The night only offered stars for illumination.

The team had grumbled that normally they would have been hitting the island after an underwater swim from the submarine. The civilian they were assigned required them to change from their standard operational insertion.

The boatswain slowed as they approached the beach. Al could barely make out the rocky headline in the dim light. Off to his right he could see the surf line of a long beach. A large headland was outlined on the horizon where the stars were blocked.

A similar beach with surf was visible to his left. A larger hill rose up from the beach indicated by the large expanse of darkness before the stars reappeared. Al remembered the satellite images and knew it was a short

300 yards along the small headland to the main house. He tensed as his boat rose over a small wave and scraped up onto the beach.

The Seal Team was already out of the boats and pulling them up under a small rock outcropping. Four team members sprinted up the rocks with their head-mounted night vision leading the way. Al didn't have an earpiece to listen to the Seal tactical radio but watched the lieutenant as he waited on the beach beside Al.

From Al's perspective, Butch obviously received good news. The Navy lieutenant put his hand up to Al's face to motion him to stay put. Then he stood and followed the route his men had taken heading west.

Al settled down as best he could and waited. He thought of his pictures safely ensconced in the dry bag strapped to his back as he leaned back and thought of its contents. With the rhythm of the waves washing onto the beach and a drop in adrenaline from the initial landing, he drifted off.

A loud crack awoke him. He snapped open his eyes, only to have them blinded by a bright blue light. He blinked and turned his head away from the source of the light just as it died out. Standing, he looked in the direction that the Seals had taken. *What the hell was that?* he thought.

He stood and waited for someone to return but no one came. Al waited, his anxiety rising. *That crack of light wasn't good,* he thought. If it was the same blue light that had vaporized North Korea, Al knew it would be catastrophic. Al stood frozen as to what he should do next.

He checked his watch. It had been four hours since he and his team had come ashore. And it had been about thirty minutes since he'd been rudely awakened. Sunrise would be in another hour or so.

Al decided he needed to find out if the Seals were still on the headland. *I'll just move down toward the main house until I can see it,* he thought. *Then I'll wait.*

He stuffed some food packs in his pack and climbed carefully up the rocks. About twenty feet up, the ground leveled off and offered an easy walk under large trees. There was enough underbrush to conceal him as he slowly approached the house.

Al watched for any Seals as he got closer but there was no sign of Butch's team. *Maybe they moved onto higher ground?* he thought. That didn't make sense, though, since that area was reserved for Captain Grinkis's Delta Team.

Knowing he must be close to the house, Al dropped onto his hands and knees. He used the underbrush for concealment as he crept ever closer. He pushed one branch carefully aside. Sitting 150' in front of him was the main house. Al dropped onto his stomach and froze.

The sky to the east grew lighter and Al looked around under the increasing daylight for any Seals. *Nothing visible,* he thought. As the sun broke the ocean surface, the rays lit the hillside above him into a golden hue.

The sunlight started its steady crawl down the hill. As the brightness neared, Al realized that the brush he was hiding in wouldn't offer good cover in full daylight. He started to slither backwards toward more dense foliage, being careful not to make any noise.

No human activity in the house was visible and Al hoped that the inhabitants would remain asleep until he was safely hidden. He turned as he crawled and immediately slid through some gray dust.

Al stopped and looked around the area. Small markings in gray dust were all around him. He studied the dust patterns that were obviously different than the surrounding dirt. The hair on his neck stood up and sweat suddenly ran down his armpits.

*My God, the dust is shaped in a human form that had been lying on the ground,* he realized. He looked for any other evidence and noticed scrape marks on the ground leading up to each dust mark. It was the mark that a crawling human would make in the dirt. But still there was no other sign of any Seal Team members.

Finding a large tree with roots intertwined with some rocks, he stripped off his gear and squeezed between the roots. He pulled in his equipment and adjusted his body to his hiding place. He had to think.

# Chapter 17

Karen stood by the window looking toward the beach and the main house. It had been a restless night and she had had had a difficult time sleeping. She surveyed the main house and the small point that extended out toward the sea. She heard rustling behind her.

"Han, are you awake?"

"Yes. I tried to get back to sleep, but the light and explosion last night made that impossible," Dr. Brody said.

"What was that? I bolted right out of bed it was so close."

"I don't know. I've never heard lightning before on the island. When I looked out, all I saw was stars in the sky. Without any clouds, I don't know where the lightning came from."

Dr. Brody stood up and walked over to Karen. He placed his arms around her. They leaned together and stared out the windows.

"Maybe I'll get dressed and go check on Wu Who. Make sure they're OK. And see if they know anything," Charles said.

"Can we still go to the cove and snorkel today? It's Sunday and we planned all week."

"Of course. But just let me check." Charles slipped on his shorts and a shirt. He disappeared down the trail toward the main house.

Walking up onto the veranda, he noticed Dr. Who standing off to the east. Dr. Brody walked over to him. The two men looked at each other. Dr. Brody shrugged his shoulders and got a shrug in return from Dr. Who.

Dr. Who retreated to the porch as Dr. Wu came out of the house. Charles noticed both of them looking up into the trees. He lifted his head in the same direction. *Nothing unusual up there,* he thought as he looked at the large tropical tree canopy.

The professor was about to return to his cabin on the hill when something caught his eye. On the ground in front of him were several gray dust patterned shapes. They appeared to be in an outline of a prone human being. He looked to each side and saw several more dust patterns.

Bending over, he grabbed a stick on the ground and ran it through the dust. The dirt underneath was a reddish hue and when disturbed, mixed with the gray dust. *Strange,* he thought.

The professor got down on his hands and knees for a closer examination. He crouched down so his face was inches from the gray dust. Looking carefully, he blew slightly. The dust rose at the slightest breath just like ash from a wood fire.

He put his nose closer and sniffed. His body froze and sweat broke out. The smell sense is very powerful in humans and an elementary fear came over him. A fear that had developed in humans thousands of years ago. A fear that was based not in the conscience, but was deeper in the subconscious. The professor sniffed again and his subconscious reacted again. It was a smell humans had developed a primeval fear of millennia ago.

Dr. Brody stood, turned around and without even acknowledging Wu Who, walked briskly back to the cabin.

*Things had changed last night. And they had not changed for the better,* he thought. *The crack of light had announced it.*

\* \* \*

Captain Chet Grinkis had his men in loose formation. Weighed down by the extra provisions they were carrying, they had made reasonable time clearing the landing beach area. The sun brought daylight and required them to seek concealment.

Two of his team had been sent ahead as soon as they had landed and Chet had received an hourly report. But the last hourly check had been missed. The tactical headset each team member wore had limited range so he wasn't overly concerned. The ridges coming down off the hill to the right would add to the dead zones.

As the main team climbed up onto a bench overlooking an enclosed lagoon, his ear piece came to life. "Dirt 1, this is Dirt 5. Do you read me?"

"Dirt 5, this is Dirt 1. What's your sit?" Chet asked.

"Dirt 1, we're under cover on the hillside above the garden. We have a clear view of the cabin but not the main house."

"Any activity? Any word from Wet 1?" Chet asked. Wet 1 was the call sign for Lieutenant Goring. From the hillside location, the tactical radio should have been able to reach between the two teams.

"Negative. No Wet 1 contact. But movement in the cabin. One male, one female. Advise?"

"Stay put Dirt 5. We're moving up toward your position. Keep us informed of any changes." Chet double clicked the transmission to indicate he was done. He pulled out his map and checked his location. He was on schedule but was nervous about being out in the open in daylight.

He motioned his men to move up hill and seek cover. The heavy supplies would be left as he took one of his men to reconnoiter ahead. The remaining team was to stay put.

Using the hillside vegetation as cover, Chet and his troop worked their way toward the observer team. They hadn't gone far when his earpiece came to life.

"Dirt 1, we have movement. The couple in the cabin is heading our way. Repeat. You are about to have company."

Chet clicked acknowledgement. The two Delta Team members moved back toward the main group to wait.

* * *

Karen led the way as she and Charles walked toward the lagoon. The Sunday excursion the week before had been exhilarating to Karen and she had announced that she was anxious to get back in the water.

Dr. Brody worked hard keeping up with the younger woman in front of him. With just her small bikini on, he enjoyed watching her lean body work its way along the rocky trail. With her boots on, he wondered why they even bothered with clothes at all. Wu Who only ventured into the garden and recognized the cabin was off-limits. And the Chinese couple would never venture out by the lagoon.

Dr. Brody was imagining his trail buddy naked when they reached the top of the hill above the lagoon. Scrambling down the ravine leading to the beach, Charles dropped his pack on the sand. He retrieved the snorkeling gear and then spread out the blanket.

Reaching for their towels, he noticed Karen had already stripped down. Her boots were laying by the blanket along with her bikini. Charles stripped down.

They raced into the water throwing on their snorkel gear as they swam out into the warm water. The sun beat down on them as they watched the sea life dart away upon their approach.

Their sea turtle was back and they hung in the warm water watching it feed on the bottom. An eel darted out at them as they swam over a shallow portion of the reef and Karen jumped. She swam back to Charles for support from the threatening black creature. Life was warm, wet and sensuous.

Dr. Brody tried to focus on the lagoon's sights, but his thoughts raced back to what he had smelled. Fear continued its grip as his partner swam up and tried to entice him into other activities. They had arrived at their favorite rock on the reef and Karen moved her body for male attention.

Dr. Brody tried to accommodate her desire but his mind was elsewhere. His body confirmed the distraction.

"Hey, what's up? We had a wonderful time on this rock last week. I thought you'd be excited to get back here," Karen said. She stroked her hands along his slippery body trying to gain his attention. The lack of response stopped her.

"The Wookiee under the weather?" she asked.

Dr. Brody pulled his brain from the dark place where it was stuck. He looked into the eyes of the woman in his arms and tried to make sense of what he was thinking. Charles could tell from her expression that she suddenly realized that something serious was up. She waited patiently as her body gently rocked in his arms from the current flowing over the reef.

*This is torment,* he thought. He wanted to take this woman in his arms and let the pleasure wash all the other feelings away. He was on a tropical island with a beautiful woman who wanted him and he was stuck on his primeval fears. *It wasn't fair,* he thought. *But she was being extraordinarily patient with me. I have to tell her.*

"Karen. The crack of light last night," he stopped.

Karen looked into his eyes, waiting for more. "Yes, Han?"

"This is serious."

"I know it is, Charles."

"It wasn't lightning last night."

The mood was shifting decidedly as the two swimmers sat together on the submerged rock. The gentle wave action only added to the drama as they rocked in unison. Charles knew Karen was waiting for the bigger issue to drop.

He accommodated her as he explained about the dust marks on the ground. He described his smelling the dust and his reaction to what he had smelled.

"Charles, are you telling me . . ."

"Yes, burnt human flesh. It was as if hundreds of my ancestor's life experiences suddenly all came together in my brain. The feeling of total fear was overwhelming."

"But who? Who would have been on the island? Wu Who were still there in the morning. You said you saw them both. So who?"

"I don't know that. But somehow, many bodies were reduced to dust last night not far from the main house. We can be sure that the aliens are involved somehow. I just don't know any more."

They held each other tight as the waves increased with the rising tide. All thoughts of any amorous activity were swept away as they both contemplated the meaning of what the professor had discovered.

"Maybe we should check with Errol Flynn? He might know something," Karen said.

They agreed that would be the prudent thing to do. They both needed answers. If the aliens were killing other people on the island, it was imperative to find out. They pulled their masks down and swam for shore. They forgot about lunch as Charles stuffed gear into the pack.

Pulling on their swim suits and boots, they headed up the ravine toward the trail back to the cabin. When they reached the top of the ravine, they froze. Standing in front of them was the blackened face of an Army soldier. The soldier was in camo gear and held an assault rifle. They suddenly knew that they had one answer to their question.

# Chapter 18

New York City

The man tried not to shake as he stood waiting. He was standing in front of a large desk and the woman sitting behind it was scrutinizing paperwork. It was the man's personnel file and that's why he was nervous.

He'd been told to head upstairs to the big man. The U.S. Ambassador to the United Nations was seeking his audience. And he didn't have a clue why. He had worked in the U.S. Mission to the U.N. for two years now and had managed to keep under the radar. At least until today.

And the man wasn't enjoying being out of the shadows of ignominy. He had been nervous when he had taken the job in the first place. The title had sounded important, Under Assistant to the Mission Secretary, but reality soon burst the bubble when he found out he was just a glorified computer geek.

He was to keep the Mission's computer files organized. Along with managing the email accounts for the general public, the man had settled into an easy existence. But he sensed things were about to change.

"Vernon Randolph. You're file says you received your computer degree from Cooper Union. Good school. Why haven't you moved up to a more responsible position by now? With a degree form Cooper Union you should have been higher up in IT by now," the U.S. Ambassador said.

"I'm not sure," Vernon lied. He knew why he hadn't moved anywhere. He was deathly afraid of responsibility. He was totally content with his under assisting role. The money was good and he got to go home at five every night to his lovely Ellie. She was happy with him, so why would he risk a move?

"Well, your supervisor recommended you and I need a computer expert right now. So I guess you're it."

"I'm it? What does it entail, if I may ask."

"Confidence, Vernon. I need a computer person watching incoming messages while I sit at the Security Council meetings. You will have a secure link to the general and will clear all messages. Can you handle that?"

"Wow, the Security Council. Me. I never thought I'd-"

The ambassador was getting a little irritated with this reluctant employee. She almost barked. "Well, the world is hanging by a thread and I need someone. If you're not the one, I'll have the general find someone else."

Vernon found his reserve of courage before talking. "I'll give it a try. I want to help."

"That's the thing. Go to the Comm Center, get your secure laptop and meet me here. You have ten minutes."

Vernon excused himself and almost sprinted to the Comm Center. The general knew he was coming and handed over the laptop. After a brief discussion to determine that Vernon knew his password and access code, he released it.

He was back in the ambassador's outer office within seven minutes. He waited until the ambassador came out.

"Good to go, Vernon? Right, lets head down to the car," the ambassador said. She walked briskly past Vernon. On the way, the security team picked them up and they all climbed into the Suburban.

The days of walking to the U.N. building were long gone. Large crowds were constantly outside the U.N. property demanding that their home be included in the human selection in the alien game. Police had installed concrete barriers around the entire East Side neighborhood with fencing to control the mobs.

Each week the people grew more violent in their demands to the U.N. As Dr. Brody made his selections, countries that were being left out organized demonstrations.

As the fourth week of the Endanger Species Game Show was about to air, the world was struggling to maintain control. Large hordes of people were on the move as they headed to the areas already selected for human use. The animal sections were losing civil control as people reacted to their land being taken from them.

The Security Council had attempted to open up a line of communication with the aliens but had been rebuffed. And now there were reports of the aliens eliminating people. Fear was building and the U.N. was powerless to control it.

"We have a good picture of the alien victims now. The first week of these yellow green light attacks has shown us what they are after," the Russian Ambassador said.

Vernon sat nervously behind the U.S. Ambassador and watched his computer screen intently. He was ready for any critical messages to come through and barely lifted his head to survey his surroundings. Vernon's sudden urge to use the bathroom upon entering the Security Council Chambers had visibly irritated the ambassador.

But Vernon was silent now. As the meeting went on, his nerves eased a bit. *These people were just like anyone else,* he thought. His wife Ellie had always told him to envision people sitting on the toilet if he wanted to reduce his nervousness. Her advice was definitely working as he worked his way around the room with his gaze. He envisioned the Russian Ambassador sitting on the toilet, and he became just another human being.

He almost jumped out of his chair though when the buzzer of an incoming message went off. The room turned its attention to the new man holding the computer. His sweat increased as he printed out the message on his portable printer. He handed it to the ambassador.

"Good news. We've made contact with Dr. Brody."

* * *

When Dr. Brody had climbed out of the ravine overlooking the lagoon he hadn't expected to run into U.S. Army Special Forces personnel. But he wasn't particularly surprised either. The human-shaped dust he had found by the main house had to have come from someone.

That the world had located their island hideout seemed only a matter of time considering the electronic resources available. That the Americans had discovered them first was logical. But now, he and Karen were sitting under the trees trying to explain the situation.

"Captain Grinkis. Let me explain again what you have stepped into here. Ms. Price and I were both transported here against our will by some means I can't explain. The aliens want the two of us isolated from the world for a reason. Now that the world has found us, I'm afraid of what the aliens will do," Dr. Brody said.

"Let us worry about that. The main reason we were sent here was to determine how the aliens are controlling you. The President, along with the other leaders of the world's nations, are nervous about this whole Endangered Species Game you designed," Chet said.

"And they should be. But I don't think the aliens are open to discussion. I've gotten some concessions out of them, but their price for those has been high."

Sergeant Aubin walked up and leaned over to whisper in the captain's ear. The strain on Chet's face told Charles everything.

"You're missing some men, aren't you?" the professor asked.

"How did you know?"

"They were landed to the east of the main house and were to observe the people there, correct?"

"Professor, what do you know?"

"I believe they're all dead." Dr. Brody watched the facial expression come over the captain and knew he had guessed right. He continued, "We were awakened last night by a crack of thunder and a lightning bolt. At least I thought it was lightning. When I went to investigate this morning, I found the outline of humans that had been laying on the ground not far from the main house. There was nothing by gray ash left. The smell was of-"

"Burnt flesh. Vaporized. Just like the Koreans and the Iranians. My God, the whole team."

"What's this about the Koreans and the Iranians?" Karen asked. Her voice broke as her anxiety showed.

"You don't know?" Chet asked. "When the aliens arrived they demonstrated their power by vaporizing every human in North Korea. Then in response to a Russian missile attack that they threw back, they vaporized all the Iranians."

Karen took quick breaths at the news. She teared up as she leaned onto Dr. Brody for support.

"We didn't know. We have no link to the outside world. The aliens tell us what they want us to know."

"So do you have a theory as to why we weren't taken out last night along with the Seal Team?" Chet asked.

"All I can think of is you're not a threat over on this side of the island. The others were very close to the main house and posed a threat if they were armed. The Chinese couple that shares our island aren't what they appear. They know too much about what the aliens are up to," Charles said.

"Are they aliens then?" Chet asked.

"I wouldn't discount it. They certainly seem to be able to take on human life forms. We deal with an Errol Flynn lookalike every day."

"And we've seen Betty Davis and Cary Grant among others. How do you think we should proceed then Professor?" the captain asked.

"Carefully. I would suggestion you keep out of rifle range of the houses. I wouldn't want to bet my life on the alien's good intentions. Maybe if you aren't a threat, you can survive."

Captain Grinkis offered that he would hold his men here at the lagoon, well out of rifle range of the north end of the island. He stated that he would work his way up to his two observers and relieve one of them. That troop would return with their weapons so he and his other observer would be unarmed.

Dr. Brody agreed that might work. "It's getting late and we need to get back. We don't need Wu Who out looking for us."

"Wu Who?"

"I'm sorry. Our island companions. Dr. Wu and Dr. Who. Wu Who is our affectionate name for them," Charles said.

The professor and Karen told the captain they would make an effort to stay in touch during the week but told them they would be busy with the game show and the garden.

Walking up the trail, Charles felt the eyes of unseen soldiers watching them the whole time. Their tropical island paradise had suddenly become very crowded.

He wasn't sure about the captain's intentions. What options did the world have besides playing the aliens' game? *None,* he thought. He was about to find out that no options could become very complicated.

# Chapter 19

Al Worthington was scared. In fact, he was beyond scared. He was petrified. The sun was setting on his first day on the island and he was feeling very alone.

*And that dust on the ground outside his hideout. Dr. Brody had knelt down and smelled the dust,* he thought. Al recognized human fear when he saw it, and he had witnessed that on the professor's face. And it was a primeval fear that had taken over the man. The look on the man as he surveyed the area put chills into Al.

If the Navy Seals had been eliminated, as he feared, could the Delta Team have survived? Al was convinced that he was suddenly very alone on a very hostile island. And now the night was adding to the terror. He heard noises that hadn't been there in the day time.

Al clutched his pack to his chest for protection from what his mind was envisioning. Gone were images of a lusty young woman swimming naked in the ocean. Now, his mind envisioned bodily mutilation by wild beasts or aliens doing indescribable things to him.

As he sat in the dark with the thought of his life being snuffed out at any minute, his sight caught something. A light. A light on the hill. A light on the hill where he knew the cabin was located. Her cabin. The woman who had brought him here.

He stared at the soft yellow light and took strength from it. Just a short distance away was serenity. Or at least he hoped it could be serenity. Then he saw a figure flit by the open window. There she was again. And then a figure that must be Dr. Brody. They were going about their nightly routine and he was witness to it all.

The light called to him and he crept out of his hole. The brush around him was still as he crawled forward toward the light. It disappeared from view and would then reappear as he moved forward under the tropical trees.

Then he froze as the main house came into view. It had been blocked by the low brush near his hiding spot but now he moved to the side as he crawled around the house. He watched as two people did their nightly duties inside. But these people, whoever they were, weren't who he sought.

The beautiful woman on the hill kept him moving forward. He reached the beach and he crawled toward the cliff. In the faint light, he found the trail that wound up the cliff and followed it. Reaching the top, he slid into the bushes near the cabin.

Al Worthington had made it. He was within earshot of the most beautiful woman he had ever seen. As he watched from across the lanai, she and Dr. Brody ate dinner at their table. Her sarong covered her upper body but Al was focused on her legs.

Tanned fit legs that he hadn't seen before. He only had seen her upper half. And now, she was in front of him. He relaxed as he gazed at the object of his desire.

* * *

Karen woke with a start. She had been restless all night. The thought of multiple strangers on the island unnerved her.

Even last night during dinner, she had felt the hairs tingle on her arms. She knew people were watching her from the hill. She had insisted that Charles shut and lock the patio doors before they went to bed. Now she wished for curtains on the expanse of windows that exposed the interior of the cabin.

She nuzzled up to Charles lying beside her while trying to keep below the window sill. She didn't want any prying eyes on her. She even had slept in her sarong, not trusting that the soldiers would stay on their side of the garden.

\* \* \*

With early morning light streaming into the cabin, Karen climbed out of bed, waking Charles. Asked what she was up to, she replied that a toilet break was needed. He closed his eyes.

When she opened the doors onto the lanai, she stopped. She looked around carefully. *Nothing amiss,* she thought.

Walking across the lanai, she pulled the gated door shut to the toilet room. As she turned around, she was confronted by a man. He quickly placed his hand over her mouth and grabbed her around the waist.

Karen struggled to get free as she tried to scream, but the hand held tight on her mouth.

"I'm not going to hurt you. I was sent here by the President of the United States to help you, but I think all the men that were with me are dead," Al said. As Karen settled down he added. "If you don't scream, I'll take my hand off your mouth."

Karen nodded agreement and Al released his grip. But he kept his arm firmly around her middle.

"Who are you and how did you get in here?"

Al was about to answer when he felt a sharp pain in his back. He froze as a voice said, "Let her go or the knife takes out your heart." For emphasis, Dr. Brody applied more pressure to the knife point.

Al immediately released Karen and she scrambled away from her antagonist. Al raised his arms above his head. "Dr. Brody. I've come to help you. I was sent by the U.S. Government."

The knife was removed from Al's rib cage and Al turned to face the professor and Karen.

"And what if we don't want your help? You being here endangers all our lives," Dr. Brody said.

"The world is at stake and the U.N. needs to be involved in what is going on here."

"Wrong answer. If the aliens wanted to play their game with the U.N., they would have. They chose me. And they added Ms. Price as my assistant. That's it as far as I'm concerned. You and your soldier boys can go back where you came from."

"Then some of the team survived? Where are they? I need to contact the Pentagon right away."

"You need to step outside right now so we can use the facilities. Then you can hide out here till it gets dark. Then we'll take you to them."

For Karen, the day dragged on. She wanted these men gone from her life. She wanted the simple life back that she and the professor had before their arrival.

But first they had to do their Game Show selections. She readied herself for her world-wide audience. It was a routine to her now. The actual meaning of the game had been shunted aside as too horrible to contemplate. She wanted to just enjoy her life on the island the way it had been.

\* \* \*

Vernon Randolph, Under Assistant to the Secretary, was waiting outside the U.S. Ambassador's office. He had been on his new job for a week and had overcome his state of fear. Starting to actually enjoy the notoriety of sitting behind the U.S. Ambassador at the Security Council meetings, he monitored the communications between the U.S. Mission and Washington D. C.

He had even brought his wife Ellie into the discussion of what was going on at these important meetings. Vernon knew it was against regulations to talk about his work outside the office, but he was intrigued by his new position and had to talk to someone about it. His wife was the logical choice.

They had a good marriage and over the years had shared most everything between them. *What could be the harm in talking about work?* he thought. *These were certainly momentous times for humankind and to be at the focal point was heady stuff.*

He was taken back to the meeting by the vibration of his computer. He had switched off the buzzer as the information had been so steady the sound had grown into an annoyance. Now when the computer came alive with a new communiqué, Vernon would send it to his portable printer and then lean forward and place the note on the table in front of his boss.

It seemed as if he was passing notes three or four times an hour as events happened in the world. The latest transmission had been a shock as he read it over. He knew that this one would change the mood in the room.

He leaned and slipped it onto the table. He had marked the heading with his highlighter. The ambassador had instructed him earlier in the week to highlight any critical message so that it wouldn't be lost in the volume of reports.

The U.S. Ambassador to the U.N. noticed the highlight and quickly read over the paper. "Mr. Chairmam, I've just been handed a most important message. If I may?"

"The Chair recognizes our colleague from the United States."

"The Department of Defense has compiled the data on the alien activity that we've witnessed this week. We have an answer to the green and yellow lights that have been circling the Earth. I'm afraid the initial reports are turning out to be true."

"Your prisons are empty too?" the Chinese ambassador asked.

"Not only are all our prisons empty, but all former prison internees have disappeared. Or I guess I should say, vaporized. Gray dust has been found in all our jail cells, similar to the North Korean and Iranian attacks," the U.S. Ambassador said.

"Same as our jails, just dust," the Russian Ambassador offered. "But our medical wards have been cleaned out of patients also. Our high incidence of drug-resistant TB patients are gone. Our security people checked at the homes of those out-patients suffering with TB and they're all gone."

The British Ambassador turned to the US Ambassador to ask, "Our health officials are reporting all our antibiotic-resistant disease patients seem to have been targeted. Does your report show a similar result?"

"I'm afraid so. Our Federal, State and local governments have been out straight the whole week trying to determine the extent of this green yellow light attack. Along with all prisoners and former prisoners were all health-compromised individuals. Not only the drug resistant carriers like you've found but patients in long term-comas were vaporized. Also, dementia and Alzheimer's Disease sufferers are missing."

"It appears the aliens mean to reduce the human population commiserate with splitting the world in half. I would say they just did a first pass and took out the 'low hanging fruit'," the New Zealand Ambassador said. Along with the five permanent members of China, Russia, France, Britain, and the USA, the Security Council contained ten members appointed for a limited term. New Zealand, Argentina, Morocco and Bangladesh were among the non-permanet members for this session.

"Do you think so? The aliens never mentioned eliminating any people. Just dividing the Earth between us and the animals," the Argentine Ambassador said.

"Makes sense. They haven't vaporized any humans in the grids that have been selected by the animals. My computer game expert says the game doesn't go past the selection process. When all the squares are designated, the computer adds up the totals and issues a score. We don't know if the aliens will let us move the populations to the human squares in the end," the British Ambassador said.

"Makes no matter. The people are already voting with their feet. We've all seen the reports of hordes of people in loaded-down cars and trucks making their way to the human squares. It's all we can do to keep order. And these are all Americans trying to shift locations. I can't imagine the small countries that have been completely lost to the other side and those people trying to move into a totally different country," the U.S. Ambassador said.

"I'll tell you how it is, it's murder. Plain and simple. Luckily Morocco was recently chosen for the human side. That damn panda went for Libya in the next move. I have no idea why. There's no wildlife in that desert. But the stream of Libyans heading west out of the square is being met with resistance by Tunisia and our country. It's mayhem out there."

The Council had been receiving such reports from the beginning of the game. The grids selected by the animal side were being denuded of people as they headed to the human squares. Left behind were billions and billions of dollars of property and possessions that were now worthless.

One of the reasons that the Special Ops team was sent to Dr. Brody's island was to attempt to communicate with the aliens. The Security Council was the only body that the aliens had contacted directly and then only to issue edicts. The humans had never been given an opportunity to communicate back.

"Any more news from your team on the island?" the Chinese asked.

The Pentagon had decided to keep what was transpiring on the island secret. That a team had been sent there was known among the Council, but any news on what had transpired was being withheld.

*Part of the team seems to have been vaporized. We are waiting for more news from the remaining team,* Vernon thought. Vernon had read the reports and knew there was much more to tell. But the rest was marked 'Top Secret' and he was just glad that his security clearance level had been upgraded with his new assignment.

He still didn't have the highest clearance, as that was reserved for the ambassador himself and the Mission's general. But what he did know kept him busy with his wife. He knew he shouldn't be talking to her about any of this, but he couldn't help himself. And he didn't talk about everything.

He had begun to realize just how much his ego was becoming involved in this whole affair. And it sure had enhanced the excitement between him and his wife that had been lagging over the last few years. Their bedroom activity was enhanced as his wife came alive the more she heard about her husband's role in world affairs. *It is almost like a 'James Bond' effect,* he thought. *All I need now was a Walther PPK pistol to complete the image.*

"Well, I'm just glad our Dr. Brody finally started adding the major cities to his human selections," the Russians said.

As the 'Endangered Species' Game approached the half way mark, Dr. Brody had begun selecting the squares holding the larger world cities. New York had finally been added, much to the relief of millions of people. Many that had packed up and left were now returning.

London, Paris, Moscow, Shanghai, San Francisco, Rio de Janeiro, Cairo, Rome, Madrid, Mumbai and Sydney had all been chosen. But the giant panda had struck terror into millions when it added many large cities to the animal side.

Dacca, Glasgow, Chicago, Vancouver, Los Angeles, Tokyo, New Delhi, Vienna and Buenos Aires were now under threat of being on the wrong side in the struggle between human and animal. Many other smaller cities were also among the lost.

The demonstrations outside the United Nations had increased with each selection. Army troops had been brought in to keep the violence from spreading. In other large human selected cities, intense confrontations were taking place from people that had moved away from areas on the animal side.

"So, has anyone analyzed this green yellow light that the aliens are using? We know what the blue light does. And we know the red light effects." Everyone turned to the Russians at the reference to their major cities being destroyed. That Moscow had been selected for a human square was sort of ironic, since most of the city was rubble now. "Has the Pentagon come up with an answer?" the British asked.

"I think all of us have a pretty clear idea of the green yellow light. We've seen the green light immobilize all electronics as the yellow light searches out and vaporizes individual people. The yellow light is amazingly accurate. We have seen ten people in a room and the yellow light will take out three individuals among them. No one else even has a scratch. Just a short spell of blindness from the bright light," the American said.

"And total trauma for those nearby. The blinding light and then the smell of burnt flesh pushes many over the edge. Our hospitals are full of people out of their minds with fear," the Kiwi offered.

"Agreed. We've all seen the results. It's brutal stuff. I hope your Special Ops team can get us some answers," the French ambassador said.

# Chapter 20

Al Worthington was tormented being so close to the object of his desires. But, he couldn't act on his emotions. Karen walked by continuously in her daily tasks as he hid in their toilet building. He so wanted to go out and tell her of his feelings, but he knew if he was caught out in the daylight by the aliens, he risked the same fate that his Navy Seal companions had suffered.

The thoughts of being turned into gray dust kept him safely entrapped with the toilet. Only at noon when she brought him some food did his heart leap. Then when she had to use the facilities and he sneaked into the nearby shower stall, again he was titillated. Her sounds as she did her business added to his desire.

How she could have hooked up with the professor was beyond him. *The man is old enough to be her grandfather,* he thought. Al was 34 years old, just the right age for a 27-year-old woman. He was Harvard educated, with a law degree from Georgetown University. That had been where he had made his political connections as he clerked for a Supreme Court Justice. Then into public service as he climbed quickly up the State Department food chain.

Landing a plumb job at the United Nations was the final step to a top-notch appointment very soon. But then he had seen her on the television. This woman had stolen all control as he had thrown himself into making sure he was on the team that would find her. And now he had accomplished that task.

It was time to show her his charm and pedigree to win her over. And competing against a sixty-something college professor from some second-rate university should be easy. Al had been a hot commodity in New York City and had been rumored to be connected to any number of New York society's chosen ones.

"Hey, its time," the voice whispered.

Al recognized the professor's voice. He had watched it get dark and knew that it would be time for the three of them to make their way to the Delta Force Team on the opposite hill. Al stepped out of the toilet building and was greeted by Dr. Brody. Standing behind him was the most beautiful woman he could imagine.

It scared this Ivy League graduate at the emotions this woman caused in him. He had certainly been with many beautiful woman in his life. Any Harvard man drew them like flies. But he wasn't sure why he was feeling such attraction to this particular woman. *Maybe it's her position of power in shaping the future of mankind?* he thought.

Al knew that it was Dr. Brody who held the power, or at least the power as doled out by the aliens. He just couldn't put his finger on the exact reason of his desire. But it was overwhelming, and he wasn't about to lose his opportunity to snatch her away from the professor.

They began walking south toward Captain Grinkis's position. Using a small flashlight to help with the hike, the three walked in a close column. Al took up the rear so as to be in a position to watch Karen. With the professor leading with the flashlight, Al would catch glimpses of her body as she walked in front of him. Al had to suppress his urges as they reached the Delta position.

"Captain Grinkis, we need to pull you and your observers back to the lagoon. It's much too dangerous here for you," Charles said.

"OK, but we need to talk when we get back to the other troops," Chet said.

"That's fine. But let's get out of here now."

With five people in line, Al made sure he held his position behind Karen. He even enjoyed the occasional bump in the night when the lead would stop and the others would stumble in the dark. *She didn't seem to mind the contact,* he thought. *This should be relatively easy.*

Chet called for Sergeant Aubin on the radio when they reached the area above the lagoon. The sergeant responded from a location in the brush as everyone gathered on the edge overlooking the water.

"Dr. Brody, let me contact the Pentagon. I have to report in on what we've found here," Chet said. The captain took the encrypted military computer and entered his secure access code. The satellite dish set up next to the computer transmitted the code and a link was established. The pack holding the solar array for power sat beside the sergeant and would be used during the daylight to recharge the batteries.

Dr. Brody sat down on one side of the captain. "I have reservations about this, captain. I'm not sure how the aliens will react to any link between this island and the outside world."

Karen sat down to watch the computer screen on the other side of the Delta commander. Al took a place next to her. He moved in so their bodies were touching. Karen maintained her position and didn't move to give Al more room. *She's not moving over. She must like the contact,* he thought.

After several screens of government warnings, a uniformed figure came on the screen. The three stars on his shoulders denoted his importance and hence the critical nature of this mission.

"Captain Grinkis, 3rd Special Forces, reporting. We have Dr. Brody here and his assistant, Ms. Price."

"Excellent job. Please put the professor on, Captain."

Chet swiveled the laptop toward Dr. Brody slightly. Al strained to stay within sight of the screen. The movement brought him even closer to Karen. She again didn't move at his increased intrusion into her personal space. Al's skin tingled at the closeness.

*"Dr. Brody, we need to know some answers. The Security Council of the U.N. is very concerned about your selections. Their experts on this game seem to think you're not up to this."*

"You and the Security Council can have all the concern you want. The aliens picked me for this job and I intend to carry on to the best of my ability. After the fact I'll be willing to answer for my decisions. But till then, back off."

*"Now hold on, Professor. As a good American, you should be willing to help your country at a time like this. We're just asking for a little cooperation, that's all."*

"That I'm talking to you at all is all the cooperation you're about to receive. I'm certain the aliens are fully aware of this contact and I'm not sure how they'll react. If the fate of the Navy Seals is any indication, I'm not totally optimistic."

"Listen Brody," the general said. "Your attitude stinks. Millions of people are dying around the world with this damn green and yellow light. Women and children are among them. Don't you have a conscience."

The professor stood up so fast he knocked Chet into Karen. Al absorbed the resulting woman landing in his arms. She lingered long enough that Al knew he had to have her. The soft yet tight body in his grasp drove his desire. He helped her up as they joined the professor.

"Charles, what was he talking about?" she asked.

"You don't know what's been going on out in the world, Ms. Price?" Chet asked.

"Captain, you do not have the authority to intrude here. You need to stop right now," Dr. Brody demanded.

"Stop what Charles? Are you keeping something from me?"

"We need to head back to the cabin. Some things you don't need to know."

"Excuse me. I've been at your side through this whole thing. I need to know what has been happening. And I want to know right now," she said.

Al felt the tension of the discussion between the professor and his supposed assistant. *Obviously, some things had not been shared. This could be my opening,* he thought. Silence hung over the small group when Karen broke the spell.

"Captain Grinkis, can your computer show me what's been going on in the world?"

"Affirmative, ma'am." But he hesitated as he studied Dr. Brody in the gathering morning light. When the professor didn't say anything, Chet sat down and typed on the keyboard. Soon international news accounts were running on the computer. Karen sat down to watch the reports.

The carnage that the aliens had caused around the world was displayed over and over again. Al noticed the tears flowing down Karen's face. While television had difficulty showing the little wisps of gray dust where before had been humans, the reporters interviewed relatives who told of the nasty work the green and yellow lights had done.

Dr. Brody stood quiet and watched. Al noticed no sense of feeling overtaking the professor. *He knows all about this. He's not reacting like this is all a surprise,* he thought.

After what seemed forever, Karen asked the captain to turn off the computer. She stood and faced Dr. Brody.

"You knew all about this, didn't you?"

The professor stood stock still and stared at her. Al could see his lower lip quiver slightly as he seemed to want to say something. But nothing came out.

"And I think you had a hand in all this. You said something way back when we got Sundays off from the game show. You told me then that there were things I shouldn't be involved in. This was it, wasn't it? The killing of millions of innocent people. You didn't want me to know."

Still, the professor said nothing in his defense. He switched his gaze out onto the lagoon, and away from Karen. Al knew suddenly that she would be his. Whatever

197

connection these two had up to now was disintegrating before his eyes. He smiled inside at his luck at being alive here at this point in time.

"Did you have a hand in this?" Karen screamed.

No answer came her way. The rage in her body strained her muscles as she seemed to try and reach a conclusion. Al watched the two intently and waited for the final blow. He knew it was coming.

"I thought I knew you. But you are a monster. You will go down in history as humanity's most evil perpetrator. Charles Brody will be spoken for centuries as the man who sold out mankind. I never want to see you again."

The joy in Al Worthington's body soared to the stratosphere at those words. He held his unemotional poise as the woman of his dreams set her heals, turned and walked off south. He waited as Dr. Brody closed his eyes in resignation. When the professor turned and headed toward the cabin, Al moved.

He quickly caught up to Karen and placed his arm around her to console her. He didn't say anything but just let her release her frustration.

"How could he? I thought we had something special." Karen spoke to no one in particular.

But Al was there to offer a soft shoulder and a caring ear. They walked along the cliff in the morning sunshine together. She, lost in her imploded world, and he in his glorious victory.

* * *

The next few days were torture for Dr. Brody. Now alone in his cabin, everything reminded him of her. Her words had torn his heart out as she accused him of the most horrible deeds. If only he could tell her the truth. But that would risk all.

Luckily, Sunday had allowed him a respite from his alien business. The next few showings on the game show were dialed in with little enthusiasm. He made his selections, waited for the show to end and retreated to the cabin to await the next day.

As he finished up an episode of Endangered Species, he waited while the wrap-up portion was completed. He then knew he was free until the next day. As he stood up to leave, a voice came over the computer. Errol Flynn materialized on the screen.

"Dr. Brody, sit down. We haven't talked for a few days." The professor followed instructions and sat down. "We know what transpired between you and the woman. It is affecting your performance and we can't let that happen. Meet Dr. Who at the main house tomorrow, early."

Before he could ask why he was required to be at Who's house, Errol was gone. Dr. Brody sat and thought about his instructions for a while and decided he didn't have a clue what the aliens were up to.

* * *

He rose early the next day and grabbed some bread as he headed down the cliff trail toward the beach. As he reached the porch of the main house, Dr. Who was sitting in a recliner waiting for something. The two men acknowledged each other and Charles took up a seat next to Who. Whatever was about to happen, Dr. Who sure couldn't enlighten him. He would just have to wait.

Dr. Wu brought tea out to the two waiting men and retreated back into the house. Dr Brody sipped the hot tea and as he lifted his face up, he thought he noticed movement down the beach. He set his tea down and focused. The movement was where the tent was staked.

This was the same tent in which he had arrived on the island. And the same tent that Karen had found herself in one morning. Now he stared as he saw the tent flap open and someone climb out. The person stood and stared at the ocean before they turned down the beach.

Charles realized that the person was female about the same time the woman seemed to recognize the house in the distance. The professor stood up and realized if history was repeating itself, he knew in what stage the woman would arrive.

Dr. Wu walked up behind him and handed him a sarong. He stepped off the porch and walked down the short path to the beach. As she came closer, he could definitely tell she was female. From her blonde hair down to her colored toenails, she was all female.

"Where am I?" she asked as they approached each other. She was making no attempt to cover up any part of her body. Charles ran his gaze down her and recorded that this twenty-something was about six feet tall, a natural blonde, naturally well-endowed and had legs that would suck any man in that came near her.

He held up the sarong as his gaze shifted up to hers. She took it from him and wrapped it around. She pulled it tight and tucked one end into the fabric just above her breasts.

"What is this place and who are you?" she asked again.

"I'm sorry. I'm Dr. Charles Brody. This is an island in the South Pacific. I'm afraid you've been transported here by the aliens now encircling the Earth."

"Holy shit, I can't be here! I've got a bathing suit photo shoot today. How do I get back to LA?" she demanded. Then Charles noticed a light bulb go off in her eyes. "Are you shitting me? You're Dr. Brody, who the whole world is looking for. The guy on that game show picking squares for the humans."

"The one and the same. And I'm afraid you won't be going anywhere real soon. If the aliens have something in mind for you, you are here till they decide otherwise."

"No way. Really? I'm Miss May. You might have seen my centerfold picture, Doc. Maybe hanging in a dorm room. My professional name is Brandi. That's not my real name though-"

Charles cut her off. He wasn't really interested in this woman's life story. Her looks certainly fit the centerfold image. He suddenly realized what the aliens were up to. From their view, Karen was now out of his life. They were providing a new female companion for him.

And they had changed their parameters from the last selection. He smiled slightly at the alien perspective of human attributes. They had tried the young, attractive and intellectual approach. In their mind, that hadn't worked. Now they were providing a more obvious choice to what they thought he desired.

Dr. Brody gave Brandi another glance. She certainly was built for what the aliens had acquired her for, but they didn't fully understand the human heart. A replacement human body couldn't be randomly plugged into a human emotional void. The aliens would never understand that human need.

"Come on, let's see if we can find you some clothes."

"Thanks Doc. I like the sarong. In this climate, I don't need much else."

Brandi swung her arm under his as they walked down the beach. Dr. Who was standing on the trail by the beach.

"Who's this?"

"You guessed it," Charles toyed.

"Guessed what?"

"His name."

"Who's name?" Brandi was confused.

"That's right," Charles played with her.

"What's right?"

"Who."

"Who where?" she asked, frustration showing.

"No, Who here."

"Doc, you're playing with me. What are you trying to tell me?"

"Brandi, meet Dr. Who." As his partner came out on the porch he added, "And this is Dr. Wu."

Upon hearing their names spoken, Wu Who both bowed. Brandi returned their bow, exposing her ample attributes. She snugged up her sarong and Charles noticed a smile on Dr. Who's face. As he started to lead her up the hill, Dr. Wu motioned that she had a box for them. Charles carried the large box up the hill and dropped it on the cabin floor.

Brandi walked in and exclaimed about the view the cabin offered. She marveled at the accommodations as she walked around the room testing everything. She sat on the bed and bounced twice while Charles opened up the box.

"It seems Dr. Wu knew you were coming." He pulled out a top and threw it at Brandi. Brandi stood up and dropped the sarong onto the floor. Without the least bit of modesty, she slipped the shirt over her head and pulled it down. It fit perfectly.

"Any pants in there?" Brandi asked. She bent over and started rummaging around in the box.

Charles backed out of the way while Brandi intently searched through the box. Standing back, her rear came around in front of him. Her shirt rode up her back, exposing her naked lower body. Charles sat down on the edge of the bed to enjoy the view. Locating some underwear, she stepped into them and pulled them up. A perfect fit. Shorts were located next and added to the cover up.

She found a sports bra and pulled her shirt off. Pulling the bra on, she replaced the shirt. Now fully clothed, Dr. Brody walked over to the kitchen area.

"Can I get you anything? You must be starving."

"Not really. But do you have any tofu? That and hummus. I could go for some hummus right now."

"I'm afraid not. We have lots of fish though, being an island and all."

"Oh, I love sushi."

"No, I wouldn't recommend raw fish. We have no medical facilities if you get any fish parasites. We cook all our fish here," Dr. Brody offered.

"And I can't get off this island, eh? Shit, I had a real good offer from Sports Illustrated. I was going to be on the cover of their swimsuit issue. Damn, I should have brought the swimsuit they had for me. Man, let me tell you, it would have driven those prepubescent boys wild."

Charles stared at her as she paced the cabin like a tiger, looking for an unlocked cage door. He wasn't sure exactly what had just landed literally in his lap, so bent to the task of making fish sandwiches for them.

"Oh no, Doc. No bread for me. And is that mayo? I can't have that. Celery's good though. And carrots." She instructed him on her dietary needs. He suddenly was understanding the demands of modeling on a woman's eating habits. Stopping to stare, he couldn't argue with the results. *At least she isn't one of those 'heroin chic' models that are nothing but skin and bones. No, this woman has ample flesh where it counts,* he thought.

Dr. Brody returned to his culinary duties as Brandi paced the room. She was looking out the windows constantly, as if a ship would suddenly appear.

"So, how long do you think the aliens have planned for me?" She flopped backwards onto the bed. "Hey, you have a comfy bed at least." She rolled onto her side, staring at Charles. He noticed the intense scrutiny as he sliced and diced the celery. Brandi took on a provocative pose as she slid her shirt up exposing her taut stomach. Her long legs moved suggestively across the bed.

Dr. Brody sliced the end of his finger off. Or at least it came close. Watching the suggestive blonde on his bed had distracted his focus and the knife had cut into flesh.

"Oh shit. Damn it!" He grabbed his finger as blood poured into the food. Brandi leapt to the rescue and grabbed a hand towel on the counter. She wrapped it around his hand and led him to the sink. Turning on the water, she held the exposed finger under the water.

"What the hell happened Doc? You need to be careful. As you said, there's no medical stuff here."

Dr Brody wanted to yell. *What the hell do you think happened? You were undressing me with your eyes while your tongue ran around your lips,* he thought. *I'm lucky I didn't cut off more than my finger I was so excited.*

The professor pointed out the first aid kit he had in the cabin and she bandaged up his wound. He sat and let the tenderness she was exhibiting wash over him. She was very careful with him and Charles knew that he was more satisfied by this attention then by what she was enticing him with before.

His feelings for Karen were still paramount in his mind no matter what suggestive position Miss May took. Although he certainly could understand his weak resistance if Brandi displayed too many such offers.

After eating dinner Brandi asked, "So Doc, where do we sleep tonight?" They both turned to look at the sole bed. Brandi walked over and sat on the edge. Her look was one of complete submission. He felt his knees go weak. *Where did the aliens ever find this woman?* he thought.

"You can have the bed. Its too claustrophobic in here for me. I haven't slept inside since I got here. I sleep on the lanai in the hammock," he lied.

The look of disappointment on her face shocked him. She looked absolutely broken-hearted that he had rejected her not-so subtle-invitation. *She'll have to get over it, at least if I can hold her off,* he thought.

"OK, Doc. Your call. But if I get too hot inside, I might have to join you." She lifted off her shirt and placed it on the table. Removing the rest of her clothes, she stretched naked out on the bed. Charles quickly killed the light and was grateful for the relief. He decided he'd better sleep in the hammock fully clothed.

Charles sat on the swinging hammock and laid down. The sway helped ease his tortured self-control. As he lay staring out of the lanai toward the hillside beyond, Brandi voiced one last utterance.

"These winds are marvelous on my body. They just soothe you to sleep. Good night Doc."

"Good night Brandi."

# Chapter 21

Vernon Randolph had been busy as the reports of gray dust spread across the globe. After the 'low hanging fruit' had been consumed by the alien death rays, the next human installments had been extracted.

The green and yellow light returned to scour the Earth in its regular search for victims. Each time the lights would eliminate certain people and leave others unharmed. The terror that the world was experiencing was consuming. No one knew who were going to be the next victims.

And the mental casualties were mounting as people woke up to find small gray piles of dust in spots previously occupied by loved ones. And that was if anyone could sleep. A typical night when the green yellow lights were reported consisted of humans shivering in terror until the lights had passed them by.

Once gone for that night, people slept from spent adrenaline. Then the daylight would bring an awareness of who had been targeted the previous night.

Across the Earth, homeless people disappeared. Then drug addicts and alcoholics were consumed. But people noticed it wasn't addicts who had been clean and sober for an extended time. Only current abusers of drugs and alcohol were vaporized.

The demand for the nightly game show had fallen significantly. Before the halfway mark was reached, the complement of land squares had been chosen. With the entire land mass of the world now either in the human side or the animal side, Dr. Brody and GP started picking the remaining ocean squares.

Some of the critical grids holding important shipping lanes had been chosen early by Dr. Brody. On the animal side, the sea of Alaska had been an early addition considering the wildlife it held. Now the show picked five squares per night.

* * *

"Dr. Brody, it's time for your third selection this evening. You picked two ocean squares in the middle of the Atlantic, where do we go now?" Bob Barker, emcee of 'Endangered Species' asked.

The crowd behind the contestants continued to cheer their enthusiasm, even though most of the real humans were exhausted and wanted the show to end. But the alien-generated supporters continued supporting Dr, Brody.

The professor was tired of the whole thing too. He wished they could just sit, he and GP, and finish out the whole deal. *Get it over with,* he thought.

At this rate, the show still had two weeks to run until the entire Earth had been divided. *Then what?* he thought. The aliens had hinted at what would happen but hadn't expressly said anything.

And the way they were demanding more people to vaporize, he wasn't sure where that would end. *Sure, they had made assurances,* he thought. *But could they be trusted?*

While the 'totalator' on the game show was holding steady at two billion dead, he knew the larger truth. That was just the number that the computer software had determined would perish if the selections he had made held true. Those two billion people had been located in the animal squares at the start of the game. Now, with the land squares chosen, millions of people were fleeing the animal squares.

The carnage was mounting as the locals in the human squares fought to keep the displaced people out. Human kindness to strangers was in short supply as the world's population struggled for survival.

On top of all of that was the winnowing out of humans as selected by Dr. Brody. The aliens had made a deal that he couldn't walk away from. It might be a deal with the devil, but it was the only one he'd been offered.

And the deal was tormenting him. Already, his selections had resulted in the actual deaths of close to five hundred million people. Some of these the aliens had chosen on their own, like the Koreans and the Iranians. But the vast majority had been his responsibility. Although with the gun that the aliens were holding to his head, he tried to push the blame on them.

Given a choice, he would have chosen no one. But he had no choice. He imagined what type of world could survive best in the future as conceived by the aliens. Dr. Brody fought his impulses to end it all. *Let the bastards do their own dirty work,* he thought.

But then he'd remember what the aliens had told him, and he returned to his duty. It might cost him his sanity, but it would be his gift to his fellow man. Or woman if that case arose.

And now the last couple of days he had a new tormentor. Miss Provocative strutted around the cabin and garden doing her chores. But she had given up wearing the clothes Dr. Wu had provided, happy to be naked to the world.

At least she understood the power of the tropical sun and partially covered up while out in the garden. She found a large sun hat to wear along with a long-sleeve cotton shirt. As to the rest of her, that was exposed. And whenever she bent over, her woman's body was revealed in great detail. And the woman seemed to be always bending over wherever Dr. Brody happened to be working.

This day he had finally had enough. After lunch he announced that he was going fishing to restock their supplies. Turning down Brandi's offer to accompany him, Charles loaded his pack and headed out walking south.

His real intention was to see Karen. And to talk to Captain Grinkis. He surmised they were still on the island although he had not seen anyone from the Special Ops Team. Reaching the area by the lagoon, he got his answer.

An encampment under the trees had been carved out for the troops. A fire on the rocks held fish cooking as Dr. Brody walked into camp. The captain walked out of the trees to greet him.

"Dr. Brody, good to see you. What can I do for you?"

"Captain, is Ms. Price here still?"

"I'm here. I told you I never wanted to see you again. Nothing has changed. I would have left if I could,"

Karen said. She stood a short distance away. Charles noticed that the guy called Al was standing near her. *What's up with that?* he thought.

"Karen, I need to explain. I-"

Before he could get another word out, he was cut off. "I want no explanation from you. I see you've continued with your human death choices even after I told you how I felt. The captain says that another two-hundred million have died since then. How could you?"

She turned and bumped into the ready Al. He placed his arm around her as they disappeared into the trees. Charles noticed that Karen placed her arm around him as they walked.

Charles stared at her until his eyes watered up. He blinked quickly to retrieve his composure when he noticed the captain still standing nearby. Turning away from his torment, he studied the young Army captain.

"Captain, I've decided that if you and your computer to the outside world wish to return with me, you may. The rest of your troops need to remain here however. As well as Ms. Price and what's his name."

"Why the change of heart, Professor?" Chet asked.

"Very soon the game show will end. I don't know what's going to happen after that. I have some inkling from the aliens, but nothing concrete. I figure I may be in need of fast communication with the human world. And you're it," Charles offered. "But your men must stay here. More than you at the cabin may enrage the aliens. And you can't bring any weapons with you."

Captain Grinkis motioned to the professor to wait as he talked to Sergeant Aubin. The two discussed something that Charles couldn't make out and Chet returned. He watched as the captain packed up the computer and all its accessories and hefted it on his back. Nodding to lead, Dr Brody headed back toward the cabin. He glanced over his shoulder as he left for any sign of Karen. There was none.

The two walked along silently as Chet worked in the hot afternoon sun with his heavy load. Dr. Brody set a quick pace and the Special Ops Commander was sweating profusely when they reached the garden. Dr. Brody turned to notice the captain frozen in place. Then he noticed the half-naked Brandi walking out of the corn stocks.

"Miss May, what are you doing here?" Chet exclaimed.

"Oh, you know me? How nice. Hey Doc, you didn't tell me we had soldiers on the island."

*Just what I need. Like I don't have enough to deal with,* he thought. "Brandi, this is Captain Grinkis of the United States Special Forces."

"Chet, ma'am, at your service."

"Oh, a Green Beret to boot. You held out on me Doc," Brandi said.

Dr. Brody noticed the stares of the captain at Brandi's lower half, exposed to the world. And Miss May was making no effort to cover anything up.

"Brandi, the captain and I have some business in the cabin. Finish up with your chores, take a shower and get dressed. We have company for dinner."

"Anything you say, Doc. Hey, you didn't bring any fish back."

Charles realized he'd forgotten to catch any fish in his excursion. They had plenty of food to eat on hand, but it meant that he would have to go out in the morning before the show.

He joined Chet as the captain set up his computer link just off the lanai. Dr. Brody motioned that they needed to talk before he made any link back to civilization. While they were talking, Brandi walked up from the garden.

She dropped her hat and shirt on the lanai floor and stepped naked into the outdoor shower. With the water running, she washed the warm water over her body. Charles noticed that the captain's attention was trained on the fully exposed woman showering a short twenty feet from him.

Dr. Brody stood up, walked over and swung the privacy gate closed. When he turned, he saw a smiling captain staring back at him.

"I didn't mean to interrupt anything here Professor," Chet said. He winked a knowing wink at his counterpart.

"Captain, you're not interrupting anything here. We do have work to get done if you're ready."

"Sure Professor."

But before they could get started, the shower stopped and Brandi walked confidently out of the enclosure.

"Sorry, I forgot a towel." She walked into the cabin and retrieved her towel. With Chet's gaze fixed on her, she dried off. Charles sat and watched the captain's stare follow every motion as she made sure every part of her was dry. Then retrieving clothes from her box, she proceeded to get dressed.

She walked out onto the lanai soon after with three orange drinks from the local trees.

"Captain, you look hot. How about a cool drink?" She bent over in front of him fully reveling her bra-less state.

*The woman has no scruples,* Charles thought. He was in his sixties struggling to maintain control. He could only imagine the thirty-something warrior beside him and what contortions Chet was going through right now.

Brandi disappeared into the cabin to fix dinner. Chet slowly returned to the job at hand but constantly glanced at the happily singing food preparer.

Charles gave up his attempt to have any conversation with the captain. They settled into watching 'Miss Hot and Ready' make dinner. *Eating was just an aforethought,* Charles thought. The captain had received all he would need just by the pre-dinner floor show.

Dr. Brody finally gave up after dinner in his attempts to corral the captain. Brandi had totally derailed any work he and the captain could accomplish. Feeling depressed by the whole thing, he excused himself and took a walk.

He was afraid of leaving the two alone, but he needed some time to think. Brandi's intrusion into his life had distracted him from his loss of Karen, but it had also confused his feelings. And now the captain was transfixed by the woman.

The professor walked along the cliff edge as the sun set over the ocean. He reached the point that plunged into the enclosed bay below, walked out to the edge and sat down. He had been here before and knew why he had returned. But last time, Karen had interrupted his destiny and had pulled him back to the living.

Now she was gone and he was left holding the blood of millions on his hands. He stared down the cliff face while his feet swung in the air. All it would take would be to place his hands by his side, pick himself up slightly, and rock forward.

The one hundred and fifty foot fall onto the rocks below would be over in a split second. He'd made sure he went down head first so death would be instantaneous. Yes, that would be the answer. *Let the aliens finish their task without me,* he thought.

He sat in the dark contemplating his future, or lack of it. Charles knew any future he would have would be a constant torment from all the souls that had died. The hundreds of millions that had already been vaporized was enough. He couldn't bear the job that still lay ahead. It was time.

"Doc, are you OK?" the voice in the dark asked. "Seems a little dangerous out there." The voice was a little closer.

The professor heard the word 'Doc'. But it wasn't her voice. It was a man's voice. Dr. Brody slunk lower, the more to disappear in the gloom. He didn't want to be disturbed.

A hand grabbed his shoulder with a man's strength. Again the voice, but louder and closer this time.

"Come on Professor. Why don't we move back and talk things over."

*No, I don't want to talk about anything,* Charles thought. *I want to stop thinking and talking forever. I've had enough thoughts for any man's lifetime. It's time to switch it all off.*

A gentle pull moved him back slightly. Then two hands firmly grabbed him under the arms and around the chest. With one big pull, the professor was lifted bodily and carried back from the edge.

"Captain, it's you." The professor spoke as if the intervening moments had been a dream. "What are you doing?"

"Let's step back a little, shall we? There's a flat rock over here we can sit on."

Charles followed the captain's lead to a large rock. He knew this rock. It was familiar to him. Somewhere he had fond memories of this rock that were warm and soft to his brain.

"Yes, this rock is a nice place to sit," the professor said as he sat down. The Army captain sat next to him. "Where's Miss May?" He remembered his tormenter of the past few days.

"She went to bed. She offered to help look for you but I said it would be better if she stayed put."

"Yes, I think that was a good idea. Nice girl, our Miss May, but she's very distracting."

"I have to agree with you on that, sir. But why were you out here sitting on the edge?"

"Well, my good Captain. The entire world is on the edge, I just wanted to join them," Dr. Brody offered.

# Chapter 22

"You want to talk about it, Doc?" Captain Grinkis asked. As a Special Ops commander he had been trained to look for suicidal behavior in his troops. While not an expert in such matters, the Army had given him enough skills to at least handle battle condition depression. *And if Dr.Brody wasn't suffering from battlefield stress, who was?* the captain thought.

"Captain Grinkis, I'm not sure if I want to unload on you. One person dealing with what the aliens are asking is enough."

"Why don't you call me Chet? I think we're in this too deep for any formalities, Doc. And as to sharing the burden, I think you have way too much on your plate to handle alone."

"Yes, that was what Karen attempted to help with," Charles said. Chet noticed Charles start to break down at the mention of her name and the loss it had caused him. "And look what happened to her."

"She's still out there. Why don't you fill me in on what the aliens are asking? I've been trained for such battles sir. I know I can help you take on some of it."

Chet waited as Dr. Brody thought through the offer. The captain stared out at the stars and followed them down to the point that they disappeared behind the hidden ridge to the north. With no moon, the night was so dark that the two men could more sense each other than see one another.

"When I was a college undergraduate, I took a year of biology. It was required for my degree program. One of the books I remember reading was by a fellow named Garrett Hardin. I believe it was called 'The Voyage of the Space Ship Beagle'. It wasn't one of the required textbooks, but was on the suggested reading list the prof provided."

Chet sat and listened. He wasn't sure where all this was headed, but the first rule of helping a soldier overcome his demons was to let him talk.

Dr. Brody continued. "I don't know why I was doing extra reading except I was interested at the time in becoming a biology major. The book was a story of humans on a long space voyage to settle a new planet. They had to operate a large spaceship to produce the food, air and water they would need over a trip that would take decades. Generations were born and died and the spaceship still continued its passage. The book's plot revolves around the inhabitants struggling with overpopulation and pollution, among other things."

"Seems sort of relevant to our situation, space ships and all." Chet was struggling to keep up and was throwing anything out to keep Dr. Brody talking.

The professor seemed to ignore the comments and continued his story. "But it was one salient point the author made in his story of humans struggling for survival. What I'll never forget was the author's enlightened statement about biology. You know, in physics, there are all sorts of laws. The laws of motion, the four laws of thermodynamics, that sort of thing. Many were first postulated by Isaac Newton. But biology has no such locked-in concrete rules. Except Garrett Hardin came up with one. He called it the 'First Rule of Biology'. It states 'You can never do just one thing'."

"What's that mean Doc?"

"That in biology, you can't do just one thing, everything is interconnected. Someone said that a flapping butterfly in Mexico affects the weather in Mongolia, or something like that," Charles said.

"Oh yeah, Gaia. The Mother Goddess of Earth the environmental wackos refer to it. I've heard of that." Chet added.

Dr. Brody was quiet for a while as the two men listened to the trade winds blow in from the ocean. The breeze carried the sound of the surf from the nearby beaches. It was a warm tropical night that could be mistaken for paradise if not for the world's fate oppressively hanging in the air.

"I've been also thinking about another of the additional readings I did for the class. It was called 'The Forest and the Seas', by Bates, I think. It's been too many years. But I still remember his hypothesis. He made the claim that all the Earth's oxygen came from the seas and all those little plankton creatures. They sucked in carbon dioxide and converted it to oxygen."

"And places like the Amazon rainforest combined with the seas to keep our atmosphere going?" Chet asked. He was in over his head just trying to keep the professor on track. Somewhere in all this they would get to the point.

"That was what was amazing about the whole book. Bates claimed that the net effect on oxygen levels by trees was zero. That all the carbon dioxide that all the living plants on Earth took in while they were living was released when they died as they rotted or were burned. Only the seas provide new additional oxygen, plant life is inconsequential."

"Huh," was all Chet could offer. *Things you learn sitting on a rock in the middle of the night,* he thought. But he was no closer to whatever point the professor was headed.

"Just imagine. All those environmentalists working to save the planet by saving the rainforest and it means nothing. Stupid people chasing wrongheaded ideas. They look good, and who doesn't like a good stand of trees, but the oceans are our savior."

"I guess you're right Doc." Chet knew he certainly wasn't about to challenge the professor on facts.

"But it's the third book I read that scares me. I'm not sure how it ended up on a sophomore biology reading list, but it changed my life. A book that was so powerful to me that I gave up on biology and switched to economic geography. Which led me to develop the 'Endangered Species' game. And then to have it all come back on me."

"You lost me there Professor. What book are we talking about now?" Chet asked. *This guy is all over the place. It will be daylight before I can get anything out of him,* he thought.

"'War on the Weak' it was called. Don't remember the author. It was the most explosive book I've ever read. To this day, no other topic has affected me like that book."

"I've never heard of it, I'm afraid. What's it about?"

Chet almost felt the shiver that Dr. Brody gave off at the inquiry to the books subject. The long silence alerted Chet to the profound influence the book had had.

Finally, Charles opened up. "The book chronicles the history of 'Eugenics'."

"Eugenics? What's that Doc?"

"The scientific study of improving the human race while eliminating the lesser specimens."

"Like Hitler?"

"Yes, he was the end result of the whole sordid mess. But the Eugenics movement started in America in the late 19th Century. Cold Harbor Lab on Long Island was the actual center of the study of developing supermen. Or at least vastly improved humans. It started out with the prevention of the procreation of the mentally infirm and others judged less than ideal. It eventually led to forced sterilization. In the end the Germans took up the cause and with their quest for excess, you know what happened."

"But how could such a thing happen in the United States?"

"Quite easy. All the top scientists were on board. Volumes of scientific studies confirmed the need to eliminate the lesser human specimens from the breeding pool. They were like horse breeders looking to create the fastest horse. Margaret Sanger, founder of Planned Parenthood in 1916 was an early advocate. Like global warming today, eugenics was a scientific fact that wasn't even argued about at the time."

"Amazing. I never knew."

"So Captain, why have these three books forced their way into my consciences from all the hundreds of books I've read over my career?"

Chet had no answer for the professor, so offered silence in return. He finally broke the long interlude with,

"I can't offer any insight on the books, but I'm sure they're related to the alien situation somehow. Maybe if you explain that, I can answer the other."

The professor began to explain the alien demands that they had forced on him. He outlined the steps he had taken to mollify the human cost that the aliens would cause and the compromises he had extracted. The longer the professor talked, the more the captain realized what a mental load the man had been carrying. *No wonder he was ready to jump of the cliff,* Chet thought.

By the time Dr. Brody was finished, Chet was exhausted. He suggested the two men sleep on what had been discussed and they would consider their options the next day. They carefully worked their way along the cliff back to the cabin.

"There's a couch in the cabin if you want to sleep there. I'm staying out of there. The lanai is as close as I want to get to my house guest. But you're welcome."

"Doc, I've been sleeping on the ground since I arrived here. It's part of my profession. I'll just sack out here in the corner of the lanai, if that's OK."

"Be my guest. Just keep a path to the toilet clear unless you want me tripping over you."

Chet grabbed his Army issue sleeping pad and threw it down on the floor. He pulled out a light polypropylene blanket and set his pack where a pillow would go. He laid down and was out before Dr. Brody had returned from the facilities.

# Chapter 23

Al Worthington, Harvard superstar, knew he had to have his game on today. The woman that had torn him from his world and had brought him to this island lay beside him in tears. And he was the man to console her right into his arms. He just had to play it right and she would be his.

"Karen, I'm here for you."

Karen seemed to respond to Al's overtures as she sunk her head deeper into his chest. The crying continued unabated as Al held on and let things flow.

After a long time, Karen's tears slowed and finally stopped. She lifted her head up and looked around at her surroundings. The sun had set and except for the light of the Special Forces wood fire nearby, all was in darkness.

She pulled away from Al. "Thanks Al. I'm sorry I'm such a bother."

Al let her sit up but ran his hands down her back. The energy of feeling this woman drove into his body and he held his hand on her lower back.

Karen stood up as Al's hand fell away. "I think I'll join the others. I'm kind of hungry."

Al jumped to his feet and again placed his arm around her shoulders for comfort. But she twisted ever so slightly out of his attempted embrace and walked quickly toward Sergeant Aubin. Al followed in her wake.

"Sergeant, anything to eat?" she asked.

"Yes ma'am. The men have caught some good-looking fish. If you're not tired of it yet, there's plenty."

"Fish sounds good." Karen sat down next to the sergeant. Al attempted to take up the opposite side, but a pile of equipment prevented him from his goal. He scurried around the fire and took up a place opposite the object of his desire.

"I could handle some of that too, Sergeant."

Sergeant Aubin looked up from his cooking task straight at Al, "I'm sure you could, sir."

Al was taken aback by the attitude projected in the statement. He had sensed a certain strangeness from the Delta troops since he had joined them back in Hawaii. With the Navy Seals vaporized while only he survived added to the disdain they openly displayed towards him.

But there was Karen. His hopes hung on her affections. He could ignore the cold stares of all the men if she would only return his attentions. He stared across the fire at her. The warm glow of the fire only enhanced the beauty he saw in her. He had to have her.

* * *

"Now, where are we again?" the Russian Ambassador asked.

Vernon Randolph sat and listened as the UN Security Council once again fought among themselves over the world's situation. The news coming in from all sources continued to be bad for humanity and the Council's frustration only grew at its total lack of power to control any of it.

"If our American colleague could update us on their forces on the island that might clarify things. The game show is almost over, and according to our computer game experts, the human side is about to bloody well get screwed," the British Ambassador said.

All the heads of the Council members turned to their American counterpart. Vernon sat directly behind his ambassador and felt the intense gaze she was receiving.

Finally the U.S. Ambassador responded. She reminded her colleagues that the attempts to intervene in Dr. Brody's selections on the 'Endangered Species' Game Show had been for naught. The professor had adamantly refused any advice or counsel.

News from the island had been routine since then. Mainly updates on the situation as Captain Grinkis observed it. And the situation updates showed a platoon of Special Forces sitting and not doing much while Dr. Brody continued his role as human arbitrator.

"Can't we get him to at least play along on anything?" the Chinese Ambassador asked. "Have you appealed to his patriotism?"

"Asked and rejected. He is a lone wolf and the whole alien connection seems to have gone to his head. We all know what power does to people. I'm afraid that Dr. Brody has succumbed to the ultimate power on Earth. The power of life and death over his fellow man."

"That's almost impossible to resist," the New Zealand Ambassador added.

The Russian Ambassador chimed in. "Can we nuke the island? That will shut the guy up for good."

Vernon was shocked by the continued belligerence of the Russians. *Hadn't they learned anything from their last attempt at forcing the issue?* he thought.

"The game is almost over. We can't risk an alien response to such an attack. And to risk so much just for the satisfaction of squashing one man? It's not worth it. It's too late in the game. But after it's all over, we might extract a pound of flesh," the Argentine Ambassador said.

"Now you're talking. We can't let some college professor get away with embarrassing this august body. It's just not done in our circles," the French Ambassador said.

A number of the members all nodded in agreement. *Pay back would be a bitch,* Vernon thought.

He watched his computer for updates from the Pentagon. Things were quiet on all fronts. He looked around the room and noticed his counterparts were all sitting quietly. Each country had established a central Comm Center so that news of what the aliens were doing could be passed quickly to the staff in New York City.

But each computer was still. Vernon moved the cursor around the screen and checked some secure sites available to him on the military network. Everything was quiet.

\* \* \*

Dr. Brody awoke stiff from his short night in the hammock. He slowly opened his eyes to a rising sun just breaking the ocean surface off to the east. The rays of the sun streaked toward the mountain that lay to the south and Charles studied the sunlight as it marched down the hillside toward the cabin.

He rolled his head to look into the cabin and saw his new partner laying on the bed. She had pulled the sheet up over her for warmth. But as soon as the first rays of the sun hit the large cabin windows, the solar energy began its work.

Dr. Brody remained in his hammock and watched the transition inside. With the added heat, a sleeping Brandi first kicked her feet out from the sheet. Then she rolled slightly, shoving the sheet down out of the way. Her breasts were now exposed as the professor continued his vigil.

Soon the sheet was thrown aside entirely and Miss May rolled onto her back. Her body lay naked to the world as her sleep continued unabated. Dr. Brody watched and thought of the aliens that had transported her to him. *They certainly upped the ante on the companionship factor,* he thought. *Much more of this and he would be forgetting anyone else.*

Charles knew he had to move away if he was going to maintain any self-control. He climbed out of the hammock and looked around for his flip-flops. Grabbing his fishing pole and some water, he headed west toward his favorite fishing hole. He needed space to think, undistracted by others.

The fishing spot that would produce a good catch was at the end of the cliff. The bay opened up to the ocean where two headlands came together. The narrow outlet created had been discovered to be a productive fishery.

He surmised that where the bay emptied into the open sea, large schools of fish gathered to cat the nutrient rich bay water. Simply dropping a line into the water quickly produced a catch. An early morning soirée to this spot would provide a week's supply of fresh fish in less than an hour.

Dr. Brody worked slowly to earn his catch. He was more intent on thinking than fishing. He lingered over each catch consuming more than two hours in reaching his limit. Packing up, he headed back to the cabin, the sun now full in the sky.

As he passed his favorite rock that had absorbed so much emotion, he noticed a figure lying on the top of the cliff. Whoever it was was intently staring down toward the bay below. He attempted to look over the edge, but saw nothing of interest from his perspective.

Closing in on the cabin, the person on the cliff suddenly noticed Dr. Brody approaching. Dr. Who quickly stood up, bowed in Dr. Brody's direction, and scampered down the cliff side trail. *What was he so intent on watching?* Charles thought.

The lanai was empty when he walked under the roof and pushed the hammock aside. Charles looked into the cabin and the bed was empty. He looked around and saw neither the captain nor Miss May.

He placed his catch in the sink and started to clean them when his curiosity took over. *Dr. Who was very focused on something,* he thought. He wiped his hands off and walked over to the cliff edge where Dr. Who had been.

Dropping onto his knees, he crawled over to the edge and looked down. Below him on the bay-side beach were two individuals. At least they looked like two individuals. It was difficult to tell since the two bodies were intertwined so tightly.

Dr. Brody laid down on the rock to study the situation. From his perch one-hundred and fifty feet above the beach, he could make out enough details to know that it was the missing captain and Miss May.

The view improved as the two passionate players on the beach changed positions. Miss May climbed onto the captain and sat down on his lap. Since neither had clothes on, Dr. Brody could imagine what was happening. Brandi went into a strong up and down motion as the captain vocally approved her movements.

He knew he should leave and let the two enjoy themselves in privacy, but he was frozen in curiosity. This woman who had so recently entered his life for one particular reason was displaying her stuff. *And it is considerable stuff,* he thought.

While her body bounced and wiggled in the sun, the professor evaluated the performance in a rather scientific sense. He had never been a voyeur to such acts and he was finding it quite interesting.

The couple shifted positions again and Dr. Brody noted the contortions that Miss May was capable of. *Simply amazing,* he thought. *Maybe I'm missing out on something.* But the longer he watched the more his thoughts turned to Karen and the time they had spent together.

He suddenly felt guilty watching others and crawled away. Sitting at the table on the lanai, his mind longed to hold his assistant once again. Charles missed her profoundly. He drifted in his thoughts until jolted back by the arrival of two partially clothed people.

"Oh Doc, you're back," the captain said. His face grew red with embarrassment. Brandi greeted the professor and headed to the shower. She pulled the swinging half door closed as the water splashed onto the floor.

"Captain, getting in some morning exercise with Brandi?" Charles let the implied knowledge of what had been happening sink in.

Chet lowered his voice so that the showering Brandi couldn't overhear. "Was that OK? I got the hint from you that Brandi was sort of . . ."

"Uncommitted. Yes, you're OK there. She is definitely a young man's game I'm afraid."

"Whew. You just said a mouth full there Doc," Chet offered. "I haven't ever been with such a-" He stopped as the shower stopped and a towel-clad Brandi emerged.

"What are you two talking about?" she asked.

"The situation. The Captain and I were discussing our situation." Dr. Brody stammered to get out.

"Well I hope our situation includes how we get me out of here and back to LA. I'm missing jobs that I've worked hard to get. They forget you fast in my line of work."

"I'm sure they do." Charles watched as she dropped the towel on the bed and began to dress. *Not many inhibitions in this one,* he thought as she bent over to look through her Dr. Wu box.

"But Doc, about our situation. As we discussed last night, I don't know . . ." Chet stopped short.

"Captain, the advantage of fishing is it gives one time to think clearly. While others were intent on physical activity, my mental skills were working up a plan," Charles said. He noticed the sheepish grin on the captain's face. *If I was out fishing for over two hours, how long were these two going at it on the beach?* he thought.

230

"Oh good, the Doc is going to get me out of here. What do we do first?" Brandi exclaimed.

"First, I have to talk with our friend, Errol Flynn. Then I make today's selections on the show. Then we head over to Captain Grinkis's men's camp. We need to recruit some help," Charles said.

"All right, I can smell that LA smog already."

# Chapter 24

New York City

Ellie Randolph sat in anticipation of the last installment of the 'Endangered Species' Game Show. While New York City had settled into moderate calm after it was selected by Dr. Brody to be part of the human side, groups still demonstrated by the United Nations trying to address their countries concerns.

She watched as the news showed a heavy Japanese demonstration by both Japanese-Americans and individuals from Japan itself. With Tokyo and a large chunk of Honshu Island on the animal side of the ledger, the demonstrators were pushing the UN for some sort of action to save their countrymen.

"Is it on yet?" Vernon asked as he stepped in from the shower. The Security Council was meeting less and less frequent as the end of the show loomed. The members had resigned themselves to the fate Dr. Brody was setting for the human world. No amount of demonstrations by disgruntled citizens was going to change anything.

"No honey. But the news just ended, so you have time to grab a drink while the ads are on," Ellie offered. Her husband had come home early so they could enjoy the extra time together. Vernon returned with a martini in each hand and handed one to his wife.

"A toast. To the world according to Dr. Brody. May it reign supreme forever," Vernon said.

Ellie lifted her glass up and clunked the edge with her husband's glass. Both took a sip before Vernon pulled his bathrobe tight and sat down close to his wife. He picked up the remote and hit the volume button. The TV came to life as the game show graphics came on the screen.

"Good evening ladies and gentlemen. It's been a long journey but tonight we have reached the end. And as promised, we have a spectacular show for tonight's finale," the show's host said. "Let's turn right away to our two analysts who have given us so much valuable information these many weeks. First for the animal world, David Brower."

"Good evening. Yes, it's hard to believe we're to the point of making our final ten selections of this epic event. The animals are certainly poised to reap a windfall no matter what happens tonight."

"Well, hold on there, mister. Just because humankind has been held hostage doesn't mean that the animals are anything close to winners tonight. As I said, 'if you've seen one Redwood, you've seen them all', and I still stand by those words. We shall see how all this shakes out before anyone declares victory."

"Thank you, President Reagan," David said. "Those words will inspire the human world, I'm sure. But to the reality of the situation, it does appear that the animal side is on its way to a great victory. As has been widely discussed throughout the entire show, the alien choice of Dr. Brody seems to have been a poor one for the human world. We have shown you on numerous shows where he went terribly wrong. And the humans are about to pay a heavy price, I'm afraid."

Vernon hit the mute button. He was tired of the hype and just wanted the show to be over. At least New York City had landed on the right side of the game. His contented life of work and home would continue. He wanted no interruptions in his simple life.

As Ellie reached over and placed her now-empty martini glass on the coffee table, her bathrobe opened and its contents spilled out in front of Vernon.

"Not now, honey. I need to see the final choices. Not that it matters much. Hell, the ratings have dropped like a stone for the show ever since all of the land squares were picked."

Ellie let her bathrobe hang loose as enticement to her husband. Vernon put his arm around her in compensation to more robust activity She nestled into his shoulder, her exposed breast landing on his chest. With the pre-game show over, Vernon ignored his wife's invitation and hit the volume again.

Bob Barker was introducing the two game participants once again. *How many shows had it been*? Vernon thought.

"Giant Panda, good to see you once again. We shall miss your charming face after tonight. I want to tell you I've enjoyed the quiet determination that you've displayed in getting the animal world to what looks like a winning position."

GP, as he liked to be called, lifted his face and smiled into the camera. The audience provided by the aliens roared their approval one more time for the panda's fine work.

234

"And our own Dr. Brody. One more time, eh Doc? You have a lot of detractors Professor, but I'm here to set the record straight. You've played one hell of a game against one shrewd opponent. You should never lower your head to anyone for what you've accomplished here," Bob said.

Dr. Brody nodded his head in acknowledgement of the supposed compliment wrapped in an insult. The alien crowd on the professor's side roared its approval. *At least they are holding whatever human support for the Professor together,* Vernon thought.

Bob got right to the point. "OK, it's GP's first selection tonight. All we have are ocean squares, so where are you going to take us?"

The panda slid the cursor across the flat panel display. The world map was almost all red or green squares indicating to which side they were attached. The panda stopped on a square in the Atlantic Ocean off Greenland and punched his joystick. The square went green to the ecstatic delight of the animal supporters.

"A good sound choice. Now, Dr. Brody, you seem to be at an impasse. Your strategy of picking ocean squares to maintain sea lanes between continents has failed. GP has blocked you at every turn. So what do you want to do with your first selection?"

Dr. Brody quickly moved the cursor to a square in the North Pacific and hit the mouse. A red square came on the map.

The final eight selections went much the same way. Drama proved impossible at this point in the game. No one really cared if a plot of sea off Diego Garcia in the Indian

Ocean or one near Easter Island was chosen. For the human world, sea squares didn't offer much. The professor answered each pick by GP quickly with little emotion. Even Bob Barker couldn't get a word out of the human participant. With frustration at any lack of excitement for the final show, Bob tried one last time to whip some up.

Vernon had had enough. He swung his hand over and cupped his wife's breast in his hand. The martini had reinvigorated him and he knew his wife got more amorous the drunker she got. He leaned in, kissed her and was happy to find the warmth retuned in spades.

He stood up and headed to the kitchen to make another drink. *That should just about do the trick,* he thought. Not that she was a slacker in bed when sober, but three stiff drinks turned her into a dynamo.

As he returned with the new drink he saw that she had discarded the bathrobe entirely and was sprawled on the couch in a very unladylike pose. He handed her the drink and sat down. But his attention returned to the game show. Something was happening. He turned up the volume. His wife moaned in frustration.

"Well, ladies and gentlemen, don't turn that dial yet. This is a huge development. Can you repeat that, Dr. Brody?"

Vernon was mad at himself. He had missed whatever they were talking about. His wife put her empty glass down unceremoniously on the coffee table but missed the top. The glass dropped to the floor where it bounced on the carpet. She leaned back and wrapped her legs around Vernon's neck and began to pull him in.

"Stop, I want to see this. Something happened." The legs slid down his back as Ellie sat up. Her breasts pushed into his back as she reached around him. Her hands moved down his exposed chest and pushed his bathrobe open. He twitched as she reached his vital area.

"I said stop it." He grabbed her hands and pulled them free. He held them in front of him so they couldn't wander. "This is important."

Bob Barker finally got Dr Brody to repeat himself. "Well, Bob, I am challenging the animal world. I'm willing to trade two human squares for one animal squares. Two for one. Doesn't get any better than that."

"And you have approval for all this?" Bob was referring to the aliens without mentioning who was really controlling things.

"Yes, Bob. In two weeks, we'll meet for an all-day showdown. We will offer up two squares at a time and will make a trade if the animals offer us something we want. That's the deal, we both have to agree on the value of the squares offered. No sucker deals allowed."

"I like your spirit, Doc. Still trying to make up for a poor showing in the main show, I guess. But two for one really boosts the animal world's holding. Are you sure about this Professor?"

The human supporters behind the professor were answering that question with resounding boos all around. Meanwhile, the animal supporters were cheering and laughing at the professor's predicament.

"Never so sure about anything in my life, Bob." The sarcasm that Charles displayed showed his determination.

But the negative reaction by the arena crowd that was supposed to be supporting the humans told a different story.

"Ok, then, folks. You heard it. Two weeks from now. An all-day Saturday spectacle to determine humankind's fate. Is our fair Dr. Brody about to give the farm away? Stay tuned for the answer."

Vernon killed the TV. He stood so fast that his previously entangled wife hit the floor hard, her bare bottom bouncing next to her martini glass. "I need to get to work right now. The Security Council is going to go ballistic over this. Shit, where's my pants?"

* * *

Karen rose after watching the game show on Sergeant Aubin's computer. *What was Dr. Brody doing?* she thought. Right behind her was her constant companion of late, Al Worthington.

"Your professor has lost his mind. Trading human squares off at two to one. The man is crazy," Al said.

And Karen couldn't argue with the man. Al might be a little clingy, but the man wasn't dumb. They had spent numerous hours sitting and talking about what the aliens were doing. And they had talked endlessly about the role that Dr. Brody was providing in helping them accomplish their goals. And the talk had led to a decision that Dr Brody wasn't doing much for humankind.

Al had pointed out all the mistakes Charles had made. She knew that he got all his information on the game from that guy called Mel. *He was a little different,* she thought.

Karen had known other geeks at college and Mel fit the description. Totally devoted to their computers and the ethereal world of the internet, Mel was lost among the warriors that sat around her. Al certainly kept his distance from the troops also, although for a different reason that escaped her.

But he had been supportive when she had needed it. After the truth of Dr. Brody's involvement with the aliens had come out, her repulsion at his dealings made her seek an escape. And Al had shepherded her away from the horror. His shoulder was always available to her when she had needed consoling.

And that had been as far as it went. As the only woman among a platoon of Special Ops soldiers, she was in demand. But their attentions were loaded with implications which didn't interest her. And Mel didn't even come near her. He played on his computer when he wasn't sleeping. He had figured out a way to connect up to the encrypted Army computer so he could get internet accesses , as well as power.

And that left Al. Karen accepted that she needed some connection to a male just to keep the soldiers at bay. She had considered the older Sergeant Aubin, but wasn't even sure of his intentions. So Al was the default individual to offer her some peace of mind. *At least till I get off this damn island,* she thought.

She had watched the last game show episode in excitement. With the game over, they could all go home. She knew that Iowa had been selected for the human side, so she was hopeful that college life and normality would soon return.

239

That was about the time she heard the commotion among the soldiers. She looked to see Captain Grinkis walk into their camp. His men gathered around to welcome him back after his short absence.

"Captain, it's good to see you again," Sergeant Aubin offered. "You haven't been turned into gray dust yet?"

"No Sergeant, still upright and walking tall. How are the men getting on?"

"Two hours of PT every morning. We run the trail back to the beach we landed on. Then two hours of water PT in the lagoon in the afternoon. They may all volunteer for the Seals when we get out of here, they've spent so much time treading water."

"Good work Sergeant, keep it up. I'm certain we'll be ordered out of here soon. I need to talk to Mel and Karen. Are they around?" Chet asked.

Mel's Delta Force brother yelled at his brother to shake it, that the commander wanted him. Karen arrived without any prodding, Al right behind her.

"Ms. Price, I need you to gather your things. You too Mel. We move out in fifteen minutes," the captain ordered.

"Hold on Captain. You just can't walk in here and order anyone about. These people are civilians and are not subject to your commands," Al said.

"I can and I just did. Dr. Brody needs their help and I've come to retrieve them."

"That lunatic. All he needs help with is a shove off the cliff by his cabin. The man knows no shame. First involving this young woman in his perverted sick plans and

240

now this. I won't stand for it. Ms. Price will stay right here," Al barked.

"Sergeant . . ." Chet started. Before he could even finish, two of his troops had grabbed Al and held him in place. Sergeant Aubin reached into his kit bag and pulled out two plastic tie snaps. As Al protested loudly, the sergeant zip tied his hands together.

The troops forced him onto the ground and the sergeant zip-tied his ankles. As he pulled out a gag to place on his detainee, Al knew when to give up. The sergeant returned the gag to his pants pocket.

"Thank you Sergeant. Now, Ms. Price, Mel, if you please," Captain Grinkis said.

Mel hadn't hesitated once instructed of the move and had his computer packed. Karen soon returned with a small satchel holding her possessions. They both followed the captain as he led them back toward the cabin.

After a short distance, Karen asked, "Captain, can you tell me what this is about?"

"Ma'am, the professor will fill you in when we get there."

# Chapter 25

Vernon had been right that the Security Council would meet immediately after Dr. Brody had issued his challenge. Leaving his wife in the lurch, he arrived at the U.S. Mission Building to excitement that had been absent in the last few weeks.

With the game almost over, the staff had resigned themselves to humanity's fate. Now with the professor upping the ante of the game, everyone was busy. Vernon wasn't sure what they could all be doing since from the beginning of the whole affair, the U.N. had been powerless.

Small groups of people were busy talking as he made his way to the ambassador's outer office. As he was ready to sit down, the door opened and the ambassador emerged with the general. They both grabbed Vernon as they headed to the Situation Room.

Vernon was amazed at the buzz once inside the room. He had never been inside the Situation Room before as it was normally reserved for senior staff only. His recent job elevation was advancing rapidly as the alien crisis continued. *I like this, I could be in line for a raise soon,* he thought.

"Randolph, grab a seat," the general ordered. Vernon quickly complied. A woman staff member he had seen around the mission was sitting next to him.

He leaned over and whispered, "Why all the excitement?"

"Didn't you hear? That Dr. Brody has flipped. He's offering up two human squares for one animal square."

"Oh, I saw that. But what are they expecting to do that they haven't been able to do before? The aliens have blunted every attack we've tried," he said.

"I guess the general has an idea. Something along the lines that if Dr. Brody isn't around to make the deal, then the deal can't happen," she said.

"Holy cow, they're going to whack the professor?" Vernon retorted a little to loud. Some in the room turned to see who was making the noise.

The woman staffer hissed in return. "Quiet you fool! You'll get me in trouble."

Vernon sat frozen as thoughts swirled around in his head. *Kill Dr. Brody. The aliens aren't going to like that,* he thought. But how? The nukes had been redirected. The Navy Seals with their weapons had been vaporized. How could anyone with a weapon get close enough to shoot the professor? *No one could, thats who,* he concluded.

The large screen at the front of the room lit up and a soldier's face came on the screen. Vernon could see trees behind the soldier as the comm link went live.

The general barked out, "Whom am I speaking to?"

"Sergeant Aubin, sir. Delta Force, 3rd Platoon. Hurrah."

"Hurrah Sergeant. Where is Captain Grinkis?"

"Captain Grinkis is with Dr. Brody, sir. He has the platoon's computer so the professor has quick access out. We are using the backup that the sub delivered when they did our resupply."

"If that's the case, I need you to switch to Tac 2. This information can't be displayed on the other computer. You know the code and password."

243

"Yes sir. But how do we know Captain Grinkis isn't tapped in to the same channel?" the sergeant asked.

"We've got that covered. You just change up and we'll reestablish communications. Is that clear?"

"Loud and clear, General." The screen went to static as the sergeant on the far off island switched to a different frequency. Vernon sat and watched.

All this excitement for an event that would end in a bolt of lightning and a pile of gray dust. He didn't envy the man or men that would be ordered to attempt an impossible task. He sat back and thought of the Special Forces still on the island and their expected fate.

Then it hit him. Special Ops personnel don't need a weapon to kill. They are trained to kill with their bare hands if need be. A platoon of trained killers was encamped a short distance from the professor.

Dr. Brody would never know what hit him as one of them snapped his neck like a twig. Vernon shuddered at the thought. His mind turned to his very tipsy naked wife that he had left in such a hurry. Hopefully she would still have her motor running when he got home. Her image satisfied him as he waited for something to happen on the island.

\* \* \*

"Ms. Price, I need your help desperately on this. I only have two weeks to get all my information gathered," Dr. Brody pleaded.

"I told you I never wanted to see you again, and I meant it. And that definitely included doing research for you. What you are proposing makes no sense, and it seems everyone else in the world knows it."

"Ms. Price, I've talked to the Doc about this extensively. He has a plan that will work. He just needs help finding the stuff he needs to know. With your and Mel's help, he just might pull it off." Captain Grinkis added his opinion to the argument.

"Yeah, the Doc says I can get back to LA real soon. He just needs to find his stuff," Brandi added as she walked up to the small group ensconced on the cabin's lanai

"And who the hell is she?" Karen asked as she stared at Miss May. Luckily Dr. Brody had emphasized the importance of wearing clothes to Brandi prior to Karen's arrival. But wearing a halter top and close-cut jean shorts, Dr. Brody wasn't sure if Karen was impressed.

"She's the new assistant the aliens provided when you quit." As soon as he had said it, he knew it was a mistake. Charles waited for the explosion.

"Oh, I see. They work fast. No wonder you're so chummy with our space buddies. They upped their bet this time with 'Miss Lost and Confused'. I felt honored that I was first. I could never compete around here now," Karen said. Her dig hit home and Charles knew he couldn't answer her charge.

"Stop, both of you. Dr. Brody has laid out a challenge and the aliens have accepted it," Chet interjected.

"Well, Dr. Brody may have laid something, but whatever challenge he's talking about is a different matter entirely. Maybe he needs to stick with his other option here." Karen rolled her eyes toward Brandi and stomped off. She headed west toward the cliff overlook.

Chet raised his hand to stop the professor from following. He followed the angry woman out to the rock and sat down next to her. Both of them stared at the blue water of the bay before speaking.

"He really needs your help. You might not understand what he's attempting, but I can assure you, he has humankind's concern foremost in his mind," Chet said.

"I'm more worried about the other parts of his body than his mind. I think another male feature is driving his concerns. Keep the concubines coming, I think the saying goes," Karen said.

"Well, you're wrong. I can't tell you how wrong you are. You'll just have to take my word on it. If you can't trust him, then put your trust in me," Chet offered.

Karen sat for a long time. Chet waited quietly for her answer. The trade winds blew and the warm air swirled. Off in the distance, the palm trees swayed in a gentle rhythm. Finally Karen spoke.

"OK, I'll do it for you Captain. But keep that man away from me."

She rose and walked briskly back to the lanai. The captain followed quickly behind.

"Let's get it done. What do we need to research?" she demanded.

* * *

Al Worthington, Harvard stud, sat in lock ties for the first time in his life. It was extremely uncomfortable. After the second day, he started asking if he could be released. He had noticed that the sergeant had been distracted on the computer for large chunks of time and Al had been judicious in the timing of his pleas.

Sergeant Aubin had extracted a promise of good behavior that Al had readily agreed to. *Anything to get out of these restraints*, he thought. Now, still rubbing his wrists from where the ties had been, he sat around acting docile for the troops.

But in his brain he was scheming. He needed to steal away and rescue the woman of his dreams. She had obviously been taken against her will back to the maniac's cabin. It would appear that the captain had been compromised to Dr. Brody's will

*Well, I haven't succumbed to any mind control,* he thought. Nothing had ever been more clearer than that Karen Price needed his help to escape the evil forces lurking on the island.

As the time progressed to Dr. Brody's game day challenge, Al became more agitated. But he had to hold his intentions to himself so that he wouldn't be strapped up again. Plotting, he held himself ready.

Five days before the big event, he obtained his weapon of vindication. The soldiers had their rifles but kept them close. Their personal handguns they kept closer. Only during their PT times were the weapons gathered and stored where Al had a chance to grab one.

*But then what?* he thought. *If one of the troops failed to notice one of his weapons was missing, which was doubtful, then the vaporizer would get him.* Al hadn't forgotten the fear that had overwhelmed him hiding in the tree well close by what was left of his Navy Seal companions.

While he loved the woman of his desire, being vaporized didn't get him any closer to her. *There had to be another way* he thought. That was when one of the troops walking by happened to provide an answer.

The soldier was nonchalantly carrying his combat web gear over his soldier with his K-Bar knife attached. As the soldier walked by Al, the upside down knife fell out of its sheath. It made no sound as it landed in a large patch of grass.

Al quickly glanced to see if anyone else had seen anything. As no one was looking his way, he scooted forward the few feet, grabbed the knife and slid back to his original position. He quietly slid the knife under some grass and waited.

Soon the soldier came along looking intently at the ground. "Hey, did you see me drop a knife around here?" he barked at Al.

Al just shook his head, "No knife dropped around me."

"Shit, Sarge is going to bust me bad for losing it." The soldier muttered to himself as he continued his search.

Later in the dark, Al secured the knife under a tree in a small opening in the root ball. It would be safe there until he needed it. And that time was quickly approaching. He slept soundly that night, the first since Karen had been taken from him.

# Chapter 26

The first week of research for the team went quickly. Karen and Mel worked the computer link gathering the information Dr. Brody needed. With only two weeks until the final showdown with the animal world, everyone worked long hours getting things prepared.

Chet teamed with the professor on the Special Ops secure link. Chet knew that he needed to keep some distance between Dr. Brody and Karen. The promise of help she had offered had been to him specifically. *The less time the two former partners spent together, the better,* he thought.

Brandi was assigned support duty. She kept the food and drinks flowing as the days wore on. She tried to keep the garden going but complained that she didn't know much about growing plants. But she picked the fruit for juices and gathered eggs from the chickens.

She received no complaints for her efforts, since clothed the entire time, the level of coverage was scanty at best. Chet noticed the long stares she was receiving from the only other woman on the team. Karen gave Brandi long stares at times as Miss May pranced around.

Chet was certainly distracted whenever she showed up with refreshments. After their fling on the beach, the two had been forced to abstain from further activities due to the workload Dr. Brody kept demanding.

Mel appeared oblivious to Brandi's style of dealing with men. And Dr. Brody seemed downright embarrassed at times with Brandi's behavior. The professor went out of his way to not even look at her when the food was being passed out. In fact, the professor avoided both women as much as possible.

Work kept Dr. Brody sustained, at least by Chet's recognition of the amount he was delegating to everyone else. Chet had been partially privy to the professor's plans but couldn't grasp the strategic attack he had planned for the giant panda.

The first week of work was soon completed as announced by Dr. Brody. The team sat back and waited for instructions. With another week to prepare, they knew something else must be in the plan.

"OK, you've all done good work. While you've been pulling together all the information I need, I've been outlining what we need to do this week," the professor announced.

The group of four tired workers groaned in unison. Chet made eye contact with Brandi and she locked on to his gaze. She rolled her eyes to indicate her displeasure at the 'all work and no play' regime that had become their routine.

Chet noticed that Mel was resigned to his fate. He was at least doing what he lived for, hanging out on the computer and the internet. *Nothing new for him,* Chet thought. But Karen was non-responsive the whole time. Her continued rage at Dr Brody was self-evident. Chet made a mental note to take her aside after the meeting to reinforce the importance of what they were doing.

"This next week will be different than last week however. This will sound strange, but I don't want the women involved in it at all. I'm going to ask Brandi and

Karen to move down to the main house till we need them again," Dr. Brody said.

The death stare that Karen suddenly gave the professor was evident by everyone at the table. Chet wasn't privy to the initial reason that Karen had moved in with the professor, but he heard it now.

"And be around Dr. Who? Not me thanks. Been there, done that. Or don't you remember?" Karen challenged. Her voice screamed sarcasm.

The whole team watched as the professor and Karen seemed to square off. None knew the history between these two. Chet was just hoping he could hold them together long enough to complete whatever the professor had in mind. He was reverting back to his command training in keeping a team working on a common goal.

"Maybe with Brandi there with you, it won't be like last time?" Chet offered.

Karen turned on Brandi with a death stare. "Yes, maybe Dr. Who's proclivities are more in keeping with Miss May."

"Pro what? Is there something I need to know about Dr. Who?" Brandi asked.

"It will be fine for both of you. Just keep your clothes on around Who," Dr. Brody offered.

Chet cringed at the ham-fisted attempt to mollify the two women. *I need to step in here before this all implodes,* he thought.

"Say Doc, how about I take them down to the main house and sort of make my presence felt? Intimidate Dr. Who a bit. I think I can get my point across without speaking the language," Chet offered.

"That's fine. While you're doing that, Mel and I will get started on our new research," the professor said.

Karen reluctantly joined Chet and Brandi as they walked down the trail along the cliff. Passing the shed where the final game show would be broadcasted, the three walked up onto the main house's covered porch.

Chet looked inside for any signs of life and saw none. He called and received no answer. He stepped in through the open French doors and searched the house. No one was present. Stepping back outside, he told the women to sit and wait while he looked around. A half hour later he returned with no news on Wu Who.

"I guess you two can just wait here. If either one shows up, come and get me. I need to get back to the Doc, but I'll tell him we seemed to have lost our overseers."

Karen continued her resistance to being anywhere near Dr. Who. Chet asked nicely that she keep her promise to help. They had been asked to wait here and Chet implored that they cooperate.

The attitude didn't diminish but the nod of agreement sent Chet on his way. *I don't know how long she'll keep her promise,* he thought. He sprinted back up the trail and joined the two other men busy at work.

* * *

"Why are you so mean to me?" Brandi finally asked after the two had sat in silence for a long time. "You're like all the others that think they're better than me."

Karen was taken aback by the bluntness of the question. She stopped her long stare at the beach stretching out in front of them.

"People are always assuming I'm stupid," Brandi continued.

"Well, it's just that you act so . . ." Karen started.

"I act, that's right. And I'm very good at it too. Last year I earned a half-million for my little act."

"A half-million ... dollars?" Karen was now staring at Miss May.

"No, chestnuts. Of course dollars! At least most of them are dollars. I'm smart enough when I model in Europe to get paid in Swiss Francs. I have a substantial sum all set aside in a bank in Zurich, thank you very much. But don't tip off the IRS, as I'm not sure my accountant fully declares all my off-shore work."

Karen attempted to speak but her mind was mush. *What was this beauty queen trying to tell her?* she thought.

"So what was your net income last year?" Brandi asked. "My agent said I was on track to break a million this year. That is until I was whisked to this island paradise. Do you really think what the Doc is doing will get me back to LA?"

"I have no idea. But he better have a plan to get LA back on the human side or you might want to reconsider Tinseltown."

"Yeah, that would be a bummer. Land back in Hollywood and that's all that's there, hollywood. And animals. Well, I could tell you a story or two about the wild animals of Hollywood, and I mean the two-legged kind," Miss May said.

Her voice trailed off as she said it. There was a sadness in the woman's voice that spoke volumes to Karen. While Karen had chosen the academic career for her life, she had not missed the male attentions college campuses provided.

"Bad huh?"

"Things I had to do to break into the big show," Brandi said.

Karen waited for her to elaborate, but nothing was forthcoming. *She must have had some terrible times* Karen thought.

"I know how bad male college professors can be. Put out or watch your grade go down. We had a small network of women on campus. We kept each other informed about which professors to avoid. Luckily I never . . ." Karen was stopped.

"You were lucky then," Brandi said. "But after what I went through in Arkansas with my step-father, at least what the Hollywood pigs did got me paid."

A feeling of shock hit Karen. *This woman had led a life very different than mine. She had real tough choices to make to survive,* she thought. Brandi had not only survived, but had flourished it would appear. It made her simple life being raised in Iowa with two loving parents seem Pollyannish. Nothing bad had happened to her in her whole life, and Karen was suddenly grateful.

"I'm sorry if I acted so mean to you before. I didn't know."

"Thanks. No one assumes that models have paid a lot of dues to get where they are. I guess some get there without all the baggage, but no one that I've ever met did."

"So Hollywood lived up to its reputation then?" Karen asked.

"You wouldn't believe half the stuff that goes on. The big shots keep it under wraps so the American public will continue watching the stars do their thing. Keep the money train flowing at all cost. Once in awhile a Charlie Sheen character will get caught with their pants down, but the money greases the local scene to keep the officials looking the other way."

"So why not go for a normal life then?"

"What's a poor uneducated girl in Podunk, Arkansas going to do? Keep getting abused by a drunk step-father until I get pregnant? Then a life of abusive drunk boyfriends popping out kids while living in a single wide by the rail road tracks? That was the life all my girlfriends got handed. And some by their own Daddy."

"What?" Karen said.

"But I said I was uneducated, not stupid. I quit in the ninth grade and got rides west to California. God blessed me with this body and I figured it would be my ticket to the promise land. By seventeen I had modeling jobs. I never succumbed to the porn peddlers, though many tried. I don't mind being naked in front of anyone, but I got enough church-going from my mama to know where the line is."

"I never knew," Karen said. She was fascinated by this side of life that she had never been exposed to before. But all this was raising the big question in her mind. "So, have you ever found love in all of this?"

"There was a cute boy back in Arkansas. We were 14 at the time and I drove him crazy. I was totally innocent.

But then my mama remarried and all of that innocence went away. I couldn't barely look at him after that. I left soon after," Brandi said. Karen noticed that she stared down for a long while, lost in her thoughts.

"Nobody since then?"

A smile came over her downturned face. She beamed as her thoughts obviously went to a different place.

"Yes. There is someone. But not in Hollywood. Nothing but pigs there. Love doesn't exist there, no matter what all those magazines try to tell you. Money rules peoples lives there and any semblance of love is just a connection to money."

"But there is someone. Who?" Karen was totally fascinated now for the answer. Who could struggle through the scars of this poor woman's life to find her heart?

"I'm not sure its reciprocal though, so I'm afraid to say," Brandi said.

"Its OK. We're stuck on this island. They'll never know."

"But he's on this island. He was wonderful and caring and knew just what I needed. He never demanded and never rushed me. It was unlike any other time I've been with a man. I was hooked immediately. I never knew such feelings existed."

Karen's soul sank. *Someone on this island,* she thought. She's never been near the troops on the other side of the island so that left three men. *Mel, no way,* she thought. *That left Captain Grinkis and . . .*

She froze. And Dr. Brody. But which one? She scrambled to find the answer. "Someone here. That was fast."

"I'll say. I never expected it. Land on this island and find the man of your dreams. He's so gentle with me." Brandi was almost cooing with pleasure as she recalled what had been obviously a moving experience. "And so important too. Why the world is fighting for survival and he's here defending it. It's so ..."

"Stimulating, I know," Karen's heart was sinking. Brandi was in love with Charles. It had to be. Karen remembered the tenderness of the man who had nursed her back to health when the parasites struck. And then the gentle lover he had been while they had been together. *But he had obviously shown the same to this other woman,* she thought. *But why am I so concerned about this?* she asked herself.

Karen fought her emotions as the conflict in her surfaced. She still despised the man who had been involved with so many deaths and now seemed bent on killing more. Why was she feeling the tug that the woman opposite her had thrust into her life?

*If Dr. Brody and Brandi had found love, good for them,* she thought. *Brandi certainly deserved it from her story.* She would just push down the conflict and wait for the endgame. Finish up here and get off the island became her objective. Feelings to the contrary would be shoved aside.

# Chapter 27

The disappearance of Dr. Who and Dr. Wu raised a concern when Dr. Brody got the news from the Captain. The two men had searched the end of the island to no avail. The two seemed to have vanished.

"Is that a bad sign?" Captain Grinkis asked.

"I have no idea. I'll check with Errol Flynn later, but I don't know if they are connected or not. I only surmised that Wu Who were really aliens."

Mel had been on his computer the whole time and finally joined the conversation, "I don't know if this is relative to what you are discussing, but isn't the windmill looking different?"

The other men whipped around and stepped out from under the lanai. Two-hundred feet away was the old-style wind mil that kept them supplied with fresh water. Like the ones shown on old Western movies, the creaking blades spun slowly in the trade winds.

Water was pumped out of a well and lifted into two elevated tanks. One fed the two households and the other was used for irrigation water in the garden. It had been doing its job steadily since Dr. Brody's arrival on the island and had become background noise until now.

No one paid any attention to the tower and the windmill attached. *It was just one of the things always there working,* the professor thought. But Mel had noticed something. Where the tower had previously ended in a tip, something now protruded. The three men walked closer for a better look. Standing at the base, the object took on a more defined shape.

"Looks kind of like a camera," Mel offered.

"Or multiple cameras," Chet added.

They stared at the device. It was round with small windows around the lower side as if surveillance cameras were monitoring them. On the upper half of the globe were small protrusions. They were too far away to make out any details.

"I can climb up and check it out," Chet said. He walked to the tower and grabbed the first cross tie. Going up one of the four legs using the cross ties, he quickly reached the bottom of the windmill. As he reached for the bracket supporting the drive action for the pump, a loud hum stopped him.

"What's that?" Dr. Brody asked.

Chet backed off and the hum stopped. He then reached for the bracket and the hum came back. Ignoring the noise, he pulled himself higher.

"Captain, stop! The protrusions on the top just moved. They are definitely sticking out now and they're aimed at you," Mel yelled.

Chet stopped and lowered himself to below the windmill. Mel announced that the protrusions just shifted back to where they had been.

"Captain, maybe you should climb down," Dr. Brody said.

After he reached the ground, the three all huddled, still watching the ball device.

"We can assume that the aliens left it there. Maybe as a replacement for the Wu Who team. Things are almost over and they may be planning their exit," the professor said.

The men returned to their research work as Dr. Brody drove them hard. This new information was vital and he wanted to make sure he had what he needed. While the first week had been about researching the trades he would offer the animals, this second week's work concerned his deal with the aliens.

At first Mel and Chet balked at what Dr.Brody was asking of them. The professor finally had to enlighten them of the risk humanity was facing. No one else knew the compromise the professor had gained from the aliens. *I wonder if the world will ever know what had been planned for them?* Dr. Brody thought.

* * *

The Situation Room at the U.S. Mission to the U.N. was quiet as Vernon Randolph finished up his work. He had been busy working with the U.S. Ambassador and the general assigned by the Pentagon.

Plans were being made to present to the other Security Council members that would affect humanity. After the game show had placed the animal world in a superior position to the humans, the U.N. was working hard on attempting to correct the situation.

And Vernon knew the key to any correction was the elimination of Dr. Brody. The Security Council had convinced themselves that after Dr. Brody had been eliminated by the Special Ops team located on the island, the aliens would turn to them for a replacement.

And the final day for the game show fit perfectly into their plans. But instead of that fool Dr. Brody trading away squares in some harebrained scheme he had concocted, the Security Council would retrieve the situation from the animal world. *Couldn't be simpler, they had said,* Vernon thought.

But he was a bit more skeptical. In fact, he was a lot more skeptical. The aliens hadn't shown any weakness so far, and he assumed they would hold that position to the end. But he was just an observer to the great 'game'. International power politics was beyond him. Intergalactic power politics was incomprehensible.

"Vernon, do you have our report to the full Council ready?" the U.S. Ambassador asked.

"Yes, Madame Ambassador."

"Good, let's get over to the General Assembly Building and get this all laid out. Our agent on the island should be about ready."

Vernon followed his boss, dutifully carrying the fifteen copies of their plan. As he worked hard to keep up with the ambassador and her security detail, his mind wandered to Ellie. His wife had almost become a nuisance over the last two weeks.

The announcement by Dr. Brody of the 'Showdown at Sunset', as the final day of trading squares had been dubbed, seemed to have thrown his wife into a drunken frenzy. Vernon could barely get in the apartment door after a long day at work before her sexual demands forced him to either pleasure her or reprimand her.

And lately, he had been spending more time at home reprimanding her. *She was insatiable,* he thought. All she seemed to think of was sex. Whatever was tormenting her, Vernon had decided that what once was a good thing was now torment.

He had taken to lingering at the Mission to avoid the distractions at home. That only made his wife seek him out more. The formerly loving couple was spiraling quickly out of control. He longed for the final game show and perhaps his life would return to normal. The simple job that he had held before this whole alien crisis called to him.

The ambassador broke his day-dream as they entered the meeting room. The other Security Council members and their staffs were settling into their assigned seats, ready for the session to start. Vernon distributed the plan the Americans had developed. By the time he sat down, low whistles were emanating from those that had read the executive summary.

"Are you quite sure about this?" the Chinese Ambassador asked.

"We have made contact with our Special Forces on the island. We have made it very clear what needs to be done. Our troops are trained and are the best. They will carry out the mission, I can assure you."

The New Zealand Ambassador jumped into the discussion. "If they don't . . ."

"If they don't, we're all dead," the French Ambassador said. The remaining members all nodded their agreement.

"Then we won't fail. That is not an option as I see it," the US ambassador said. Her confidence didn't spread to the others. Vernon could tell by the strained looks that the Council wasn't sure this was the correct course of action. But he was busy thinking about his wife. *I wonder if she'll find someone else to satisfy her?* he thought. He knew that the world situation needed to resolve itself soon or his marriage would be over.

* * *

Sergeant Aubin knew immediately that he was gone. Snapping awake in an instant, he grabbed his flashlight and scanned the area where Al Worthington had been bedded down on. *Nothing,* he thought.

The sergeant got his troops awake and went to locate the two sentries he posted each night. Even with no presumed threat, Sergeant Aubin had kept the normal routine of life in the field. He located his first guard and receive the answer that he wanted. The man was wide awake and had seen no one.

Locating the second guard, the sergeant had been able to sneak up on the man without his presence being detected. A K-Bar knife on the man's throat woke him. The sergeant left it biting into the man's windpipe long enough to make his point. Sleeping on guard duty in Sergeant Aubin's troop was not acceptable.

"Stand up, soldier."

The now wide awake soldier scrambled to his feet. Standing at attention, he started to utter an excuse.

"Shut your pie hole. Because of your slacker attitude, we lost someone tonight. Our diplomat is missing."

"Sergeant, I don't know what-

"I said shut it. I want all of you turned out in five. No guns. Just knives. We are heading to Dr. Brody's cabin tonight. I have a bad feeling."

When the guilty soldier didn't immediately fall out and follow the sergeant's order, Aubin vented his wrath.

"Sergeant, I need to report that I lost my K-Bar. Last week. I've been searching like crazy for it ever since. That was why I was so tired."

"Well son, that's unfortunate. You will remain in camp and guard our weapons until our return. At that time I intend to make you wish you had never landed on this tropical isle."

*At least now I know where our diplomat is going and what he's carrying,* Sergeant Aubin thought as he got the other men ready to move out.

\* \* \*

Al crawled another two hundred yards through the underbrush. He was sure he was far enough away from the Special Ops camp to stand up, but he was hesitant. *Those guys are good,* he thought.

He decided he better keep crawling uphill and away from his intended target. It wouldn't do to get himself captured. Karen was relying on him to save her from that whack job professor. He touched the Army knife safely jammed in his pants waistband. Some tree bark and a small vine made a rudimentary sheath.

The knife had already cut him twice with its razor sharp blade. The blade needed protection or it would gut him as he carried it. But he knew it would make fast work of his nemesis.

Al's mind focused on sneaking up behind Dr. Brody and hearing the gurgle of the dying man's last breaths. The thoughts sustained him as pain pulsed through his body from crawling over the ground.

Deciding to stay on the high ground, he swung around to the opposite side of the island. He would approach the cabin from the side least expected. It meant crossing close to the main house, but he couldn't help it. Al would just use the cover of darkness and watch for those two Chinese characters.

Sunrise caught him still traversing the hill. The ground was incredibly rugged and he was moving so slowly he would have to wait out the daylight hours before preceeding. If he recalled the sergeant's comment, that would place him by the cabin the night before Saturday's final show. He would eliminate Dr. Brody before he ever stepped onto the game show. The world would be saved and he would have his Karen.

Al found a dense clump of brush near a small stream and settled down for Friday's passage. It was all he could do to force himself to sleep while fighting the adrenaline of the escape mixed with the anticipation of the kill.

* * *

The three men on the lanai finished their work and sat back exhausted. It was Friday afternoon and the week of work had kept them from any other tasks. Food had been grabbed occasionally as the kitchen supplies dwindled.

Dr. Brody raided the shed for supplies to complement the few things they took time to gather from the garden. The women had followed Dr. Brody's wishes and had kept their distance. They had been overheard numerous times swimming in the surf on the beach. Their laughter and squeals of delight broke the grim task that the men were forcing themselves to endure.

The contrast couldn't be plainer. *That was why I didn't want the women involved in what we had to do,* the professor thought. He now felt vindicated in his decision. The three men may have nightmares for the rest of their lives, but the fairer sex would be free of that torment.

And soon the entire world would discover the results of their work. Dr. Brody shuddered at what was coming, but knew it was the only way. The alternative was unthinkable.

Out of the corner of the professor's view, he saw it coming. Sergeant Aubin stepped out from behind the toilet building holding a knife. The professor moved but it was too late. Just before the knife reached Dr. Brody, Captain Grinkis sprang out of his seat and caught the sergeant's arm.

"Sergeant, stand down," Chet ordered. "What is the meaning of this?"

"Captain, I'm sorry. I couldn't really do it anyway. Not the Professor."

The sergeant dropped the knife and sank to his knees. "The Pentagon ordered me. I knew it wasn't right. But . . ."

"The Pentagon. What the hell is going on out there? Do they know what's about to happen? Those fools." Captain Grinkis suddenly realized that the entire troop may be under the same orders. He scanned the area looking for more threats. "Where are the men, Sergeant?"

"Looking for that Worthington guy. Seems he's loose with a K-Bar."

"Is he part of the Pentagon plot?" Chet asked.

"No, and neither are the men. I'm the only one that's after Dr. Brody. Sorry Doc. Duty called and its hard to resist."

"That's OK Sergeant. But that Al fellow. Who's he after?" Charles asked.

"Probably you," the sergeant said. "All he talks about is Ms. Price and how you are holding her against her will. The guy is a few bricks short of a full load if you ask me."

Captain Grinkis added, "Sergeant, are you squared away now with where your duty lies? Can we rely on you not to inform the Pentagon of your change of heart."

"10-4 on that, sir. I was never on board with taking out the Doc. But years of service takes over some time."

"Hey guys, I wouldn't do anything sudden-like," Mel injected. "That device is rotating and those protrusions are activated. I think it senses a threat to Dr Brody."

The two soldiers turned to see the globe on the windmill locked onto their bodies. Captain Grinkis carefully kicked the knife away from them toward the shower. The protrusions retracted.

"That was very close. I think we almost found out what that thing is up there for," Mel said.

Chet spoke, "Sergeant, go locate the men and get them back to camp. It's much too dangerous for them around here. I'll take up the Al watch."

Sergeant Aubin marched off toward the opposite hill. As the three remaining men began to discuss the implication of the Pentagon orders, Karen appeared, winded.

"Brandi has the parasite. I need help getting all the supplies for her to make her comfortable." Dr. Brody started to get up but Chet stopped him.

"Karen, tell me what you need," Chet said. "Doc, you got lots on your mind. Take care of business so you're ready for tomorrow. We need the best day of your life. Mel, you watch and help the Doc with whatever he needs."

* * *

Karen gave Chet his orders and disappeared back down the trail to the big house. With Wu Who gone, the professor knew that the two women had taken over the house. Karen didn't know that Chet would sneak down each night and spend his spare time with Brandi.

The alcove in the main house that had once been hers was once again her room. Without Dr. Who on the scene, she didn't mind the small space without a door.

But now there was a new torment that kept her awake. Each night, after she was asleep, she would be awakened by nighttime activities in the master bedroom. The thin walls muffled the sound, but the moans and bed shaking carried across the house.

268

Each night, Karen lay and stared at the ceiling while Brandi experienced undivided attention. Before first light, the noise would end. The morning brought a disheveled Brandi staggering out of the bedroom, a smile radiating.

Since their work wasn't required at the cabin, both women would spend the afternoon napping, Brandi for energy for the night time Olympics. Karen napped from lack of sleep.

But even her naps were fitful. The thoughts of her Dr. Brody next door in the arms of Brandi tormented her. All night her feelings would swing wildly. First, from one of rage at the person she thought the professor had become. *An evil worse than Hitler,* she thought.

But then her feelings of the love she once held for the man would take over. Tears would flow as she listened to the rhythm of love next door. *Her man with someone else,* she thought.

At least he had been her man at one point. And it had been wonderful. Better than anything she had ever experienced. But Brandi received all of what once had been hers. She deserved such true love after all that she had been through. *It's all too sad,* she thought. Karen suffered as her feelings were torn apart.

But tomorrow was Saturday and hopefully the end of it all. She would leave the island and try to get her life back. But the world had changed. *What was there to get back now?* she wondered.

Brandi had finally succumbed to the island crud. Luckily, Captain Grinkis had volunteered to help with her care. Karen had dreaded that Dr. Brody would have taken up the job as Karen would never be able to watch the two of them in close personal contact.

Karen remembered the close contact she had had with the professor when the parasites had attacked her. It was that close comfort by Charles that had released her inhibitions and led to their closeness.

The captain showed a short while later with the required supplies. Fruit juices and soup were the main requirement. And tenderness sponging off the fever along with carrying her to the toilet. *Yes, the captain could handle all those task much better than Charles,* Karen thought.

Karen felt the sleepless nights catch up with her. She knew she needed sleep. *Brandi was in good hands and I need some rest,* Karen thought.

She grabbed a blanket and headed out on the headland in front of the main house to a quiet grassy knoll overlooking the ocean. Nestled under the tropical trees, the trade winds blew over the area. *It was perfect for sleeping,* she thought. Settling onto the blanket, Karen was soon asleep.

Karen awoke in fear. A hand covered her mouth, an arm gripped her tight. She struggled to free herself.

"Quiet, it's me. I didn't want you to yell out," Al said. He slowly removed his hand from her mouth.

"Al, what are you doing?"

"I've come to save you." Al released her and sat back to examine his prize. Karen felt his gaze undress her. She slunk back away from him.

"Where are you going? I came to rescue you from that madman professor. You know he's mad. What about those millions of people he's killed? Don't forget them. What about the children? Millions dead."

"Al stop. I don't want to hear it. It's too horrible."

"But you must hear it. The man must be stopped. Now he's going to trade away even more human life. For what?"

*Maybe he was right,* Karen thought. *Millions dead. He was right about that. And what was this Saturday deal going to do? More millions dead I suppose. And for what? Miss May. Was that what Charles was after? Trading mankind for the titillation she heard each night. How could anyone sacrifice millions for moments of flesh? It was madness,* she thought.

She didn't know what to believe anymore. But she knew she had to be careful.

*Al is next to her and he seems as crazy as Dr. Brody,* she thought. *What was it that attracted such losers?*

"What are you planning Al?" she asked. Her tone implied an alliance.

"That's better. I risked my life getting away from those soldier boys. They would have killed me if they had caught me. But I evaded them. Me, Al Worthington, evaded Delta Force."

Karen sat on the blanket and let the man ramble on about his accomplishment. It was when he leaned over to kiss her that she showed that she might not be fully on his side.

"What the Hell is that about? I came here to save you and you spurn me?"

Karen suddenly knew what Brandi had experienced in her life. Male power demanding favors. To resist such a

271

demand meant . . . She shuddered at the thought. Karen changed tactics.

"I'm sorry, Al. It's just so scary. To be so close to such a man as the professor and know what he is perpetrating. It doesn't lend itself to romantic thoughts."

Al tried again and Karen accommodated his kiss. He changed positions and pushed her back onto the blanket. His tongue found her mouth and she resisted the gag reflex.

When his hand reached her breast, her heart was racing. *What have I've gotten into?* she thought. As his hand moved lower she tried to shift her body but his embrace tightened to keep her still. His mouth shifted lower, following his hand. She had to do something.

"Al, I can't. I can't be with anyone till he's gone. He and I were, you know ..."

"I know you two were involved before I got here."

"Then you'll know why I can't be with anyone else until he's gone. I've tried to wash his smell off me. I'll always smell him until he's dead. Kill him, Al. Help me." Karen lied. *Anything to get this psychotic off of me*, she thought.

Al stopped his groping and pulled back. "Is it that bad?"

"Worse, Al. You can't imagine how my skin crawls just knowing he's there in that cabin. It crawls, I tell you. You have to save me," she lied again.

"Yes, I came to save you. You're right. He needs to die now."

Karen relaxed slightly as Al stood up. She sat up, hoping to watch her attacker walk off to do his deed. Instead, he quickly returned with a vine. As she realized what was about to happen, panic hit her. Al grabbed her hands and tied the vine around them. Then he gathered up her ankles and hog tied her on her side.

"There'll be no change of plans now." Al disappeared into the bushes. Karen watched in horror as Al retrieved his knife from his pants as he left.

# Chapter 28

"Ladies and gentleman, welcome to our Grand Finale of the Endangered Species Show. Today we're about to experience the 'Gunfight at the Sunset Corral'. Will today be curtains for humankind? Is man about to ride off into the sunset of extinction? Or will they fight and save the day? To answer these questions for our viewing audience are the two best analysts the world has produced, President Ronald Reagan for the humans and for the animal world, David Brower. Gentlemen, how do you see today playing out?"

Vernon sat down behind his ambassador in the Security Council room, tense in anticipation. Word still hadn't been received on whether Sergeant Aubin had been successful in his mission of eliminating Dr. Brody. The talking head portion of the show would lead into the main event. That would be when the Council would discover if their mission had been successful

"Well, let's review for everyone where we are right now," Reagan started. The Security Council groaned at the delay in discovering Brody's fate. President Reagan carried on, oblivious to the concerns of the world's leaders. "Dr. Brody did an admirable job saving the humans. He made sure some of the richest farmland was safely on the human side. The entire Mississippi River valley is safe as well as the Eastern US seaboard. He missed blocking the other side in their attempt to gain the old bison range down the east side of the Rockies. The West Coast was a mix. At least the Professor gained the Central Valley and the Columbia River country."

David Brower chimed in. "But cutting North America in two was a brilliant move by GP. From the wilds of the Canadian tundra all the way down to the Mosquito Coast near Panama, the animals have uninterrupted free range."

The host added, "Yes, Mr. Reagan. That seems very important. Humans are cut off from each other in the Western Hemisphere. With the animals controlling the Amazon Rainforest and most of Venezuela and Columbia, South America is isolated from the North. Even the sea lanes between all the continents are blocked."

"There you go again. As host you're supposed to be neutral in these proceedings. The human side has some difficulties, and the blocked sea lanes are one critical one. But look at Europe," Reagan offered.

Europe had been a tough one for the animals. With limited natural land still intact along with the highest human population density of all the continents, only a few squares had been picked by GP for the animal side.

But the animals had made up for Europe in Africa. Whole sections of the second largest continent had been added to the animal's side. The entire central portion of the continent, from Tanzania on the Indian Ocean to Senegal on the Atlantic were colored green.

Only on the northeast corner and the southern tip of the continent had humans picked up any valuable squares. The expanse of the Sahara desert had been selected late after most of the other land squares had been committed. The patchwork of red and green squares told the story of neither side having much interest in the desert.

Much of Asia suffered a similar fate. While Siberia and a swath down through western China into Thailand had been picked by the animals, the large population centers of China and India were human squares. The desert country of Southwest Asia was picked late in the game and showed a checkerboard pattern.

Australia had been moderately simple. Dr. Brody had picked most of the urban areas of the country while the animals had selected the outback. Antarctica had gone almost all to the animals.

The ocean squares had been the real battle zone. As Dr Brody attempted to pick squares that gave him a continuous area between continents, GP had blocked every move. The world would be a very limiting place if humans could only fly and not ship cargo between continents.

"So, we have laid it out for you. You be the judge. Did Dr. Brody fail in his first attempt? Will today bring redemption? Will the offer of a two-trade entice the animals to give up critical squares to the humans? They seem to hold all the cards today. We'll be right back with the answers after these commercial announcements," the host ended the prelims.

"Hit the mute switch somebody," the British Ambassador yelled. With quiet in the room, he demanded, "Good god man, don't you have any word yet? That bloke should have completed his job and reported in. If it had been the SAS doing the job, we'd all know that it was fininshed."

The U.S. Ambassador ignored the taunt. "No word yet. I guess we'll know soon enough." Her resignation to events showed. Vernon slouched in his chair to stay hidden behind his boss. He wasn't liking the attitude that these other ungrateful countries were exhibiting. *At least the United States had tried to do something,* he thought.

As the ad for funeral services continued on the screen, everyone mumbled that America wasn't the can-do place it had once been. The last President had ignored the vital needs of the country while on a noble mission of changing America. And now when it mattered, America was the country that 'couldn't shoot straight'.

Dr. Brody appeared on the screen as the ad faded out. The groans of the Security Council were pronounced as the volume button was hit.

Bob Barker stood between the professor and GP. Giant Panda waved his paw at the screen when he was introduced. Dr. Brody nodded his acknowledgment to the moderator. He held a large three-ring notebook in his hands.

"Wow, Professor. You did your homework over the last two weeks. I hope GP is ready for your onslaught. Shall we begin?"

Vernon jumped as his computer link with the U.S. Mission Situation Room came alive. A message popped onto his screen and he read as it printed. A smile attempted to break out on his face but he did his best to suppress it. His boss turned around as the paper fed out of the small printer.

"Well, we know your boy bloody well blew the deal. What do they have to say for themselves?" the New Zealand Ambassador demanded.

Vernon could see the U.S. Ambassador turn red in anger while she read the short message. She turned around to see if there was anything more. Vernon shook his head.

"Come on. We're all in this together," the Moroccan Ambassador insisted.

"From Sergeant Aubin, Delta Force 2nd Platoon. To U.S. Commanding General, the Pentagon. I quote, 'Screw you', unquote. That is all."

"What is 'screw you'?" the Russian Ambassador asked.

Someone leaned over and explained the meaning to the man. He turned red in anger at such insubordination.

"I believe events are out of our hands," the U.S. Ambassador stated. *I think so, too*, Vernon thought. *We'll have to wait to see if there are repercussions.*

The members sat back to watch Dr. Brody's attempt to save the day. GP tried to act magnanimous as he began a trade of one animal square for two human squares.

The initial deals involved the human side getting clear sea lanes between continents. The green animal squares multiplied as the professor traded away human sea squares. Finally, 500 mile wide travel zones were obtained so ships could transit safely between continents.

Then Dr. Brody started dealing for populated areas. GP resisted at first, but he finally began to bargain. The two-for-one trading increased the green squares on the large electronic display behind Bob.

"Boy, we need to change the name of this show to 'Let's Make a Deal'. I've seen more property change hands in the last three hours than a sooner wagon could cover in a homestead stampede." Bob realized that most of the audience was staring at him after his bit of excitement had brought out his Oklahoma upbringing. Bob attempted to recover. "Dr. Brody, your next trade offer please."

"Bob, I'm offering up square 4544 and square 3343 for the Tokyo square," Charles said. The ocean squares all had numbers on them and the game show staff lit up one square near the Azores and one square off Greenland. Neither one held any land or were vital to any sea lanes.

GP hesitated. The animal supporters behind him yelled to hold out for more. The island of Honshu held the majority of Japan's population. Almost devoid of any natural resources, the play was strictly a human one, ocean water for people.

The panda shook his head. He wouldn't deal. His supporters cheered his toughness. The professor had anticipated this dilemma.

Luckily he had been able to use the two-for-one enticement to gain access routes around the globe for human shipping. While merchant shipping would be limited to defined zones, at least ocean shipping between continents could continue.

But now GP was playing tough. He anticipated that the professor would up the ante. But Dr. Brody had to be careful. He only had a limited number of spare ocean squares left to trade and had determined that trading land squares was out of the question.

Humans couldn't live on the ocean, so those ocean squares were expendable. But land was vital to humans, even marginal land like the Sahara. There were few places on the high and dry portion of the Earth that didn't hold some individuals clinging to existence. Dr. Brody wasn't about to easily give up land squares.

*But some marginal squares for Tokyo. That seemed worth the trade,* he thought. He indicated that he was willing to add a Sahara square to the two ocean squares., three-for-one. GP continued to hesitate. Dr. Brody knew the pressure was on him to deal, not on the panda. The animal shook his head. The environmental supporters roared approval. *Time to change tactics then,* Charles thought.

"Well, Bob, I guess we don't have a deal then. But I've been the one proposing these trades. Seems a bit lopsided. Maybe there's some squares that might interest the other side." Charles watched GP blanch. *Well, maybe they weren't ready for that,* he thought. He knew that he held squares on the human side that the animals desired. Early in the game, Charles had chosen some key squares for just such an eventuality.

"Well, Professor, you seem to have hit a nerve. I guess your opponent was ready to sit back and let it come to him. You've turned the tables on him."

As GP thought of his next move, his supporters started yelling at him. Squares that they thought should be grabbed were yelled out. The panda nodded that he was ready to deal.

The human supporters cheered on the professor for his shrewd move. One of Dr. Brody's optimum picks had been the square containing the mouth of the Amazon River. While the animals had quickly scooped up the rest of the vast rainforest, the river mouth had eluded them.

GP highlighted the Amazon square. It turned yellow to indicate it was in trade. Then he clicked on an ocean square off Florida. He sat back with a smile and waited. His supporters went wild in anticipation. Such a trade would be a steal for the animals.

"Oh come on. You're going to have to go a lot further to get that trade to work," Dr Brody challenged.

The panda's expression turned to a frown as the people behind him jeered at the rejection. The professor waited. He knew by the rules of today's game, the animal side only had ten minutes to complete a trade or the square would be gone forever. He watched as it seemed the panda's forehead started to bead sweat. The pressure was on. It was the only chance for them to complete their total hold on all that rain forest.

Two more inconsequential squares were added by the animal side. Dr. Brody shook his head and looked at the clock running.

"Come on GP, time is winding down. The most important piece of the Amazon and its slipping out of your hands forever. I'll guarantee you that the chainsaws will be running five minutes after the show ends."

John Muir was about to blow a gasket he was screaming so hard behind GP. The panda was in a panic. He threw in two more squares of Sahara sand. Bob Barker raised his eyebrows at the now five for one offer highlighted on the map.

"No deal. You offer me junk for the number one square on your side. You better get serious. One minute left. I can hear those wood chippers warming up already."

Rachel Carson and Aldo Leopold picked up their chairs and began banging them on the arena floor, they were so mad. Thoreau was being escorted from the stands with what looked like heart palpitations.

GP quickly swiveled his joystick to the Tokyo square and it turned yellow. He waited for an answer. Dr. Brody shook his head. The clock was draining.

Suddenly GP totally panicked and highlighted the LA and Melbourne squares. Dr. Brody quickly hit the confirmed button.

"Wow, eight for one. You folks at home, I hope you could feel the tension in the room at that one. Well played Dr. Brody. We have an hour left. After that one, do we have any other deals to make?"

In his research, Dr. Brody had stumbled on the Seven Wonders of the Natural World. He had accidentally picked three of them during the course of the regular game. Hoping the animals would want them on their side, he also knew that the three squares wouldn't command the tribute that the Amazon square had extracted.

He was right as GP lit up one of the listed natural wonders, the Great Barrier Reef of Australia. The professor had tried to pick up just Queensland but with the 500 mile squares, had ended up with two hundred miles of ocean off Queensland. Consequently he had the reef also.

"I would like to propose something to my worthy opponent. He is interested in the reef. I'm primarily interested in the land. I propose we have the ability to split squares to our liking," Charles said.

"Mr. Producer, can we accommodate that request?" Bob asked the man in the booth producing the show. After a minute, he had his answer. "Dr. Brody, the man says he can do that. They just need to reconfigure the software. You should know about that."

Dr. Brody let the mistake go by him. He hadn't developed the actual game they were playing, only the original concept. The software company had offered to buy his rights and had developed the final game. But he waited while the screen behind him jumped into whatever mode they were choosing. Bob gave the participants the thumbs up.

"OK. I would propose that the reef portion be included. We keep five miles out from shore. In exchange for that I would ask that the animals give up three access corridors across North America, east to west."

"No, no, don't do it." John Muir yelled.

GP started to shake his head to kill that proposal. Charles jumped in to explain.

"Humans need a connection between the two coasts. The access I propose would be 80 percent underground with the occasional short depressed areas for ventilation. The depressions would be strongly fenced. Only trains would move through the tunnels. Trucks and cars would travel if loaded on the train. Buried pipelines for gas and oil would also traverse these same corridors," Dr. Brody explained.

"No way. Save the bison. Think of the prairie grizzly bear. And the wolves, don't forget the wolves. Keep it free of humans," John Muir screamed.

GP was frozen. He didn't seem to know what to do, as the Barrier Reef represented a huge marine life sanctuary.

"Time again is winding down. I'll be putting in a call to Brisbane as soon as we're done. They've wanted to dredge the entire thing for road base. Coral works real good keeping cars moving through the wet season up there," the professor taunted.. He thought he almost saw GP faint at the idea of all those little marine animals crushed with human cars speeding over their carcasses.

Small yellow lines across America had been put up on the board along with the truncated square off Queensland. The animal supporters sat in stunned silence as they also contemplated the worlds largest reef turned into road base. GP punched the joystick in agreement. The human supporters went wild.

The last two natural wonders of the world were summarily traded off for valuable human squares. Each time, Dr. Brody used threats that each natural site would be obliterated by humans if they didn't trade. By the end of the show, things looked decidedly better for the human side

Dr. Brody ignored the cheers from his side as he awaited the end of the broadcast. From his shed on the island, he turned off the monitor and slumped in the chair. *That was the easy part,* he thought. Now he knew he had to endure the 'night of the living dead'.

# Chapter 29

"The son of a bitch did it. I can't believe it. The stupid bastard actually pulled his nuts out of the fire," the Canadian Ambassador yelled. As one of the non-permanent Security Council members, he drew looks of admonishment for his lack of social graces in such a decorous setting.

"I believe the proper phrase should be he pulled our nuts out of the fire," the New Zealand Ambassador corrected his British Commonwealth partner. "And to think we tried to take this bloke out. Our bloody good break, I'm sure."

The entire room all mumbled agreement with the Kiwi assessment. Dr. Brody had definitely saved the day considering the position the humans had been at the beginning of the final show.

Vernon was among those congratulating themselves as he chatted up his neighboring staff members from the adjacent countries. With the United Kingdom coming alphabetically next to the United States, the woman staffer for the British Ambassador had been making overly friendly advances on him since he had been tapped for this assignment.

With his wife acting crazy for whatever reason that was eluding him, Vernon was enjoying his new friendship with his neighbor. *Keep your options open,* he thought.

As the giddiness of the accomplishments of Dr. Brody settled over the entire room, people relaxed. Suddenly the giant screen at the head of the chamber flashed on. Staring out at them was a 10' image of Jack

Nicholson. Vernon instantly recognized the Nicholson lookalike in the courtroom scene from 'A Few Good Men'.

"You've messed with the wrong frigging Marine!" He screamed at the instantly stunned audience. Vernon slinked down fearfully into his chair from the rage directed at the assembly.

"I'm coming to rip your frigging head off and shove it down your hole! You don't know who you're messing with," the alien-inspired Nicholson clone screamed.

The Security Council was frozen in fear of what the threat entailed. They had attempted to interfere in the alien game show and they knew that retaliation was a distinct possibility.

An earsplitting crack and a flash of light blasted the room. Vernon dove for cover holding his ears. He thumped into the British woman staffer as she fell out of her chair. The two grabbed each other and waited for the noise and brilliant light to subside.

With their eyes shut tight from the brightness, they clung to each other shaking. Vernon pulled her tighter and he felt her respond. They were suffocating each other but it seemed the only way to survive.

Soon a brimstone smell wafted into their noses followed by a sickly burnt flesh odor. The entangled staffers gagged at the stench. Slowly, Vernon opened his eyes and relaxed one arm from his death embrace. He seemed to be still alive. Vernon checked the woman in his arms and she responded. *A second one alive,* he thought.

As she opened her eyes, she asked, "What's that horrible smell?"

Pulling his shirt up over his nose to stifle the awful smell, Vernon stood and surveyed the still smoky room. Others around the room were moving as they recovered from the alien attack.

"Oh my God," the British woman exclaimed. She pulled her blouse up to cover her nose as she continued to hold onto Vernon for support.

He took her in one arm as they walked toward the exit and fresh air. The other surviving staffers joined them in the scramble to escape the foul smell. Reaching the outside, the survivors all gathered in a small group.

Less than twenty people had withstood the attack. Vernon began scanning the people standing in front of him and none were ambassadors.

"Did you see the gray dust everywhere?" one of the New Zealand staffers asked.

"I think all of them are dead. Vaporized. The entire diplomatic corps of the Security Council. What will we do?" a Canadian staffer said.

"We lost some of the staff people also," Vernon added. He didn't know everyone in the room, but he had been in enough planning sessions to surmise which staffers had been killed along with the ambassadors.

As many of the survivors collapsed on the United Nations lawn, the darkness was shattered by the green and yellow alien lights. Everyone cringed as the lights began their dance over Manhattan Island. The flashes and constant cracks forced everyone to hit the ground screaming.

A few minutes and the lights moved on toward Brooklyn. Vernon twisted from his face down position in the grass and eased his eyes open. The green and yellow lights were everywhere. The aliens were methodically working their way east as the sky over Connecticut glowed in an almost constant green yellow blur.

Turning toward New Jersey, Vernon witnessed the same blanket effect. The sky was alive with the searching lights.

"What is happening? Why are we being killed? I thought that after the game things would be settled. I don't understand?" the British woman asked. She continued her vise-like grip on Vernon's arm.

"But its not the blue light. The blue light killed everyone. The green yellow light kills selectively. We're still alive, and the lights are fading. Look, they're moving on," Vernon said.

All of the remaining staffers from the Security Council were back on their feet straining to see the fading alien lights. They agreed with Vernon's assessment that the alien lights were retreating. But awareness of their surroundings grew as they realized that it seemed that the entire city was screaming.

Vernon, with his woman friend still attached, walked over to the security gate leading to First Avenue. They witnessed people pouring from the high rise buildings in fright. As the street filled with survivors, Vernon called to some.

"What happened in your building?"

The constant answer he received was that any number of residents had been vaporized into dust. He asked more questions and began to get a picture of who had died and who had survived. *Amazing,* he thought. *I need to return to the Mission and check on people.*

At the U.S. Mission he witnessed a building in shock. Gray dust swirled as Vernon rushed by the front desk. The security team was present but in a state of shock.

Reaching the Situation Room, he entered his password for admittance. The smell struck him as he shoved the door open. Staff members sat crying with shirts pulled up over their noses, dust everywhere.

"Where's the general? We need to get this information off to the Pentagon now," he said.

"Gone. They're all gone," one Army corporal said. Vernon recognized him as one of the communication staffers the Army had sent.

"What do you mean, gone?"

"Turned to dust. Vaporized. All the senior people are dead. We already contacted Washington. Same thing. The green and yellow lights struck there too. Only the staff are still alive."

*Well, that was at least something,* Vernon thought. *The aliens seemed to be taking out the ruling class of the country.*

"Mr. Randolph, sir. I believe you're senior now. You are in command."

The words struck Vernon like a hot poker. *Me, in charge? That can't be true. I'm just a lowly bureaucrat sliding through life and waiting to go home each evening,* he thought.

"What should we do?" two different staff people asked at once.

The panic swelled into his throat and he thought he would vomit on the spot. He fought for control as he noticed the entire room staring at him. They were waiting for instructions and he was the one they were looking to for leadership.

Vernon forced every ounce of strength in his body and steeled himself. He would rise to the occasion. His country needed him at this crucial time and he could do it. The transformation took mild-mannered Vernon Randolph to a new level.

"Contact Washington. We need to report our condition here in New York. Has anyone done a head count yet on who survived in the Mission?" As Vernon spoke a woman staffer quickly volunteered to run through the building and list the survivors. "Get as much information as possible from all points in the country. I'll contact the other missions and see if we can organize a meeting. We need to know the extent of this attack on the world. And somebody open some damn windows and air out this place."

By daylight, Vernon had contacted the surviving delegations and an ad hoc Security Council meeting was set. He waited in the now empty ambassador's office for the U.S. Mission staff to collect as much information as possible before the meeting.

The secretary stuck her head into the office to announce the British Ambassador, Acting. Vernon stood up to greet his guest and froze. In walked the woman who had been his survival companion through the alien attack. She was showered and dressed impeccably, any post-traumatic stress missing.

"Madame Ambassador. A pleasant surprise."

"Mr. Ambassador. I congratulate you on your elevation, considering the circumstances. But please call me Cecily. I think we have met the test to be on first name basis, Vernon."

"What news do you have from London? My news isn't good I'm afraid."

"Mine either. It seems the ruling class took the biggest hit last night. Reports are still sketchy, but except for a few members of the House of Commons, the entire British Government was wiped out."

"Exactly like us. Five Members of our House of Representatives survived. The senior one has been sworn in as President. The U.S. Constitution lays out a list for secession in the case of the death of the President, but it never envisioned this."

"We have a Prime Minister which, like you, was appointed from one of the surviving members of the former ruling party. But our military command structure was devastated down to colonel level. Do you think the aliens are weakening us for attack?"

"I hope not. If they had wanted to finish us off, the blue light would have vaporized all of us. No, there's something else at work here. And we may not know what that is for some time."

The two new ambassadors stood at the open window and scanned down First Avenue. The crowd in front of the U.N. building continued to build.

Television trucks that had been stationed on the side streets during the entire alien encounter noisily ran their generators. Cameras and reporters lined the outside of the U.S. Mission. The world wanted answers.

Vernon realized that he was the man in charge. *I have to provide some answers,* he thought. He instinctively reached out to Cecily's hand and gripped it for support. He felt a tingle rush through him as she returned the sentiment. The two leaned into each other as they both realized what their new positions entailed. They would need each other in the coming days.

# Chapter 30

As the world endured the green and yellow lights of the alien attack, the South Pacific island was quiet. The almost constant trade winds blew in off the ocean. The wind chimes added to the low rattle of the nearby windmill. Leaves on the numerous tropical trees rustled in the warm breeze.

The subdued noise was matched by the somber mood of the individuals on the island. Each had worked hard in preparation for the final game show and had watched on Mel's computer as Dr. Brody deftly skewered the panda. Any happiness at the results were dashed when the professor emerged from the shed.

Everyone could tell that it wasn't over yet. Dr. Brody had retreated to his rock at the top of the cliff in silence. Not sure what was coming next, each had taken a spot to wait.

Chet was back at Brandi's side nursing her through the effects of the island parasite. Mel sat alone on the lanai and awaited news from the world media. And Dr. Brody sat on his rock, overlooking the spot where twice he had nearly ended it all.

Chet was the first to realize. *I haven't seen Karen return,* he thought. *I've been so busy with Brandi, I forgot all about her.*

After checking that Brandi was resting comfortably, Chet walked onto the porch and studied his surroundings. *She had headed off that way with a blanket,* he thought.

The headland lay in front of the main house and Chet scanned it for any sign of life.

Dropping off the porch, he jogged out toward the easternmost point of the short headland. Halfway to the end, something caught his eye, a slight movement in a patch of grass. He drifted toward the spot.

Stepping through some brush, he saw her. Karen was tied up with a green vine and laying on her side. When she heard his footsteps, she started struggling against her restraints, her voice muffled.

Chet raced to her and pulled the gag from her mouth.

"Stop him. He's going to kill Dr. Brody," she screamed.

"Don't worry, I've already stopped him. The professor is safe."

Karen relaxed as Chet untied the vines. He rubbed the spots where they had cut into her and helped her stand up. Karen immediately collapsed. The effects of the long confinement prevented her from walking. Chet swooped her into his arms and headed back to the main house.

"You should be all right. As soon as the blood gets moving again."

"Thank you Captain." She relaxed against the soldier's chest as he carried her. "I missed the final show. How did it go?"

"The professor was great. He saved the day. All our hard work paid off. The animals still have over half the Earth but the human half is very livable. And we have shipping lanes between all the continents. And most of the islands, too."

"He did it? I'll be, he really did it."

By the way she said the words, Chet could sense Karen's feelings toward the professor. He looked in her face and his assessment was confirmed.

"The Professor is a special guy, isn't he?" Chet added.

"Yes, Captain. He is very special. I wish . . ."

She stopped mid-sentence. Chet noted a switch in her tone. Almost one of melancholy at the loss of something. Chet glanced down again and saw that Karen was staring out, deep in thought.

Reaching the main house, the captain carried Karen into the bedroom and placed her next to Brandi. Brandi stirred with the disturbance.

"Oh, hi. How long have I been sleeping?"

Chet explained to Brandi that she had missed the big show and filled her in on the results. She smiled weakly. Chet leaned over and gave her a kiss. She reached up and pulled his head closer.

"I'm feeling much better. I think I can get up," Karen said. She moved slightly on the bed trying to not interrupt the two embraced people close to her.

"Oh, sorry. No it's OK. Stay as long as you want," Chet said, his face slightly red. Brandi pulled him back to her and snuggled in close. She wrapped both arms around him. Karen watched the two carry on.

"Hmm. May I ask a personal question?" Karen asked. "You two seem very close. Captain, have you been sneaking down each night last week."

"Guilty, ma'am. Sorry if we disturbed you."

"So, you two are. . ."

"Totally crazy, I know. But what a feeling it is," Brandi raised her head long enough to utter the words. The strain of the parasite took over and she flopped onto her back, moaning.

The captain checked her forehead and reached for the pan of cool water to help fight her sudden fever attack. Karen watched Chet lovingly administer care with a tenderness only reserved for someone in love.

"Thank you, Captain. Thank you very much," Karen said as she struggled to walk, headed for the trail up the hill.

* * *

Mel was studying his computer monitor intently when a wild woman ran into his midst.

"Where is he?"

Before Mel could even answer, Karen spotted Charles sitting on the rock. But before she could sprint to him to correct everything that had come between them, Mel literally tackled her from behind.

"No. He doesn't want to be disturbed. He's been out there since the show ended."

"But I must tell him everything. It's OK now. I know he was right. He'll want to know that," she said.

Mel pushed her into a chair with a forcefulness that meant it. Karen sulked at the rude behavior she was being shown by an obvious intruder. *Where had he been when she and the Professor were tackling all of this alone?* she thought. *It had been Charles and me against the world then.*

After a long silent spell broken only by Mel's fingers punching the computer keyboard, Karen asked. "So where did the captain put Al?"

Mel looked up in confusion. "Put Al where? What are you talking about?"

"When he stopped Al from killing the professor. Where did he put him afterward?"

"Al didn't try to kill the Doc. It was Sergeant Aubin the captain stopped. He had been ordered by . . ."

Karen was gone like a shot, running towards Charles. Mel leaped after her. As the two ran urgently to the professor, Al Worthington, face and upper body smeared with mud, stepped out of the brush. Shirtless and with a Rambo like bandana around his head, the diplomat-turned-assassin ran from his concealed position toward Dr. Brody.

Karen watched in horror as Al closed the short distance between his protective cover and the exposed rock. A K-Bar knife came up in his right hand, aimed at his nemesis. Running like a wild man, Al aimed his weapon.

Knowing she could not intercede in time, Karen screamed, catching Charles's attention. He turned his head slightly to see her running in the distance. Karen tried to warn him of the impending attack approaching behind him.

Al was within ten feet of his mark when a loud crack and a blinding light stunned everyone. Karen stumbled blindly and crashed onto the rocks. Her ears throbbed as she screamed in pain. She lifted herself anticipating seeing the professor stabbed.

Instead, smoke lingered where Al had been. Dr. Brody cringed on his rock from the noise and blinding light. Karen picked herself up and hobbled over to Charles.

"Are you OK, Han?"

"You called me Han," the professor said.

They stood and looked around. Gray dust floated down onto the ground. Mel arrived and pointed to the globe on the windmill. The protrusions on the top where now receding back into the body.

"I guess we know what they do now," Mel stated dryly.

The trade winds gathered up Al's remains and gently carried them across the island. Some drifted out over the cliff, to settle in the bay. Soon, there was no evidence that Al Worthington had ever existed.

"He was crazy as a loon, but he didn't deserve that," Karen said finally.

"He was going to kill the professor. What do you mean he didn't deserve that?" Mel asked.

Chet arrived carrying Brandi on his back. She looked the best she had in the past two days and announced she was hungry.

"That's a good sign," Dr. Brody said. He reached down and took Karen's hand in his. She felt the electricity that had once been there. "I think we could all use a bite."

Chet placed Brandi in the hammock of the lanai. The professor and Karen went to work in the kitchen putting a substantial meal together. None had eaten properly over the last two weeks and suddenly everyone seemed famished.

Mel was back on his computer trying to gather information as Chet busied himself fussing over Brandi.

"So Mel, now that the big event is over, what are your plans?" Dr. Brody asked.

"Gee Doc, I hadn't thought that far yet. Why are you asking?" Mel asked.

"I need help here on the island with communications. The aliens will be leaving soon and their data link will go with them. Any interest in helping me?"

There was a long hesitation as Mel stopped typing. Finally he said, "Dr. Brody, you were a legend before. Now, my God, your status in the world is . . ." Mel stopped. He was speechless.

"I'll take that as yes, you'll stay. And you, Captain Grinkis. I need a good security man. I'm afraid I might have created some enemies over this whole thing. And I'm not certain the alien devices will remain after they leave."

Karen noticed Chet's look to Brandi for an answer. Their gaze locked as they communicated without speaking. Smiles exploded from their faces as Chet answered, "If Brandi can stay also, I'm your man."

"Of course Miss May can stay. What would our island be with only eleven months?"

"Now that we have that settled, I still need a good assistant. And we know the aliens only pick the best. What do you say Ms. Price?" Charles asked.

"Oh Han, I thought you'd never get to me. I'm sorry I ever doubted you. The pressure you were under and the way I treated you. You should-"

"You talk too much," Charles swooped Karen into his arms and they kissed. She threw her arms around him as she felt the moment wash over her. She closed her eyes to keep the distractions away.

"Hey you two, we're hungry," Chet admonished. "Move aside and let me take over. You two take a walk for awhile. Dinner will be ready in half an hour."

Five minutes later found the two lovers on the beach. They stripped off their clothes and plunged into the surf. After the gray dust episode, it felt divine to wash the world away. Charles found her and pulled her under the surface. The two caressed each others bodies as they floated in the luxurious warm water. *The feeling is coming back,* Karen thought.

The torment she had suffered thinking that Brandi had stolen him away washed out to sea. Her accusation that the professor was throwing the game to gain sexual favors from the aliens washed away. The whole sordid business of dealing with the space invaders was cleansed from her body.

The waves carried the two up onto shore. Finding solid ground in which to settle, Charles took Karen in an embrace, their bodies moving closer.

"Oh Han, I missed your attention," Karen moaned on the sand. A wave washed over them and rocked them slightly. But it didn't interrupt the continuing attention Dr. Brody was giving his assistant.

The Princess and the Wookiee were soon reintroduced to each other. It was as if they had never left. Karen writhed in ecstasy as another wave crashed over her. Karen figured they had missed their half-hour window until dinner and threw any time schedule away. As the two lay spent on the beach, they let the waves continue their cleansing work. *Everything could wait while we put the past away,* she thought.

# Chapter 31

When Karen and Charles returned to the group, many half-hours had passed and the night air had finally driven them from the water. Not that it was cool, but it finally dawned on them that they were still hungry. The beach activity had tempered the feeling for a while, but now both of them could wait no longer.

Reaching the cabin, they were greeted by a solemn bunch. Gone was the celebratory feeling when they had left. Karen felt the tension immediately as she walked up to the lanai.

"What's happening?" she asked, her thoughts of hunger once again shoved aside.

No one spoke. She looked from person to person for an answer. Still no response. The professor walked up and stopped. Without even speaking, he quickly turned and left, headed for his rock. Karen saw him leave and suddenly realized what had just transpired between them was about to crash to Earth.

"Tell me," she demanded.

"Sit down," Chet ordered. "You need to be prepared for bad news."

"Tell me right now what is going on. Cut out the bullshit of bad news. What did he do?" The aim of her accusation was evident in her voice.

"He had to, Karen. You don't understand," Chet continued.

"I understand plenty. He knew this was coming and yet he just tried to pull me back into his little evil scheme.

And the fool I am, I was ready to jump with both feet. Well, no more."

She walked over to Mel's computer. Mel scrambled to quickly move out of her way. She sat down and her gaze locked onto the screen. Watching intently as the media coverage of the night's work by the aliens was reported, her eyes grew bigger and began to tear up. Soon, tears flowed down her cheeks.

Mel disappeared along with Brandi. Just Chet remained with Karen. She continued her vigil on the events that her fellow humans were suffering through.

"You knew, didn't you?" she asked.

"Some of it. But he didn't let on to the entire thing. It came as a shock to Mel and I, I assure you."

"How many so far?"

"Three billion and counting. That's almost half the world's population. And it hasn't stopped yet," Chet said. Mel had been keeping track on a spreadsheet program he had quickly put together.

Karen's head slumped as she began sobbing at the news. *How could I?* she thought. Her mind raced to the man who had just held her tenderly on the beach. *How could such a man be capable of such atrocities?* she thought. *Eva Braun lying naked with Adolf Hitler, did she have these same feelings?*

"Karen, I think there's more than any of us know. Perhaps you need to wait for an explanation from the Doc."

"How do you explain half the world's population going poof? I hit the wrong button, sorry." Her sarcasm hit hard. "No, the only explanation is that we've all been duped by the biggest con man in history. And now we have the blood of millions of men, women and children on our hands." She looked down and stared at her hands. Her sobbing grew louder.

* * *

Vernon Randolph, U.S. Ambassador to the United Nations stood on the Mission front steps. The crowd clamored to reach him as opposing groups of protesters shoved each other for visibility. The news media took the tumult in and sent it out to the world.

The ensuing week had been difficult for the Mission staff as news of the alien attack emerged. It appeared that almost five billion human lives had ceased to exist in one night from the green and yellow lights.

While some countries suffered huge losses, others were relatively spared. China and India had been devastated. Estimates placed the number of people still alive at around 200 million in each of those countries. Considering their population prior to the attack, nearly 2 billion Chinese and Indian souls were lost between the two countries.

The third world had also suffered. The poor had added another billion to the total. One billion people had been consumed prior to the night attack, with criminals, the infirm and elderly suffering almost total extinction. The final billion of the total was squeezed out of the rest of the world as the aliens looped off certain segments of society.

But this demonstration was more single minded. A worldwide demand exploded for Dr. Brody to be brought to justice as the perpetrator of the greatest crime against humanity.

On the opposite side were the true believers in the professor. They were now convinced that he had saved mankind from certain extinction. In cities all around the Earth, similar confrontations were raging.

It was into such an atmosphere that Ambassador Randolph was about to step. The cameras zoomed in as he stepped to the microphones.

"Ladies and gentlemen. A week ago the world suffered like it never has before. The greatest loss ever seen of human life has staggered the globe," Vernon staid. In the background he could hear the protester's demands for justice. They called for Dr. Brody's head on a pole in front of the U.N. Building.

Dr. Brody's supporters yelled down their opponents as both sides drowned out the speaker. Finally, Vernon gave up and retreated into the Mission Building. Guards closed off any access as the demonstrators pushed forward.

Police worked to keep the protesters separated, but soon shoving matches turned into fist fights. Makeshift weapons appeared as the crowd became violent. The police retreated to wait for reinforcements while the news people fought to escape the carnage.

\* \* \*

The island had become a battle zone also. The women had retreated to the main house while the three men remained in the cabin. Mel kept the news flowing while Chet tried to contact headquarters.

Chet continued to sneak down each night to Brandi's bed. She didn't seem to hold the captain personally responsible for what had happened. But the feelings between the two had taken a hit. Now each were planning their life away from the island.

Mel also was anticipating a return to college life. He commented that with his experience through the whole thing, his blog site would rocket into the internet viral zone.

Dr. Brody worked in the garden and tended his chickens. Chet had noticed he had resigned himself to a life of solitude on the island. Everyone had seen the growing protest calling for Dr. Brody's arrest. A return to normalcy was out of the question for the professor. *Only the alien 'bug zapper' could keep him safe,* Chet thought.

Sergeant Aubin and the Delta Force men continued their vigil by the lagoon awaiting orders. Chet knew that most of the command structure in the United States had been destroyed. While he had contacted the staff people manning the command center, no one of authority was ready to make any decisions so everyone sat and waited.

Being careful to keep the news from the professor, Chet had informed everyone that the sub still stationed near the island should be receiving orders any day to take them off. It was just a game of waiting.

But the wait was straining everyone's dispositions. The world seemed to be coming apart by the day and being stuck on the island didn't help. Each one was anxious to get home and check on loved ones.

Chet sought out the professor as his guilt grew over his impending departure. "Doc, I was thinking. Those books we talked about way back when. You used the Forest and the Seas in your bluff, didn't you?"

He knew Dr. Brody had been right, but just didn't know why. *I want some answers. Lord knows the Doc won't survive after we leave,* he thought. Chet knew that with the professor's demise the answers many in the world wanted would be lost forever.

The aliens continued to just sit in their space craft orbiting near the Space Station. No lights of any kind had been displayed since the night of the attack. And no transmissions had been received. *They just sat up there waiting. But for what?* he thought.

"What did you ask me?" a distracted professor asked.

"Remember, we talked about three books. I think they were critical to your plan to deal with the aliens. I was just thinking about them, is all."

"Oh, I see. Yes, the 'Forest and Seas' reminded me that the oceans are our life blood of oxygen. Humans just needed access across them. Our sea lanes between continents cover both shipping and fishing. The rest of the ocean was just space I could trade away. Humans don't require large areas of the sea set aside for their exclusive use. Oxygen just comes up out of the sea water and moves to where we need it. The animal side certainly won't interfere with that."

"That was a great plan. It threw the other side off completely." Chet wanted to keep the professor engaged. "And the 'Voyage of the Spaceship Beagle' book, what did that give you?"

"Like I told you, the First Law of Biology. You can never do just one thing. Threatening GP with ripping out thousands of years of coral growth to build roads turned him into a compromiser. The threat to do that one thing would have repercussions around the entire world. Same as cutting down our part of the Amazon rainforest. Especially a large square at the river's mouth. Terrible consequences. He panicked at that point."

"Would you have followed through Doc?" Chet asked.

"Of course not. I'm not an environmental moster. But GP didn't know that. He couldn't take the chance. He had to deal."

"So bluffing worked."

"But I knew more than GP. I knew what was coming afterward." The professor stopped as he remembered the billions of dead. "He thought I would attempt to save as many humans as possible. I knew we were going to get creamed after the game was over. That let me bluff with places like Tokyo a lot easier. Small consolation, Tokyo, when considered in the total scheme of things."

Chet noticed the professor slip into a melancholy mood. The deaths hung over Charles like a cloud. Whenever the subject of the dead arose, Dr. Brody would retreat into his own world. Still, Chet wanted to learn the truth so continued.

"Doc, about that night. You knew how bad it was going to be, didn't you? That's why you sent the women away when we started researching the second week."

A long pause preceded the professor's response. He chuckled at something in his mind. "Captain, I'll tell you what came to mind when the women were banished. I thought of the movie 'As Good As It Gets' starring Jack Nicholson. Nicholson plays an obsessive compulsive trying to find love. As a romance novel writer, the character played by Nicholson meets with his publisher. Upon leaving the office, a secretary asks how he, as a man, could write so well about a woman. Do you know what his response was?"

Chet shook his head. He remembered the movie but not the scene.

The professor continued, "He turned to her and said 'As I write, I think of a man and then take away reason and accountability'. I remembered that line. When we went to determine who lived and who died, we had to use reason, not feeling. And we men had to be accountable for what we did. Something as horrible as what we did shouldn't be placed on any female. That had always been the male role before feminism took it away."

Chet knew why the professor had recalled the book 'War Against the Weak'. Dr. Brody had become the ultimate Eugenics practitioner. But something bothered him about the reports that they were getting. Every country had lost many of its top leaders. Governments and industries around the world were floundering in the aftermath of the alien attack.

"What I don't get in all this, Doc, is ... OK, I get the criminals, infirm, elderly, addicts, and disease carriers getting it. Fits with the whole Eugenics manifest as I understand it. But why those rich people. A lot of powerful people got it in the neck that night."

Again Dr. Brody paused. Finally he offered, "I set a standard that no large country could have more than 200 million. Hence the haircuts that China and India took. Then I set a limit of 100 million for medium countries. Again a lot of countries took a hit. For the small countries we made a list of the ones that were too densely populated for their resource base. They took a hit."

"But that wasn't enough, was it?" Chet asked.

"Captain, when you have to eliminate five billion people with some semblance of a goal in mind for the aftermath, a lot of decisions have to be made. Luckily, the green yellow light weapon the aliens have can be dialed to be very precise. I set that the bottom 35 percentile would be eliminated, the poor if you will. In most countries, that consists of the unproductive takers of society. But just as bad are the takers at the top. The rich who spend more time working the system than producing goods or services."

"Crony capitalism?"

"One word for it. There are many words for it around the world. They all mean the same thing. Leeches on society that take, usually from the government, and pay favors to the same government. They produce nothing and help humanity not a whit."

"That was why you wanted the information on the top 10 percentile."

"Exactly. If you make more than $110 thousand a year, you're in the top ten percent of people in America. We'll use that as our example. I eliminated the top five percent, which puts one in the $160 thousand per year range. I exempted such people as doctors and engineers, people who add value to society. People like politicians, lawyers and financiers weren't exempted because generally they are dregs on humanity."

"So that was the list Mel and I worked up. I didn't know I was condemning people to their fates by adding them to one column or the other," Chet said.

"Five billion people had to go, thats a lot of eggs to break to make an omelet, as they say. I'm sure we screwed up in places, but humanity survived. It will make the necessary adjustments now."

Chet watched as the professor drifted off. The conversation was over. Dr. Brody retreated into his own little world. The captain had seen such behavior before in combat soldiers after an especially deadly fight. The professor was definitely suffering post traumatic shock. *Hell, we all are,* he thought. He and Mel had been part of it. And the whole world had suffered through it.

But something the professor had said stood out. 'Humanity had survived' had been Dr. Brody's words. *I want more of the answer to those words,* he thought. *The professor is holding something back.*

# Chapter 33

Vernon gathered the other members of the Security Council in the meeting room as requested. His new friend, the British Ambassador, sat beside him along with the other newly appointed ambassadors.

With the violent deaths of so many elites in each country, the Council was now populated by the staffers that had been left standing. Like Vernon, greatness had been thrust upon them.

But an ominous message had been received from the aliens. They were requesting a meeting of the entire Council and had set the time and date. The entire world would receive the same message as the gathered group. Vernon just hoped that the 'vaporizer' wasn't going to be put back in operation.

He smiled at Cecily as they waited. They had become very close over the last month. Late night planning sessions had led to other late night activities as Vernon began to feel his place in the world. Not only did he keep his wife satisfied, now he had a mistress. It was an example of the old world style he had read about.

Vernon's thoughts turned to his last late night encounter with the British Ambassador. It had included his office desk and a view of the East River worthy of his new position. *Or worthy of her position, at the time,* he chuckled to himself. *Yes, life might be the shits for some, but he was enjoying his fully.*

He almost wet his pants when the screen came on at the appointed hour. Glaring down at the room was a Darth

Vader lookalike. Heavy raspy breathing filled the hall as Vader waited for his presence to be fully felt.

"People of Earth. We have established separate zones on your planet so all species may enjoy a life without fear. Humanity has taken a heavy toll for its irresponsibility over the eons in not providing good stewardship of the planet."

"We came here with directives to set human development back in order that the animal world might recover. To that end, we were prepared to eliminate all but one-hundred million humans."

Vernon looked at Cecily. Both had the same shocked expression.

Breathing heavy, Vader continued, "But your human representative worked out a Great Compromise. We have abided by that agreement. We expect you Earthlings to abide by your word. As we leave you to your fate, your human representative will provide an explanation. Tomorrow, Dr. Brody will tell you the terms of the compromise. Pay close attention because there can be no transgressions. I repeat, no transgressions will be tolerated."

Vader stopped to let the threat sink in. Everyone in the Council chambers looked around at the challenge presented.

Continuing his lecture, Vader said, "Further, Dr. Brody will be issuing directives to all human inhabitants as to your behavior toward the animal world. We have witnessed humans retaliating against the animals as they leave the animal zones. This will not be tolerated. You are two separate worlds now. Hopefully your stewardship of your half of the planet improves significantly. Finally, be forewarned that we have added Earth's humans to the Galaxy's Endangered Species list. Have a nice day."

The screen went blank.

Vernon recovered from his initial shock. "Have a nice day, what the hell was that?"

"Good God, we have to put up with this Brody character still! I thought we were finished with that asshole," the new Canadian Ambassador said. His language in polite company had not improved from his predecessor.

"I guess we'll find out tomorrow," the Chinese representative offered.

* * *

"One last hurray. Then we can get out of here, finally," Karen said. She had been waiting for the final word that they could all leave. *Whatever the professor had to say, at least it should be over,* she thought. *Anything to get away from here.* She had successfully avoided Dr. Brody since that awful day when she watched the reports of billions of human deaths on Mel's computer.

Even after a month, she still hadn't slept through the night. The torment of all those lost souls tore her mind in all directions. Leaving the island would be one step in putting the whole sordid mess behind her.

"Karen, I think you need to talk to Chet. He's gotten out of the professor what the topic of his speech tomorrow to the world will be," Brandi said.

"There's isn't anything he can say that would change my mind."

"Don't be so sure. I'd talk to him before you do something you'll regret the rest of your life."

Karen wanted to avoid the nagging so left the main house and walked out onto the beach. The trade winds were blowing as usual, the palm trees swayed. A thump of a coconut hitting the sand reminded her of her first morning on the island. Laying naked and scared, she had wondered what the thump noise had been.

But it had been the soothing noise of the waves hitting the beach that had allowed her to step outside and confront her fears. And what a turn her life had taken. First the thrill of togetherness with Dr. Brody followed by the despair at the realization of what he had done.

But that was followed by the reconciliation after the final game show and the subsequent togetherness on the beach. Only to be dashed again on the bodies of billions of people.

And now her friend and confidant was telling her to open her heart once again. That there was more to the professor's story. More information that might change her mind again. *How does one justify five billion dead?* she thought. *I could never again be close to such a monster.*

As she continued down the beach she felt the warm water of the surf wash over her feet and lower legs. The sea water splashed up her legs as a large wave boomed onto the sand. Her shorts, now wet, clung to her thighs. She stopped and pulled them loose. *They'll be dry in a few minutes,* she thought.

She looked up and saw it. The tent was still by the beach. *An alien transporter device would be more appropriate,* she thought. She stared at the thing that had been the instrument of so much sadness.

"Boy, you're hard to find," a voice behind her said.

Karen wheeled around to find Captain Chet Grinkis standing there. "Captain, what do you want?" She lied. She knew what he wanted but didn't want to hear it.

"Can we walk?"

"Its a free beach." Karen turned around and continued her beach walk. Chet caught up and walked beside her on the ocean side.

The two strollers walked the entire length of the beach without saying a word. As the sand ended and the rocky cliff rose up, they turned around and headed back toward the main house. Again, no words were exchanged.

When they reached the alien tent, Karen stopped, pointing out the tent a short distance away. "Captain, do you know what that is?"

"A tent."

"It may look like a tent. But I can attest that its the Portal of Hell. Anyone coming through that is condemned to a life of suffering," Karen said. Her eyes misted up at the thought of all that had occurred since she opened that tent flap.

"And do you think that Dr. Brody is the devil incarnate?"

"If not, can you name a better candidate?" Karen asked.

"Not at the moment. But I can name the greatest living human being. In fact I'll venture to say I can name the greatest human ever, at least since Christ walked among us."

"You're not nominating our professor are you?"

"The one and the same. What he accomplished through this whole ugly alien encounter will be memorialized for millennia on Earth. And maybe someday, we can pay a return visit to our alien friends, courtesy of one Dr. Charles Brody," Chet smiled.

Karen was taken aback by his expression. "How could you say that, after what he did? Five billion dead."

"As an academician, you know the concept of examining all issues from all perspectives. You are blinding yourself to reality."

"Well excuse me, Captain. Most of my view is blocked by piles of dead human beings: people that never did anything in their life to deserve what fate gave them. Oh, excuse me, it wasn't fate. It was Dr. Charles Brody," Karen was fuming.

"You see five billion dead. I see two billion alive. I like my view better."

"That's because you're standing on the piles of dead bodies, figuratively speaking," Karen said."

"Two billion alive is better than one-hundred million. Twenty times better. But I'm just a stupid soldier, ma'am."

Karen looked at him with a curious eye. *What point was he trying to make?* she thought.

"What one-hundred million?" she asked.

"Maybe you need to listen to Dr. Brody with more of an open heart tomorrow. That's all I'm saying," Chet walked off down the beach leaving Karen stammering with questions. *What is he saying?* she thought.

316

# Chapter 34

Mel's eyes popped open in fright. He had lain half asleep for a while before he realized he was naked. He was never naked, except for a quick shower once a month. As a geek, his life revolved around computers, not humans.

Computers didn't require cleanliness by their handlers. And with the lack of female companionship, stripping naked never happened. Both conditions pleased Mel.

Machines were far superior companions. They neither talked back nor demanded much. *Well, there was the occasional tweak that any computer required, but that wasn't a chore,* he thought. *That was pleasure, pulling out wayward components and replacing them with new stuff.* Mel thought life didn't get any better.

*Human interaction is so overrated,* he thought. But as he looked down he realized he was definitely naked. And he was in a nylon tent. *What was going on?* he thought.

Then he bumped into it. Or maybe it was him, or her. In any case, Mel felt something behind him as he lay on his side. He nervously turned his head to see what was touching him.

*Jesus, Captain Grinkis,* he thought. He snapped his head forward. What are we doing in a tent together? And he looked naked too. *Man, this is way too weird,* he thought.

"Mel, is that you?" the voice behind him said.

Mel swiveled around onto his other side, careful not to touch the naked man. As they each looked at each other, they both avoided looking down.

"What's going on Captain?"

"Seems we've been transported to the alien tent. But why? We're already on the island."

"Will you guys shut up? I'm due at casting at five AM. I need my sleep," a third voice said. But this one was female. The two men looked at each other and froze.

Chet moved slightly and Mel could tell by his expression he had bumped into someone behind him. That brought another incredulous look between the two. Chet nodded for Mel to peek over him at what or who lay behind him.

Mel carefully lifted himself up on one elbow. A naked woman came into his view as he rose above the captain. His eyes gave him away and the captain carefully twisted around so he faced his other tent mate.

The woman continued to sleep soundly as the two naked men stared at their companion. She was a natural brunette with fair skin. Her body was athletic and although not as well-endowed compared to Brandi, certainly would fill the needs of any healthy male suitor. Her legs stretched down and Mel judged by comparing her to the captain that she was about 5' 7".

"What's she doing here?" Mel whispered.

"Hell if I know," Chet replied but with a bit more volume.

"Will you please shut it? A girl needs her sleep. Five o'clock comes to early for-" The voice stopped. With eyes shut tight, she ran her free hand down her side. Discovering no covers nor clothes, she reached forward.

Chet tried to dodge the extended hand, but his male anatomy stuck out to much. Her hand froze at the feel of the impact. Suddenly her eyes snapped open.

"Who are you?" she demanded. Before Chet could answer, her hand retreated to her side, and then to her private parts. "What are you doing here?"

"I was about to ask you the same things. What's your name?" Chet asked.

Mel, hidden by the captain's large body, said, "Ask her where she came from?"

This second voice in the tent seemed to set her off. The woman sat straight up and looked over the captain at Mel.

"What kinky shit is going on here? This isn't in my contract. Where's my agent? What the hell did he get me into? I don't do threesomes, no way."

"Slow down, Miss. We can explain," Chet said.

"Where's the door out of this place? That's the only explaining you can do for me. And where's my robe? The prop guy always has my robe ready."

In terror, Mel was already out the tent flap. He covered himself the best he could as Chet and then the woman stepped onto the beach.

"Where's the crew? Say, what is going on here. I was supposed to be at casting today. Where's the cameras?"

"Miss, please follow me. We can answer all your questions. Mel, run ahead and warn the women. Another one has arrived."

They both watched Mel's white backside bounce down the beach, his arms flailing. His screams alerted the two women in the main house. They disappeared and returned with wraps. When the new women got closer, Brandi let out a scream.

"Tina!" She bolted down the beach to embrace the new arrival.

"Brandi, I can see you're in on this. You've been after my acting slots since last year. Well, just give me that sarong." Tina grabbed the sarong in Brandi's hand. "Now, where's the studio geek? I need transport to get to my casting call."

A laugh rose from Brandi as Tina hustled toward the house. Karen handed Mel and Chet each a *lavalava*.

"All three of you arrive by tent this morning?" she asked.

"Yeah, but why? We were already on the island. Why would the aliens transport us from the cabin over to the tent when we're leaving in three hours?" Chet said.

Mel just stood in his spot and stared at the brunette. He hadn't ever been naked with someone so beautiful before in his life. In spite of the captain being in his way, he had received an eyeful. The view was certainly different than the female geek that he once had hooked up with. *That had been a strange deal,* he thought. *But she had a wickedly fast video board and game engine though.*

* * *

The nuclear attack submarine that had delivered the Special Ops personnel to the island had maintained its station just offshore. It had stayed submerged the entire time and only lifted its antennae to communicate with the outside world occasionally.

It received orders to surface at noon to recover all personnel leaving the island. The sub commander had been forewarned to expect a company of Delta Force along with a male civilian as well as two female civilians. The same orders had been sent to Captain Chet Grinkis, Commander of the Delta Force deployed to the island.

Chet hiked over to the Special Ops camp and informed his sergeant. They had decided to use the Navy Seal rafts still located on the beach at the end of the headland. The sub confirmed the tides and weather for an extraction.

Sergeant Aubin had the Delta Force troops packed and moving quickly. Chet led them back toward the main house. Without Wu Who in the area, the armed soldiers carried past the house and headed onto the headland.

Captain Grinkis stopped in his tracks when he reached the spot where he had rescued Karen from her captivity. Where once there had been a small patch of grass on a knoll now stood a cabin. It looked to be a copy of the cabin on the hill. A rusted metal roof belied the fact that it had not existed yesterday.

Walking inside, he admired the view of the ocean through the surrounding windows. To the south and east, a beautiful vista opened up of the coral blue sea off the rocky shore. Waves crashing against the headland filled the single room with sound as the trade winds kept the temperature pleasant.

Even the tropical trees overhanging the roof appeared like they had been there for years. *Where did this come from?* Chet wondered. His men gathered under the oceanside lanai as they examined the small toilet building with the outdoor shower just off to the side.

Peeking in the toilet, he noted the same stunning view that Dr. Brody had in his cabin. *Just lower down and in a different direction,* he thought. *But why here and why now? All but the Professor are leaving in a few hours.* Only the aliens could have put it in place so fast, but Chet didn't have a clue why.

He escorted his men out to the small beach on the end of the headland. The Navy Seal rafts were still intact where they had been stored high on shore. The troops went about checking the rafts and readying them near the surf. Chet left the sergeant in charge and returned to the others.

Chet arrived to an argument. Brandi and Tina were still in each other's face over why Brandi sabotaged Tina's screen test for a major part in a movie.

"But Tina, I had nothing to do with it. You have to believe me."

"If I didn't have a history with you, I'd almost believe you. But this isn't the first time. You've been jealous ever since I beat you out for Miss January last year."

"That's it. I've been going crazy trying to place you. You were Miss January. My roommate had you on the wall," Mel finally said.

"I just said that." Tina looked at Mel with a certain curious look as if maybe he was a little slow.

"In fact, you're Lucie Loupalova's younger sister, aren't you?" Mel exclaimed. His face was brightening with each discovery of their new island guest.

"Miss November, three years ago. Did your roommate have her on the wall too?" Tina added with a bit of sarcasm.

"No way. I did. She was gorgeous. In fact she looks just like you." Mel was in full excitement mode now. "I had to keep my friends from snatching her picture many times. They considered her not worthy."

"My sister, not worthy? Are you friggin' kidding me? She was the top vote-getter on-"

"I know. I wrote a software program that continuously filled her twitter account on the night to vote. I can't believe her sister is here, right in front of me," Mel said. "My friends didn't think she was worthy in the land of geeks. But I didn't care. And I kept her picture up even after-"

"Her accident. The worst day of my life." Tina and Mel both went silent.

Chet and Karen leaned into Brandi. She whispered back, "Killed during filming of a helicopter scene in a movie. Poor thing was hit by the rotors when the pilot lost control in a sudden cross wind. Awful."

The five individuals sat in silence under the cabin lanai. They only had a couple of hours left on the island before they would be whisked back to the real world by the nuclear submarine. The talk of Tina's sister's death brought the recent world carnage into perspective.

Millions of survivors were experiencing the shock of losing loved ones. The entire Earth's population was grieving. The five looked out as Dr. Brody sat on his now familiar rock. Alone with his thoughts, the professor was readying his message to the world's surviving humans.

As the time of the professor's broadcast drew near, Mel worked his computer keyboard so that they could all watch from the lanai. Once it was done, they would say their goodbyes and head to the extraction point. The sub would surface and this part of their adventure would be over.

*Except for Karen,* he thought. Chet knew that her feelings on the events of the past month still consumed her thoughts of Dr. Brody. She would watch with the others and then make her way to the beach and a trip home. *Iowa was still intact and part of the human world,* Chet thought. Karen had told Brandi she just wanted to find her family and return to her studies. *How that was possible, I'll never figure out* he thought.

But Chet knew everyone had to deal with the trauma of the alien attack as best they could. *The main point was to accept survival and create a better life for oneself,* he thought. *The survivors owed as much to the victims.*

Dr. Brody walked by the group, lost in his thoughts. They all sat motionless as the man responsible for so much disappeared down the trail headed to the shed. Mel connected with one of the main media links and a screen with the U.N. blue logo came on. Robust music played in the background as everyone waited for the professor's announcement.

Gone were the color flacks and talkative show hosts. The human side was now in control of the airwaves and things had taken on a serious, somber tone. No ads ran before the announcement as the world waited.

Chet could only imagine the remaining two billion people making their way to a television set. He knew that Dr. Brody's talk was being broadcast over all radio channels as well as short wave frequencies. There would be few in the world who would remain out of touch.

"I think we're about ready. There's the room in the shed and the Professor is sitting there waiting."

The other four moved closer for a better view. The shed that lay less than one-hundred feet from their position was the focus of the world. The music stopped.

"Men and women of Earth. Terrible events have played out in the name of fairness for all species on our planet. Humanity has suffered losses from which they may never recover. I want to stop and ask that we all honor our dead with a minute of silence. Whatever your belief system is, our family, friends and fellow humans deserve our silence."

A clock in the corner of the screen popped up and began a countdown. The professor lowered his head in respect. The four sitting in the lanai joined him. When the clock reached the twelve, Dr. Brody resumed.

"The aliens talked of a Great Compromise that I negotiated for humanity. They mentioned one-hundred million humans as their original target. I am here to say that as I understood their original directive, Earth's human population was to be reduced to only one hundred million souls. That would have resulted in over seven billion dead."

"As part of such a drastic reduction, the aliens would have left us alone for one thousand years. At the end of that time they would have returned to see how we had managed our new role as stewards of half the Earth. If we were judged redeemed, we would have been left unmolested by the aliens."

Chet squeezed Brandi's hand at the news. He had surmised as much from his talks with the professor. He had tried to express this to Karen but had been rebuffed. He looked at Karen now and saw a woman who was wrestling with her thoughts.

By her eye movements and her body language, Chet knew that one big fact was finally getting through to her. But the professor spoke up again.

"To save as many humans as possible, I offered numerous alternatives to the one-hundred million human mark and one thousand years scenario. After a lengthy negotiation with the aliens, we settled on slightly different terms. Humanity is limited to two billion people, absolutely no more. The green and yellow lights should have reduced our total to close to that number. But we now only have twenty-five years to prove our worth in the stewardship of the planet."

"Whew, baby. The Professor is cutting it close. The world would take twenty-five years to decide on the proper color for fire trucks. He's asking the impossible," Chet said.

But he noticed that Karen was on the edge of her chair as she watched the computer. Her expression had decidedly changed from one of open hostility to one of giddy happiness. She waited for Charles to continue.

"There were many variations to this agreement but this was the one that allowed the largest number of people to survive. I'll make it very clear. The aliens will not tolerate a human population over two billion, no matter what."

Dr. Brody continued. "All people now in an animal square have thirty days to move to a human square. No molestation of any animals will be tolerated in that move. Further rules of how the two sides will interact will be issued by me. Be forewarned that it will not be open season on animals in the human squares. We will continue to respect their existence among us with reasonable hunting and trapping laws that have been in place for decades in many countries. It is our job to see that these areas are respected."

"At the end of thirty days, the aliens will confirm all animal squares void of humans. The aliens say they will then leave."

"I will repeat, they will return in twenty-five years. At that time, if the human population has risen over the two billion limit, the blue light will clear the planet of human life. As the aliens said, we are an endangered species. Only by working together can the world avoid human extinction."

"In closing, I have attempted to save as much of humanity as possible under very restrictive limits. I will struggle with my maker for the rest of my life over what I was forced to do. I ask for your prayers that I be forgiven. Thank you."

Karen was gone the second the screen went back to the blue U.N. logo. Chet watched as she flew around the corner and disappeared below the cliff.

# Chapter 35

Karen caught Dr. Brody as he emerged from his broadcast shed. He looked spent from the strain of his announcement. As he looked up, he saw the response he had hoped for. Karen ran to him and leaped into this arms. He staggered from the impact but held on tight. She kissed him hard as she squeezed.

"Charles, I want to be the first to forgive you. What you did was nothing short of a miracle. That you could get the aliens to change their original plans will be remembered as humanity's greatest moment."

The professor took it all in. He had longed for this moment but the events continued to interfere. Maybe he could finally find the peace that he longed for. But there was one final thing.

"Karen, it's not over yet. There is one thing I need to tell everyone before they leave the island. Something that could change their lives."

"Mine has already changed, Han. I'm not going anywhere. I want to stay here with you."

"No, Karen. You need to hear me out first. Then you decide," Dr. Brody said.

Karen looked at him in confusion. He could tell that she wasn't ready for another conflict between them. They had already suffered setback after setback as her emotions were ripped apart only to be reconciled. He knew she couldn't continue the roller coaster that their relationship had become.

The two climbed the cliff-side trail to the cabin. This had been the initial site of their first encounter together. The four others all rose to congratulate the professor. He waved their recognition away.

"Hear me out first. Everyone sit. You need one more bit of information before you row out to that sub."

They each looked at each other. Some had more concern on their face then others. Tina, the newest member of the group, appeared totally confused. *She was still looking for her limo,* Charles thought.

"Some of us have experienced what we called the 'Island Parasite'. Brandi was the latest victim. The captain and Mel will develop symptoms. We should tell Tina what she can expect within about two weeks."

Tina looked at Dr. Brody in more confusion. *She's just waiting for the prop people to deliver her bathrobe and she thinks she's out of here,* he thought.

"Everyone, I have some good news and some bad news for you," Charles offered.

Chet jumped first. "Tell us the good news first, Doc. I think we need some."

"Alright, the 'Island Parasite' isn't a parasite per say. It is an inoculation that the aliens have administered to each of us."

"You mean they injected alien shit into me?" Brandi asked. "I didn't get any needle pokes that I remember."

"No needles Brandi. Its the tent. Everyone of you has been transported through the tent. Somehow the tent has the means of introducing their vaccine to each of you."

"So, are we aliens now?" Mel asked. His voice carried a certain wishful thinking to it.

"Afraid not Mel. You're still human. Well, let me rephrase that. You were human."

The silence on the lanai was stifling. Even the trade winds could not move the oppressiveness of the professor's words.

"Then if we're not aliens and we're no longer human, what are we?" Karen asked. The concern on her face melted Charles's attempt at drama.

"You are all ... what should I call you?" he stopped.

The others sat stiff and waited. The pause, as Dr. Brody searched for the right expression, was intolerable. Finally Chet demanded, "What the hell are we, Doc?"

"I guess the best word to describe each of us is superhuman."

The word hit hard. They all fell back as they contemplated what had been said.

"And just how superhuman are we? Able to leap tall buildings in a single bound?" Chet half joked.

"No, nothing like that. A more subtle superhuman. Each of you are now immune to all disease. Your immune system will be so strong that practically nothing can hurt you. Broken bones should mend almost instantly on their own. Cuts will dry up and close with no aid what-so-ever."

"Anything else?" Chet asked.

*How does he know?* the Professor thought. "Yes, there's something else. Your aging has essentially stopped."

"What, I'm going to look like this forever?" Brandi jumped to the fastest conclusion. Miss January was right behind her in adapting to their new reality.

"Yes. The way we are right now will carry into the indefinite future. The aliens didn't give me an exact number, but you can all expect a very long life. As in hundreds of years, I surmise.

"Wait till we get back to LA Brandi. We'll be richer than anyone could imagine. Looking like this forever and making money the whole time. It doesn't get any better than that. Wait till I tell my agent," Tina shouted.

"Be sure to talk to your agent's son and his son. You'll need to line up replacements as we outlive them all. Thanks, Doc, my little soiree to the island worked out just peachy keen," Brandi said.

Chet looked at her in disappointment. The professor sensed that what they had discovered in each other had just been vaporized by the thoughts of many lifetimes of acting stardom. Charles watched the captain look away.

"That was the good news."

The two beauty queens stopped their celebration as the words hit them. *They had forgotten the other part of the equation,* Charles thought.

The professor continued. "Before anyone makes plans, you need to know the price of a long life of healthy youthful energy. The effect only works on this island. If you leave, the vaccine quickly disappears and you rapidly catch up to the age and health condition that you would be if you hadn't ever been here."

"You mean I'm stuck here forever?" Tina asked.

"If you want to remain a young healthy woman you are. Only the island will provide you with the necessary environment to keep the vaccine functional. If you leave even for a day, the effect is gone. I'm afraid you'll all be here for the duration," Charles said.

"If we want to remain young, that is?" Chet said. He looked at Brandi. Charles looked at Karen and could already tell her answer. She stood up and embraced her man.

"I want to stay here with you no matter what the conditions. We've had too many interruptions to let this one stop us," Karen said. She kissed Charles and he gladly returned the commitment. They turned to see if they would have company on the island or if the prearranged departure would still take people away.

"Brandi, I'll stay if you do. I can't imagine spending a long life with anyone but you. Life back there is so much nothing. You know that," Chet said. Brandi leapt into Chet's lap and almost knocked the chair he was in over backwards. As they were busy confirming their decisions to stay, Charles and Karen turned to the remaining two people.

As Mel and Tina had been the only other two brought by the aliens through the tent, they both had immunity. They had to choose what they would do with it.

Dr. Brody noticed that Mel was leaning toward staying. He had committed before the news to being Dr. Brody's communication expert. A long lifetime of hacking would be his reward.

Everyone turned to Tina. They all knew that she had been brought to the island by the aliens for a reason. And the gift of longevity was hers for the taking. But would the bright lights of LA force her to give up the gift? *And was it a gift if she couldn't display it to more than the people on the island?* Dr Brody thought.

The news reporters gathered in the United Nations Conference Room for the big day. It had been thirty days since Dr. Brody's announcement and the world was anticipating the aliens departure. A live link with the Space Station was running on all networks as the entire human population awaited the event.

The green and yellow lights had scoured the animal zones the previous night and everyone assumed that additional people had been vaporized. Reports had come in all month of people refusing to leave areas that had been their homes for generations. Since no human was there to report their fate, everyone knew the alien death machine had completed the liquidation as planned.

As the press waited, the announcer for ZBC Networks gave a running commentary of the TV feed from the Space Station camera.

"We're still waiting for the alien space craft to fire up whatever kind of engines they have and leave Earth's orbit. We know from reports of those close to animal squares that any who had stayed in the animal zone were eliminated last night. So we are now officially two separate worlds on Earth. And with the edict that Dr. Brody issued last week, the rules are set on our interaction."

The camera in space shifted its view as something seemed to be moving across the expanse of space. While everyone watched, a portion of the giant football shaped alien spaceship separated.

"I don't know what this means, but it may be that the aliens are leaving part of their space ship for some purpose. Radar reports are that the various satellites that the aliens deployed have shifted into defensive mode. That's coming from our military sources."

The television camera shook as the view jumped on the screen. A portion of the alien ship began moving away from the Space Station and the bouncing camera zoomed in as it left. When the view had been reduced to a small shape in the distance, a flash of light shot the aliens out into space.

"Well, I do believe they're gone. A chapter in Earth's history has closed and a new one has opened. This will always be an important juncture in man's life on this planet. How long that life will continue is now the question. For an answer, we now go live to the new Secretary General of the United Nations. The man who is being described as the most powerful man on Earth, Vernon Randolph," the announcer said.

"Ladies and gentlemen. Wherever you may be at this moment, I can report that the aliens have left our solar system. They may have gone, but they are not forgotten. Too many have died from their short visit."

"And they left us with a great task. We need to resettle many which, for some, will be in new homes in a new land. Next, we need to get our world economy realigned after the losoes in territory we have suffered. New sources of materials need to be located to replace areas now behind the animal frontiers."

"But most importantly, the threat of our total extinction must be avoided at all cost. The U.N. has already begun a massive census of the world to determine the exact number of humans. Already we are searching for a secure means to identify everyone so we can adhere to the two billion person limit that has been imposed on us. The U.N. will hold one hundred-million slots at the ready to assure that we do not exceed the limit set by the aliens."

"To that end, once the two billion approved people are identified, any and all persons are subject to arrest and imprisonment upon lack of a proper numbered ID. Lacking a U.N. number ID will result in elimination. We are serious in meeting the demands of the aliens and will not tolerate law breakers. Only persons issued a numbered U.N. ID will be allowed on the planet."

"These may sound like draconian steps we are taking but humanity's survival is at stake. I think with what is at risk, all people living on Earth will agree with these controls."

"In closing, I want to continue to express the world's gratitude to Dr. Brody for his supreme gift to mankind. Wherever he may be at present, All Hail Dr. Brody."

"All Hail Dr. Brody." The entire press corps and distinguished guests reiterated Randolph's statement. Outside the U.N. Building, the gathered masses all yelled 'All hail Dr. Brody'.

* * *

Karen dropped her clothes on the small beach by the lagoon and quickly dove naked into the water. She adjusted her mask and snorkel. With her flippers adjusted, she swam for her favorite rock in the reef.

Dr. Charles Brody was right behind her. The two met at the rock and immediately embraced. This was their routine. Twice each week they would take a break from gardening and trek out to their favorite spot on the island.

With the two other couples on the island, that left each couple their own two days each week to experience the lagoon in solitude. One day each week was a free day.

Brandi and Chet were regulars to the lagoon. Although Karen didn't know if they knew the wonders of her rock or not, she was sure that they had found their own special spots among the coral and reef.

It had taken a couple of weeks, but Tina and Mel had finally settled into a life together. They had moved into the new cabin on the point provided by the aliens.

As the senior island residents, Charles and Karen could have chosen any of the houses. They chose the original cabin on the hill as it held many strong memories for them.

"So Han, ready to meet the Princess?"

"Always. The Wookiee is looking forward to a long engagement, so to speak."

They laughed at the reference to a long life together. It still seemed impossible that they would stay as they were for what would be an eternity. At night they often discussed the ramifications of such long life. *Would we get tired of each other?* she often thought. And after a good number of years, they could never leave. The cumulative effects of all the years hitting them at once meant certain death.

But would life of such longevity make death seem more appealing? The two spent many metaphysical hours discussing their new situation.

But the lagoon made them forget it all. The warm water combined with the naked smooth feeling the salty sea provided drove such thoughts away. Here there was an eternity of fish and coral. Floating, as if suspended in time, allowed them to reinvigorate their love for each other.

And then to the rock. The solid object in the middle of the reef that offered the support for the physical nature of their relationship. Karen couldn't even begin to think of love-making into a limitless future with one man. But that had been her choice.

"Hans will we ever tire of this?" she asked as the two met, their bodies coming together.

"That alien juice running inside me certainly is better than the little blue pill, thats for sure. I haven't felt like this since I was twenty years old and-"

Karen placed her finger over Charles mouth. She didn't want to know his past. The present was too wonderful to cloud with that.

"There is something I've been meaning to tell you," the Professor said.

"Not another mystery from the aliens?"

"Actually yes. But I didn't want to tell the others. If this comes to pass, the reason will be too horrible to imagine."

This froze any amorous movements and the Wookiee slinked back. *What is he going to tell me now? Jesus, it never ends,* she thought.

"I wasn't entirely honest when I said that if the Earth's population goes over the two billion limit, that the blue light will vaporize human life off the planet."

"There's more? How much worse can it get?" she asked.

"No, not bad. Well, bad for everyone else. But if that happens, the aliens assured me that anyone on this island will be immune. We'll survive."

"Six people on Earth. Three couples. Sounds like Adam and Eve all over again. Right here in Paradise."

"That would be us."

"And with all those years to procreate. Makes my juices flow just thinking about it." Karen bent over and nibbled on Charles' ear. She whispered to him an enticing proposal.

"But what about the serpent? There's always that serpent that screws up the deal," the professor said as he recalled his Bible.

Karen changed his mind back to the business at hand. Bible tales could wait.

"All this talk of repopulating the Earth has made me want to get started now. Can we continue when we get home?" Karen asked.

Charles agreed and they swam over to their beach spot. Gathering up their belongings, they quickly climbed the ravine. A brisk walk brought them up to the cabin where they ran into the other couples watching Mel's computer.

"What's happening?" Karen asked. She forgot about her offer to Charles as she sat down.

"We've been watching this supposed leader of the U.N. Mel, back up the file so they can see it from the beginning," Chet said. "Unbelievable."

Mel typed on his keyboard and swiveled the screen around so Karen and Charles could watch. He hit the arrow and the file began to run. It was a copy of the speech that Vernon Randolph had given the day before outlining the measures the U.N. was undertaking to save humanity.

Karen felt the rage flow as she watched. Holding Charles's hand as the screen played, she felt his rage overtake hers. As the tape ended, he exploded.

"Who is this pissant and how did he become dictator of Earth? I saved humanity for the likes of this?" Dr. Brody roared.

"What does it all mean, Professor?" Brandi asked.

"It means that my attempt at leaving the world with a base of people who would commit to freedom and prosperity for all has been usurped by bureaucratic tyrants. This is all wrong."

"It seems that the fear of extinction has eclipsed all other basic human desires. They are willing to give away all their freedoms for a shot at moving off the Endangered Species list," Chet surmised.

Dr. Brody fell into a deep silence as he contemplated man's fate. He finally concluded.

"It would have been better off leaving the aliens to take the human population down to one-hundred million. At least they would probably have had one-thousand years of freedom. Now what do they have? World control over everything. What have I done?" the Professor asked.

Karen held him as he sank into despair. She knew he would continue to blame himself and with their long life guaranteed, he would have an eternity to dwell on the pain.

"Doc, maybe I could offer something. It might put things in perspective. It's something you taught me," Chet said.

Dr. Brody lifted his head and looked at the captain., his curiosity peeked.

Chet continued. "As a man of science, you would agree that humankind is part of the biological world, correct?"

"Yes, Captain, I will grant you that," Charles responded.

"Then, you have just been shown the power of the First Law of Biology."

"You mean 'You can never do just one thing'?" the Professor offered.

"Exactly," Chet said.

Everyone sat and contemplated the meaning of the philosophical discussion taking place. Miss May and Miss January were less involved than the others.

Finally Karen broke the spell. "And if Vernon What's-His-Name fails in his great quest for control, which seems very likely given the twenty-five-year window he has, then we fall back to Plan B."

"Plan B?" Mel asked. The others all looked at Karen with quizzical stares.

The End

# Acknowledgments

First, there is Timothy Johns, my tireless editor. Though he works hard that my writing is presentable, place no blame on him for the final product. That all rests with me.

My proofreaders offer valuable feedback at different phases as my draft is put together. Jeanne Crownover, Dick Martin, Marsha Wiles, Larry Stoddard, Tiffany Martin, John Briggs and Rod Gravelly have all kept me from straying too far off on tangents.

Finding Morwenna Rakestraw to do the cover layout was a relief.

Mitch Press of World Book has offered his wisdom from his family's years in the book business. While not all encouraging, his guidance as publishing transforms in the digital age has been invaluable.

Lastly, and most importantly, my wife deserves recognition for her support of my writing.

Dear Reader,

Thank you for your selection of reading material. I hope this book measured up to your expectations. The most critical part for a new author is getting the word out to other readers.

I would appreciate your help in spreading the word. There are three important things you can do. You need to understand the importance of the first one to my becoming a successful writer. Amazon.com is huge in the new book publishing era. So please:

1.      Go to Amazon.com and leave a review
2.      Tell a friend about this book
3.      Tell your social network about this book.

The more positive reviews that are made in various places will help readers find me.

Again, thanks for your support.


W.B. Martin


And check out my website at wbmartinauthor.com